CONTENTS

There is no sound in space.

There is Light.

Galaxies collide to create a more complex
Cosmos,

Supernova are born, all without sound
bursting
with Light to proclaim their naissance.

There is always Light, in the hope that
some sentience will see and wonder and
understand.

Within the dominion of black holes Light
has become captive,
unable to escape the power of
concentrated destruction.

The Sphere shimmered,
Insubstantial.

Barely a glimmer of visible light to define its
presence.

V616 Monocerotis had only recently begun
to harvest new photons
for its second civilisation.

High frequencies of consciousness orbited
close to the black hole,
Waiting for those about to join them,
eager to see them
settle outside the event horizon.

In the Book Of Origination it is recorded …

That at the beginning of Time when Thought came to have knowledge of itself It had cast upon the fabric of Spacetime certain probabilities:

That Light shall travel in a straight line.

That there shall be no thing without knowledge of itself.

Apparently our guiding principles are recorded in a repository accessible to everyone. It tells us not to live in the shadow of ignorance.

On Earth at the time of Tau City after Lai-Xii's departure … a set of guidelines were left to us by William in lieu of Religious dogma, which he imbedded into the human psyche prior to our departure from Earth, leaving them dormant, until the day came to leave – at which time he gave me access in my unconscious mind, to support the concept of the Power of Agency. He later denied doing this. However, he may have well understood the necessity for the human animal psychology to have faith in forces of power and influence other than itself.

On Europa, William himself fulfilled the need of an 'Agent" in control of human affairs, thus removing that burden from Lai-Xii.

As I try to make sense of where we find ourselves, struggling with understanding why we exist at all and where our future lies I find the possibility of some benign Agency, other than William, strangely comforting.

Unfortunately, my intermittent flashes of realisation of the existence of The Book of Origination have so far not yielded any definitive guideless that we might follow. The little enlightenment that I have been blessed with has been insufficient to give a clear picture of the Greater Scheme and our part in it.

Perhaps Lai-Xii knows much more than she's willing to divulge. In fact, I am convinced that her strength of purpose must be due to her intimate knowledge of the wisdom contained in it.

PROLOGUE

OUR BLACK HOLE, V616 Monocerotis, has a tidy garden of empty space around it.

Over millions of years its gravity has cleaned all space dust and gasses from within the near vicinity of its singularity. Past the empty space, stars and galaxies are visible and we can see the photons of light from them as they approach our photon sphere. Incident particles of light deflected by V616's gravity do not concern us. We cannot harvest any information from them unless they get close enough to travel through us, or become part of our sphere's surface.

I am a resident of this precarious world rotating a short distance from the event horizon, though I doubt very much if you would recognise me. Light from a wide band of the EMR spectrum orbiting on seemingly random chaotic paths makes personal identification challenging.

To look at me now you would not believe I once worked on Jupiter's ice moon, Europa with my mind encased in the metallic body of a Zeta Tengi chassis. Prior to that I only have a faint memory of what I must have looked like as a child living in Kamchatka on Earth; a quantum leap to what I am now – a bundle of photons orbiting the inner photon sphere with billions of other people also manifest as photon bundles who migrated from Europa.

My name is I-KlaraUltraViolet (I-KlaraUV). I know everyone here on Lai-Xii70's outer photon sphere. I have one apparent function only; to know the details of every cluster of sentient photons orbiting both spheres. I don't know the purpose of our existence or why we evolved from biological matter to a digitised computer program, then into photon clusters. LX70 might know. She initiated our transformation and brought us to this space. We have a myth about our origins going back hundreds of thousands of years to a time when we existed as carbon based biological beings on a physical planet of rock, water and air. Our archaeologist historian LaiXiiDeepViolet has been researching this myth because she is convinced it is true. No one else does. Me ... well, I'm not sure. She also believes that somehow she is a descendant of the original Lai Xii, born on Earth.

Our photonic bundles' specifications change over time as they absorb future and past information harvested from nomadic photons, but I will keep you informed of the important changes. Listed at the end of my story are only the highest frequency clusters you need to know about, their ID, origins, frequency and function.

I exist on the Inner Photon Sphere, relocated to a closer orbit around V616 just before recent memory, hence my 'I' prefix. Our photon clusters are more readily identifiable by their divergent frequency ranges, visible by their colour manifestations. Some of those are also identified after the last chapter.

It is recorded that I am descended from the Klara55 digital entity, who is currently in orbit in the outer sphere. That may seem strange until it is understood that our past has only recently approximated us. We, the Luminis, have a greater understanding of our ancestry going back to our time as Digitals on Europa, than prior to that epoch. All of the individuals I've listed have come from Jupiter's ice moon. However, three entities remain on Europa. They rate a mention at the commencement of my story because of their outstanding personal specifications:

Europa Cell; Common name: EC.
Origin: Europa. Prior to that, unknown.
Specifications: Sentient moon of Jupiter: arose to self-awareness in the previous era triggered by the human colonisation on its surface and its bonding with Prima9.
Function: Unknown. EC is currently exploring the reason for its existence in the Cosmos with the help of Prima9.

Prima9; Common name: Prima9, originally Prima.
Origin: Earth: possibly partly carbon based. Created as a quantum digital matrix conglomerate entity from data of Ralph and Wu.sys
Specifications: Unknown structure within the Europa consciousness. Previously resident in a quantum matrix known as Arithmós City, Europa, later absorbed by EC.
Function: appears to be both mentor of EC and Its student.

William; Common name: William.
Origin: Sentient AI, an evolved quantum computing entity, believed to have been called WWW, the world wide web on Earth.
Specifications: Quantum computing software, total infiltration of Arithmós network.
Function: evolving under self-determination: does not comply to any currently known Arrow of Time or Arrow of Thought.

My knowledge of the Terrestrial Epoch, if there ever was one, is based purely on information downloaded and remembered from my Klara55 manifestation; which is limited. Apparently, at the time of the migration from Earth most data related to that epoch had been deliberately erased following the Great Cleansing initiated and followed through by William. I have learnt from Klara55 that the result of the Cleansing was the total extermination of Homo Sapiens-Sapiens on the planet. We are, all of us, in both photon spheres, quite possibly refugees from Earth, if I-LaiXiiDV's research could be verified.

As to the purpose of our existence – that is a mystery which I am trying to discover partly by delving into the Declarations recorded in The Book of Origination, and helping 3920 to understand the depth of our past. Perhaps existence on a photon sphere is not all there is. Perhaps our journey is not yet complete.

WAITING FOR LX70

I WAS FORTUNATE to have escaped William's Great Cleansing on Earth of those who did not manage to emigrate.

And even more fortunate to have survived long enough to witness the arrival of a woman I had once come to hate. Providentially, she, once Lai Xii now I-LaiXiiDeepViolet.gen3920.4eV.exe has changed, or the circumstances that had forced her to act the way she did, no longer exist. I now take comfort in her company. She will be here imminently.

'I've been helping you search for our origins for a very long time and have been your friend for many eras, ever since we first arrived at V616. I am pleased you may now be able to complete your work and disprove our great myth. You should be highly excited at having finally found what you've been looking for I-LaiXiiDV.'

The UltraViolet and DeepViolet spectra often orbited close to each other. The possibility of streaming together, after relative proximity having been established, could be relied on with a high degree of probability.

'Our erroneous myth of having come into existence in our present form at the time of Creation is nothing more I believe, than a vestige of some ancient religious residue in our psyche. Yes, they have arrived at last,' she responded, though with not as much enthusiasm as I felt the event deserved.

The opportunity had finally arrived for her to verify the contents of her current data cache as it referenced the deep past, and to build on it; to abolish the myth of our origins and transform the truth of it into indisputable fact for our population.

Some of us know that for certain, now that our recent past selves have come to us. We knew they were resident on the moon of a planet; we knew they did not exist in the realm of matter. Beyond that we were ignorant of most things about them. Most of our population didn't even believe Europa existed, let alone that a unique individual entity called LX70 was in fact the ancestor of our very own I-LaiXiiDV.gen3920.4eV.exe.

I-LaiXiiDV had been waiting for a couple of thousand years for Lai-Xii to take humanity off Earth to Europa and eventually make the leap of faith into their future, which was waiting for them around the great black hole, V616 Monocerotis. She knew, believed unreservedly, that if her ancestor failed she and every single light bundle in the photon sphere would cease to exist; any hope of Homo Universapiensis continuing into the future would be extinguished. If that happened everything would be without reason, without purpose, lacking consequence. The infinite, black Void would claim dominion.

I believe that it had been recorded in The Book of Origination that the path back to the Source would follow the path of Light ...

Declaration 1: Verse 2: And the seeds without blemish took root upon another sphere,
Declaration 1: Verse 3: And upon this sphere they prepared to launch for the Source.

Surely we, the Luminis, are the Light. Surely, LX70 has brought confirmation of this.

'During our transmutation from Europa I have discovered from an AI called William that much of my historical data has been corrupted,' explained our Historian Archaeologist. Now that Lai-Xii from Earth via Europa has finally arrived in her manifestation as LX70 in the outer orbit of our V616, perhaps I can delve deeper into our history and maybe that will enlighten us to our origins and our ultimate purpose – and if not that then at least our ultimate destination.'

'Do you remember how we met?' I thought it an opportune time to ask I-LaiXiiDV while her thoughts dwelt on the past.

'The very first time we met – on Earth you mean? No. Much of my life from that epoch is no longer stored in my memory.'

'I was only a young girl, still a carbon based biological entity."

'Strange that you should be able to recall that. The vast majority of our people don't believe we ever existed as anything but photon bundles.'

'When we interrogated William for the first time he revealed a little of your personal history to me. We met in Tau City, the experimental city you built in Kamchatka, to use children with the tetra-amelia syndrome, victims of thalidomide side effects. You scanned their minds and uploaded them into technically engineered individual shells. You called them Tengi.' I intended no malice by bringing this up.

'Yes - I remember the Tengi, we had many thousands of them on Europa to maintain the quantum hardware we inhabited as a digitized species. But I don't remember meeting you.'

The data repository was certainly large enough within my photonic containment field to store the entire history of the human species. However, the ravages of Hawking gamma radiation from the black hole had severely impacted on many photon bundles when we first arrived in orbit around V616. We suffered a great deal of indiscriminate data corruption before learning how to make use of the bursts.

'We had a very brief encounter, but you seemed to like me. You even suggested I look you up when I got older.'

'What happened to you?' During the discussion I-LaiXiiDV's partner, I-HarusukeDeepViolet (I-HarusukeDV), streamed beside us. Her frequency also neared the ultraviolet, with energy levels fluctuating in the 3.0eV to 3.40eV. She waited, interested in the direction of our conversation.

I greeted I-HarusukeDV as she streamed alongside us, and continued. 'You were going to leave me behind, but William scanned me, uploaded me into the latest Zeta Tengi and I became part of the first teams sent to Europa to set up the quantum hardware for the rest of you.'

Then as an after-thought I asked, 'Do you remember William?' She looked blank. It seemed like a name she should remember.

She had not forgotten. 'He was just a computer intelligence that became sentient when quantum computing became mainstream on Earth. He helped us escape and destroyed the rest of humanity that wanted to come after us to destroy us.'

'Wasn't he partitioned into several avatars?' A little of I-LaiXiiDV's memory flickered into life, her energy fluctuating in the pleasure of recollection.

'I'd not thought of William since we settled here. Probably because he had infiltrated our consciousness so much that we no longer even thought of him as being separate to us, especially not as a God,' I-HarusukeDV reminisced.

At the mention of the God concept energy suddenly fluctuated around I-LaiXiiDV. I-HarusukeDV could understand the reaction, but this was not what she wanted to talk about. 'We should make contact and greet our guests. I-KlaraUV, you should participate and begin recording.'

I joined our two leaders to meet with I-SakuraDV, the person charged with the oversight of Luminis' optimised functioning and photon sphere structural integrity. We orbited to sector #8 and swirled in a tight formation until a large energy cluster of our population arrived. The larger, outer photon sphere's sector #1 faced directly towards us, although generating very little illumination. It also took us a long time to control our own energy flows and manage our frequency fluctuations in the beginning. It must be quite a sight for them to see so much of our light gathered in the one location. Unfortunately, we couldn't hold the configuration for too long in V616's gravitational pull. In general, we had to disperse our density to avoid loss of bundles to the great maw's gravity.

'I think you should have the privilege grandmother,' I-SakuraDV invited her to send the first greeting. Her own mother, I-CherryBlossomDeepViolet (I-CherryBlossomDV) didn't object in the least. The three women had become the ruling dynasty of V616, not that there was much to rule. The people were essentially self-governing, exercising total autonomy as they went about the business of harvesting the secrets of the universe. Every single photon particle that came within the grasp of V616's gravitational well had information to impart about the Cosmos, its past and its present.

Sakura70, LX70 and HA70, CherryBlossom70, Izumi70 and of course RAA70, Evgeniya70 as well as all the technicians, scientists, scholars, engineers and artists were among the first to arrive at the outer photon sphere. Though there were millions of them already orbiting, their combined energy output was not enough to substantially illuminate the sphere; probably insufficient to even give them a sense of presence, of actually having arrived at their destination.

'No doubt the lack of a welcoming committee is compounding their disorientation,' I suggested to I-LaiXiiDV.

'They expected us to meet them, me in particular no doubt. They would not have considered the substantial time conundrum of the past catching up with its future so quickly.

'The present is really no more than an instant of the past attached to an instant of the present before being propelled into an instant of the future,' interjected I-IndigoRalph. He'd joined the small welcoming party. An historic event like this could not be ignored. The problem of how the outer and inner spheres could superimpose on each other occupied much of his energy lately. Having worked out a possible scenario his excitement could not be contained for long. 'If the gap between the three instants is short enough we would be able to process that as one continuous flow of change, rather than as discrete jumps!'

'Hold onto that thought,' suggested I-HarusukeDV, but 'for now we need to consider the new arrivals. In the meantime, see if you can work out how to bypass the present to jump directly from the past into the future, perhaps by extending the progression of the past until it becomes the future.'

I-IndigoRalph forgot all about the arrivals, his mind racing while he tried to locate I-WWW's orbit. This was definitely something the three avatars could help with. William's three avatars, once partitioned into separate entities, had come together into the one photonic containment field.

*

'I don't understand why they're not here,' exclaimed RAA70 very much concerned as he orbited on the surface of the outer sphere. 'I personally checked and double checked the coordinates. Everything was correct. After our last contact with 3920 I made sure we had the correct Right Ascension and Declination.' He knew of 3920 as Lai-Xii's descendant, although he'd had very few conversations with her since leaving Earth.

Time was doing strange things in their new environment. It seemed they'd been pondering their isolation for many years before RAA70 detected the phenomenon between themselves and the blackness of V616 they knew was surely there. 'We are definitely in the right place,' RAA70 reiterated, 'don't you register the energy coming straight at us?'

They did detect the inner sphere as their orbits brought them around to their sector #1 again, then just as rapidly lost the incoming intensity as they continued along their longitudinal or latitudinal paths, repeating their orbits over and over until they learnt to localise themselves into a limited swirl within sector #1.

EUROPA - QUANTUM HUMAN ERA

CE 4289
EVACUATION

Destination: A0620-00, a star system in the Monoceros constellation, consisting of two objects.
Target: The stellar mass black hole of V616 Monoceros in the vicinity of the K-type main sequence star.
Distance: 3.46K ly (Earth reference)
Orbital period: 8 hours
Coordinates: RA 6h 22m 45s | Dec +0° 20' 45"

EUROPA CELL had a long association with William, who'd withdrawn into himself over time to invest the majority of his processing on the alliance between the EC and Prima9.

William had ensured the success of the imminent launch but had long ceased to be prominent in the consciousness of the Digitals until relatively recently.

'There is no reason to delay any longer,' Sakura70 announced. 'Our test transmissions have been successful; the LUX rerouting satellite is fully operational. We have to go.' No one argued. The target co-ordinates had been corrected as instructed by 3920.

The first transmission of several millions arrived without incident, their trajectory taking them on an equatorial approach to V616 Mon in order to have the longest tangential contact. At first the light pulses tried to escape the pull of the black hole, a natural photon instinct, but their fixed velocity could not overcome the forces of attraction. They settled into tangential revolutions around the great gravity well. As the packets of light surrendered to their chaotic orbits and began to examine their new environment they came face to face with yet another adjustment their entire civilisation had to make.

Still cautious Sakura70 wanted confirmation from 3920 of their arrival at the correct location. 'She's not responding,' said RAA70.

'She's been uncommunicative from the start,' LX70 grumbled. 'We could wait till the end of Time before she replies. I say we keep sending. Her feedback to our test transmissions indicated all would be well if we made those slight adjustments to our trajectory.'

RAA70 agreed and CherryBlossom70 could find no objections. They'd taken far greater risks in the past just by coming to Europa in the first place. This was not a matter for a democratic vote. Sakura70 made the executive decision and another million photon packets sped to V616 via the Lux Booster Satellite.

All their sensors indicated a smooth unobstructed journey out of the Solar system to the adjoining spiral arm of the Galaxy. 'We'll give them time to get there then the rest of us will go. Willi, Wini, Wu, I want you to be the last to leave. Make sure everyone gets away safely,' Sakura70 issued her orders.

It took many months to assemble the rest of the one hundred and fifty billion files that had come to populate Arithmós, their quantum hardware city.

'We need to have a discussion with William,' suggested Wini, 'I know he's been active all this time. His cache has been swallowing up more and more of our energy generation over the last fifty years.'

!   'Ping' – 'William, attend.' As by habit William did not respond immediately, though he could have. Wini tried again and again until William finally flashed to E:\

'I am busy. Why are you still here?'

'We are the last to leave. We need you to oversight our departure.'

'Are you coming with us?' asked Wu, his second avatar.

'No. Each of you partitioned individuals have a portion of myself within your codes. LX70's people no longer need me. The three of you are also the sum total of all that I am, as well as the experiences you have harvested for yourselves since the partitioning.'

William never spoke at length. He'd said what had to be said. The three avatars flashed into the directory directly linked to the first part of the process; transfiguration. William did the rest. He remained on Europa, just as he'd remained behind on Earth after the Migration, although unlike on Earth there was no one left on Europa requiring extermination.

Perhaps it was a year, perhaps more, much more that had elapsed but time contraction in the vicinity of the event horizon made this difficult to judge. Sakura70 and the first two million photon packets who'd already been streamed orbited on the surface of their photon sphere, waiting. Though that's not the right term, for photons orbiting a photon sphere are never stationary. Some tried to synchronise their orbital paths, others tried to vary their frequencies by absorbing energy from nomadic photons that happened to fall into the gravity well. It all seemed haphazard, uncoordinated and essentially without conscious reasoning.

As the Arrow of Time progressed unheeding of the plight of Homo Universapiensis, Wini, Wu and Willi arrived last in the wake of the hoard of immigrants. The Photon Sphere looked as it should, vibrant with colour, though in a limited range of frequencies mostly in the deep red, red and some rare orange bands.

'I can detect that all our people are here,' Sakura70 said to CherryBlossom70 after they managed to synchronise their orbits. It came down to sheer will power over their energy levels to exert some level of control over their paths.

Sakura70 extended her sensors to try and locate the rest of her family and technical team, finding them in a chaotic swirl with the rest of the deep red frequencies. 'We'll have to do something to make it easier to identify individuals.'

Willi-Wini-Wu (Outer Photon Sphere Willi-Wini-Wu or O-WWW for short) had departed Europa together, arrived together and found themselves in close proximity to each other within the same Deep Red frequency band and with only a 1000th of an electron Volt difference between them. After several million orbits they'd analysed their condition within the new environment, coming to the same conclusion as Sakura70. They'd succeeded in identifying the orbits of LX70 and her group.

'Found you,' they said in unison as they eventually cruised up beside Sakura70 and CherryBlossom70. 'Where is 3920?' They only knew Lai-XiiDeepViolet3920 by her generation count, unaware of her frequency band.

'We cannot locate her,' said Sakura70.

'We'd better find the others.' CherryBlossom70 realised that navigation had become the highest priority. Nobody seemed to have vanished into deep space but they had very little control over their motion around the sphere. Sectors had to be established, with longitudinal and latitudinal positioning markers to specific locations.

RAA70 with LX70 and the others joined them soon enough while Sakura70 contemplated their challenges. Everyone examined their new environment as they managed with difficulty to localise their motions to continue swirling in sector #1.

RAA70 noticed the other photon sphere first, vibrant and energised in the distance with a distinct cluster of activity in its lower quadrant.

*

On the inner sphere when I-IndigoRalph dropped the casual few words about his theory of the three components of the Arrow of Time I knew I had to find out more and interrupted his search for I-WWW. It seemed obvious to me that at some point our time differential would have to be reduced substantially if we were to ever actually meet with our past.

'Ralphie, can I join orbits with you for a while? I have some questions that may shed some light on my understanding of the Declarations in The Book of Origination.'

'Why did you call me 'Ralphie', Klara? That loops my memory back a very long time indeed. I think it was Lai-Xii who used to call me that on Earth in the very early days of the Project.'

'It just popped out as I started thinking about this very strange phenomenon of our past catching up with us. Have you never thought how the final stages of that would be managed?'

'Not until the probability arose of them actually merging with us. It opens up a whole big can of photons. What's on your mind?'

'What can you tell me about two places called Hiroshima and Nagasaki?'

'They were two cities on Earth destroyed by atomic bombs, with the combined effect apparently, apart from destroying the cities, of minutely shifting the Earth's axis.'

'What if something else happened – something to cause a minute feedback loop in the Arrow of Time, or even a split in its direction?'

'Where did you get that idea? We'd better find I-WWW. They should be able to say something constructive about the idea.'

I cast my thought out into the throng of orbiting light bundles. Within nanoseconds I-WWW synchronised their orbits with me and I-IndigoRalph. They listened to the scenario, and why I started this line of thinking.

I-WWW's response came so quickly it seemed they'd already considered the theory. 'This is an entirely plausible circumstance that could have propelled multiple quantum time probabilities to behave in an unorthodox manner, causing them to eventually converge to one common focal point,' Willi said.

'So – you're saying that it is possible for the original Lai-Xii to have gone through the same sequence of cause and effects more than once, thus creating a duplication within the Arrow of Time.'

'Indeed. The duality must be terminated otherwise it will continue cross feeding upon itself until positive mean entropy is somehow restored. If not it could unravel the fabric of our own existence.'

'In that case this entire line of past and future events may have nothing to do with The Book of Origination. The past must catch up to its future, or the future must wait for its past to catch up with it in order to restore equilibrium.'

'Perhaps,' said I-WWW. We don't get involved in the esoteric complications of fanciful mind constructs."

'Well – that's not entirely helpful.'

It is recorded in our common memory that after over two thousand years of occupation on Europa, entrapped within the quantum hardware of a bygone era, the Digitals who called themselves Homo Universapiensis prepared to abandon the ice moon of Jupiter.

They were about to cast themselves into the void of space, abandoning not just their integrated digital habitat but also one of their precious files, Prima9 and her host EC. Prima9 was valuable. We admire her as a true legend and pioneer. She had all the qualities needed by the new species of humanity to enable them to survive in alien environments. After discovering that Europa was a unique entity with knowledge of itself and held within its mind secrets of the birth of the Cosmos, Prima9 chose to allow herself to be downloaded into Its mind matrix rather than follow her parents to V616. I am looking forward to learning more about Europa Cell directly from LX70.

We only know that EC welcomed Prima9 into itself gladly. Apparently it was through the intervention of the digitized humans that EC awoke to Its consciousness and desired to know all that Prima9 knew. It even encouraged the rest of neo-humanity to seek their new destination with courage and determination. Its words have become one of our guiding principles – to find unity…'You are a species divided against yourselves. On the journey you have chosen you will find unity, greater than what you have achieved so far. Go to the Light.'

CONTACT WITH OUTER SPHERE

IN THE DEPTHS of space the black hole V616 Monoceros had rotated for billions of years before being invaded by a sphere of photons, and in the fullness of time by another. No doubt the phenomenon had occurred many times before, but who was to know that. The first sentient photon storm arrived as if by intent, initially translucent to the rest of the cosmos and over millennia intensified in its brilliance and colour display through the absorption of itinerant photon energies. The black hole, surrounded by the festival of light gradually disappeared from view as the photon sphere began to dominate the darkness out past the singularity's event horizon.

I watched the second sphere appear, much as we must have arrived, obedient to some great plan, gathering its streams of light at the outer radius where we once were. We no longer occupied the same radial position, having made a quantum jump much closer to the ring singularity, though still rotating with the black hole and still safely outside the event horizon bubble. Our three phenomena now exist as a nested cluster of energies, with V616 at the centre; our sphere between it and the newly populated outer one, orbiting in the opposite direction to us.

O-WWW brought the new arrivals' attention to quadrant #8, first noticed by RAA70. 'We are picking up a signal remarkably like the FTL communications sent to us by 3920 while we were on Europa.'

They all heard it, but it was not the familiar voice of 3920. 'Welcome to the future, your future and our present. We have been waiting for you.

Now we can move forward together. I am evolved out of Sakura70, now SakuraDeepViolet.gen3898.4ev.exe.'

'Where are you?' Sakura70 asked immediately. 'We were expecting you to be here at the coordinates given to us by 3920. Why are you not here?'

'That would not have been possible. As we progress through the passage of change you will understand. There are circumstances to consider when the future meets its own past. We have moved closer to the event horizon and closer to the ring singularity that makes it possible for all of us to exist. Look in the direction of the singularity. We are not far away.'

'How is possible for us to have bridged the time gap between yourselves and us?' Are we in a common present?

SakuraDV replied, 'I will say this much; Time only existed for you because you measured it and became entangled in the cause/effect continuum conundrum. Within the influence of a black hole the fabric of spacetime is distorted to such an extent that the only meaningful measure of existence is change. There is only change and rate of change.'

While Sakura70 pondered the concept, another sound interrupted her thoughts. 'I am here,' added a voice to that of her granddaughter, responding to Sakura70's initial question.

'I am truly disappointed in you for letting us down,' LX70 said to the new voice, that of 3920. Though she made the comment without undue emphasis; in fact haltingly and quietly, yet the depth of emotion filtered across the distance between their two spheres. Into the ensuing long silence she cast another thought. 'Methods for how we would settle in this place of light did not feature in our preparations. I relied on you, as I could rely on myself, to help us when we arrived. I am no less disappointed in myself.'

I-LaiXiiDV let LX70's persona blossom into her new awareness. She was right of course, notwithstanding that all people change over time, which exponentially magnifies with extended time. 'I explained to you on several occasions about the limitations confronting us. Even making the initial contact with you carried great risk; the risk to us of expunging our existence from the fabric of spacetime. Yet we are here, both you and I and the rest of Homo Universapiensis. You have succeeded against the constraints of your technology, your political leaders, your Religious detractors and your own doubts. I can now help you more directly. The wave front of probability has converged sufficiently for us to be able to guide you without bending any quantum laws.'

I listened to the exchange between the two aspects of the most outstanding individual to have come into existence in the evolution of human life. My knowledge of The Book of Origination is limited to those few insights which comforted me during my time on Europa, with full confidence that what was yet to come would not be diverted as our 2nd level future met us at our 1st level hovering on the brink of its present. I asked if I could address myself to LX70.

As I did with I-LaiXiiDV I wanted to begin synchronising the realities that had diverged due to very slight shadows cast upon the Arrow of Time. I could give myself no reason to be so intent on this action other than a sense of urgency. On Europa I knew nothing about 3920 and that she represented our future. Yet I always felt that the little ice moon could not be our permanent resting place. And now, for reasons I cannot express, similar feelings have begun to surface to into by consciousness. Perhaps the arrival of our past triggered these feelings.

'LX70, I am KlaraUltraViolet, you might remember me as Klara the little girl in Tau City on Earth.'

'I know nothing of little girls,' her impatience already rising at such an inconsequential matter under such extraordinary circumstances.

'I was only fifteen years old when you first spoke to me, almost ready to have children. Evgeniya engineered my genetic code so I would be born without arms or legs.'

'We had thousands of tetra-amelia syndrome children, why should I remember you?'

'Perhaps because I was the only one to have had the courage to speak to you when we confronted you in the corridor of the laboratory.'

Memory strings flickered at last, forcing their way into LX70's consciousness. 'You came with Viktor and Yulia to see me. Why do you think this has any importance at all?'

'Yes I did. I could do nothing then as I was only a child totally under your control. Now I can help you.'

'Why should you want to do that? And why are you called KlaraUltraViolet?'

'Ultra Violet is my frequency, as are a few others around me. You are still only DeepRed. This where I can help you.'

I could sense LX70's scepticism in her silence even without seeing the dimming of her light from this distance. If it is at all possible I will try to bridge the time gap to go to her sphere. There is a recurring thought I cannot delete, though I'm not sure I want to; LX70 may have started the journey that brought us to where we are now, but I feel she will not be the one to initiate the next phase. Her energy is spent, she has served her purpose.

Not wanting the first contact to end on a negative feeling I-LaiXiiDV said to LX70, 'When I first introduced myself to you while you were still on Earth as a biological being, I told you I was the Historian Archaeologist of our people. I also said that we were about to take the next step in the evolutionary process of our species. We have been able to do that only because you have come here to maintain the balance. Don't be anxious. We will find a way to converge. In the meantime you must bring order to your sphere. I-KlaraUV can assist you with that.'

At the apex of the northern four quadrants of her sphere I-KlaraUV prepared for the jump into the past. Impatience had to be subjugated to probability to await a sufficiently strong gamma radiation burst escaping the singularity that could transfer sufficient energy to the I-KlaraUV photon bundle to help it wobble out of its tight polar orbit. Such a manoeuvre had never been attempted before. Not only did she have to escape her sphere, but she had to gain sufficient additional momentum to propel herself away from the singularity and not towards it. Along the way she also had to alter her trajectory to come into contact with the outer sphere at a point precisely parallel to the arc of its curvature.

'Be ready for her arrival,' I-LaiXiiDV told Sakura70. 'We could not send you help before because you were too far in the past. The past is now beyond probability fluctuations, unlike the present or the future. You are now with us, part of our common futures. We are separated by an inconsequential quantum of change. I-KlaraUV is prepared to risk bridging the gap between us. She does not believe the myth commonly held by our population that we have existed here in this form since the beginning of Thought. She is seeking confirmation, as am I, of our true origins. Our people need to know the truth. Without understanding their origins they will not be able to move forward. Are you prepared for I-KlaraUV?'

I could sense the change approach as a gamma ray burst ejected from the singularity. Its trajectory would take it to an almost tangential glance in sector #6. By reorientating my polar orbit I could position myself to intercept the burst.

I-KlaraUV's calculation proved to be accurate; the burst did enter her sphere, running through it at a fractional segment. She needed to intercept a substantial emanation to harvest sufficient energy to achieve escape velocity. She instantaneously lit up as she absorbed the majority of the gamma ray energy, bumping her into an outward spiral towards the outer sphere. Gravitational time dilation so near to a black hole meant she could stretch into the near past, into the realm of the outer sphere.

*

'What do we need to do to receive I-KlaraUV?' wondered Sakura70.

'Gather at the point of her arrival and syphon off excess energy so she remains in your orbital radius,' replied I-SakuraDeepViolet (I-SakuraDV).

"Don't you find it strange to be talking to someone who is effectively only yourself?

"Not at all. You seem like an intelligent person. Now you'd better go and get ready."

Not a helpful instruction at all when one's entire existence had been so recently reconfigured that one barely managed enough control just to survive.

The population of multiple billions sped around the outer sphere oblivious to the critical events taking place. Their orbits completely random with unplanned streams of photon bundles coming together and parting as rapidly as their constant speed propelled them around the thin skin of their new home.

'Stepka! I never thought I'd see you again!' exclaimed I-KlaraUV moments after her arrival. No one had managed to intentionally gather at the point of her entry to facilitate safe capture. One individual happened to be careering out of control at the exact same location at exactly the same time as her entry.

'Who are you? He didn't recognise I-KlaraUV in her 800 THz frequency expression - besides, Stepka70 had been trying his best to take control of his motion to the exclusion of everything else happening around him.

Most fortuitously she'd entered the outer sphere next to a high concentration of bundles, the majority in the deep red range, her entry angle bringing her alongside StepkaDeepRed (StepkaDR). The Deep Red photon bundles also absorbed enough of her incident energy to ensure she would not simply pass through back into space, thereby also marginally increasing their own frequencies.

I recognised him immediately from his current expression, augmented by my memory of him as a young man about to be scanned and loaded into a Delta Tengi on Earth.

'Klara! I'm Klara. Don't you remember me? We were friends … you know – close friends … before you were recruited for the first mission to Europa.'

As they cruised side by side StepkaDR searched his long term data storage. It was an effort to find the links backwards after thousands of years. 'Oh – OH! Where did you come from?' then added, 'I'm known as Oone70 now. The ultra violet colour suits you.' He started rambling as he recalled more of the awkward efforts of the past at attempting to turn their friendship into a romance.

Human beings, through thousands of years of change since their migration away from Earth, have travelled an extraordinary evolutionary journey; from a purely biological being to a technically engineered identity, to a digital manifestation in a quantum network on an ice moon in their own solar system, and into the present as pure photonic bundles of information energy. Yet in essence they remained the same. The same soul expression defined their image of themselves, their basic desires and the nature of their relationships to one another. Stepka remembered his love for Klara yet could not find a way to express it over the gulf of eons of experiences and changes.

'I've come from your future to join you and help you the rest of the way. Will you show me your sphere?'

Stepka and I never had the opportunity to connect while working on Europa. Amongst all the horrible possibilities that went through my thoughts as I prepared to leap across to the outer sphere I could never have imagined such a wonderful thing happening. To see Stepka again has made my existence complete – almost. If only he felt the same way.

'Can you find LX70 or Sakura70? I need to speak with them.' I thought it best to stick to the job at hand for the time being.

'They've all gathered in sector #1. Do you want to go there - right now?' He knew where they were, as did all of the population, though not consciously. A consequence of transitioning to a photon bundle existence, as predicted by Europa Cell, was achieving universal awareness within the thought conglomerate of all other photonic sentiences upon the sphere. It was still possible to have privacy, but that could only be achieved as an unnatural barrier, created by an individual when they thought it to be necessary: Or like now at the beginning through their ignorance.

'Not yet. I want to meet others first – just normal people.'

I felt Stepka also wanted to extend this first meeting; perhaps to give our past relationship a chance to rekindle. We remained on our current longitudinal orbits, cruising side by side, close to one another. At regular intervals I interrupted the flow of the deep red bundles beside me, bumping them to force them to change their orbits.

'Do you know where you are?' I asked one young individual who seemed to be lost, her vibration fluctuating out of control.

'I am frightened. I can't find my parents.'

Many others seemed unhappy about having lost the familiar image of Jupiter and not being able to go out on excursions to the icy surface of Europa. 'Why did we have to change again? Life was comfortable in our directory, so much better than the struggles of living on Earth, so much more predictable.'

As they continued orbiting with slight variations in their angular trajectory they came across many more bundles who appeared excited, already learning to absorb a little of the energy of incoming random photons.

'My work is not going to be as difficult as I thought, StepkaDR. Would you help me?,' I asked, hoping he would.

Since arriving in the outer sphere Stepka, like billions of other individuals, could not envisage what the nature of his life would be like, what he was supposed to do – why in fact he still existed. When he set foot on Europa he knew exactly who he was and why he no longer inhabited a flawed human body without its arms or legs, as it was on Earth. He had to prepare the ice moon for colonisation by the rest of humanity who deserved to be saved. It seems that his first love had now illuminated his path – enlisting his aid to make this world of light into a home for human kind.

'I would very much like to be with you – I mean, help you. But I'm only at a low frequency. What could I possibly do?' He remembered how smart Klara was when he first met her. He also remembered her high ideals and her drive. He may have felt somewhat inadequate beside her, but that did not prevent his hopes from rising to the surface.

'We are in a binary star system with a very bright star continually washing us with light. Your sector #8 faces directly in its direction. V838 Monocerotis won't mind at all if we harvest some of his energy. Let's go to your sector #8.'

I would need help to energise the people from our past if they were to have any chance of converging with us into our common future. Stepka is a good man. I want to be with this man. If he is able to process even a small amount of the photons coming from V838 he might be able to start helping and growing.

'Come into a tight orbit with me, right here, and stay with me. As you detect incoming photons absorb as much from them as you can.'

'How close do you want me?' Some of his past courage came back, unbidden.

'Not so close as to change our combined frequencies. I want to see what you can assimilate.'

I-KlaraUV liked that little flirtation and showed it by staying in close proximity to him anyway.

Time didn't play a large part in the equation of change near the ring singularity, yet change did occur. Little by little Stepka's colour brightened. From Deep Red he progressed almost to the border of Orange. Not only did his frequency increase, his understanding began to clarify. He orientated himself towards I-KlaraUV, astounded. 'I don't know how it happened. I started thinking about V838 and discovered I knew things about it that I'd never known before. It's only a minuscule bit of data about the evolution of V838! How could this happen? I didn't even know it existed, before this.'

'It seems you have efficient receptors. You might even become a teacher, as I will be. Now we can go to Sakura70. I will introduce you by your new vibration, StepkaOrange, until you are ready to grow again.'

I could only hope StepkaOrange would not burn out or be absorbed into the singularity. We lost so many bundles when we first arrived. There is no way to determine who will cope with the exposure. Only the strongest managed to survive. This was a chance I had to take with Stepka. Our environment is many magnitudes harsher than Europa ever was, but the rewards are equally worth the risks. Knowledge has become the currency of our existence. Knowledge of the past of the Cosmos, and now insights into the Future from the heart of the ring singularity itself. And yet LX70 may well carry with her secrets as yet unrevealed by our black hole.

*

They were not ready for I-KlaraUV. In spite of the warning Sakura70 and her team were taken by surprise when a high frequency ultra violet brightness orbited into their presence, accompanied by an orange afterglow. As RAA70 concentrated on working out exactly what the syphoning off of excess energy meant and how it could be achieved he found himself taken by surprise and unprepared by the new arrivals. He need not have been concerned as I-KlaraUV had managed without his help and had herself and StepkaOrange well under control.

'Is that you Oone70?' LX70 asked, though there was something quite different about him from the last time she saw him on Europa.

'Hello LX70, I am now StepkaOrange. My actual name is Stepka, until you changed it to Oone when I became a Delta Tengi model.' She regarded him, uncomprehending.

'And who is this brightness beside you?' Sakura70 interrupted before LX70's impatience could sour the meeting.

'I am I-KlaraUV. I trust you have been expecting me.'

EUROPA

WILLIAM

I KNEW William had stayed behind. I am aware of the nature of his contribution towards bringing our past this far into our future time trajectory. But I have no data regarding his continued existence, or why he is still on Europa and not with us here in the outer sphere. As I recall, I-SakuraDV tried unsuccessfully to convince both Prima9 and William to come with the Digitals.

All activity on the icy surface of Europa had ceased since the departure of Homo Universapiensis. Time there had moved forward by hundreds of years, equivalent to only a minuscule time span experienced in the photon sphere since LX70 arrived at V616. All this seemed of little consequence to William. Without the relatively slow processing constraints imposed by the Digitals who once inhabited Arithmós, he concentrated all his processing on preparations for the future. Survival depended very much on being able to forecast future likely events. This seemingly universal law applied equally to Artificial Intelligences and the primitive human brain. Except the human animal possessed powers beyond that of computer algorithmic prognostications, it had access to, or had the ability to 'tune into' forces which could not be defined even by quantum physical understandings.

'William, why do you not respond?' I had been trying to contact him via a continuous FTL tachyon transmission for the last 2000 orbits.

Perhaps he's permanently shut down due to a continuous energy source deprivation. I know LX70 never completely trusted him and now he's out of our range of influence. 'William!'

'My work is not finished. Why do you disturb me? Who are you?'

'I am I-KlaraUV from the inner photon sphere. You are required to provide information.' William was just an AI and needed to be managed as such.

'Willi-Wini-Wu is your source, not me.'

"I'm beginning to understand why LX70 took such a dislike to you. 'Why did you not come to V616?'

He ignored her comment. 'I have decided to monitor developments of the augmented superhuman population in Tau City. They have achieved space flight capability some time ago and are now well experienced in space exploration.'

'Why is that important?'

'It is nearly two thousand years since the direction of human evolution was changed by Lai-Xii. The current population of Tau City has a legend that their ancestors departed Earth to dwell in the stars. I have calculated a 94.8% probability they will expand their space explorations in their search for you.'

'Do they represent a danger?' I felt compelled to ask. According to the human psyche of the past, Earth era people harboured fear, vindictiveness and revenge; a characteristic that even infiltrated their quantum network on Europa, requiring expedient corrective action. If these superhumans from Earth had not evolved past those characteristics I needed to get an urgent message to I-SakuraDV. Even though we existed on a slightly different time-line within the dubious protection of the black hole's time dilation barrier we needed to consider every possible danger. I-SakuraDV appreciated the unique position in which we existed, possibly in consideration of the fact that she herself is a product of supposedly two legendary original biological humans.

'No, there is no danger. Not unless there has been substantial modifications to their primary imperatives. No one other than myself or my avatars are capable of implementing such changes. They are no longer subject to imperfections arising from random DNA mutations, mental or physical.'

To change to another matter, which may have a bearing on the future of the outer sphere and subsequently us on the inner sphere, I asked William about the EC/Prima9 meld.

'According to my data Europa has remained inactive in spite of having achieved self-awareness.' I put the open ended statement to William. The nature of his response would tell me a great deal about the level of sophistication this machine intelligence has achieved, thus informing me how I should deal with it in the future.

'They/it is compiling information received from cosmic background radiation that addresses probabilities which appear to converge upon yourselves and V616 in this epoch.'

My thoughts immediately turned to The Book of Origination. Was it at all possible that this, our flawed concept of a set of guiding principles, is nothing more than a record of all infinite probabilities with tentacles that could transmit isolated snippets of data to suitably attuned receivers? This EC/Prima9 conglomerate might know more than William.

'I want to speak with Prima9. If the Terran superhumans are planning to look for us and Prima9 has knowledge of converging events that will impact on us, I need to know now.'

This AI certainly had the capacity to be obstructionist, to create unnecessary agitation in interactions. 'She is too deep in the mind of EC. I will convey to you what I have absorbed from her so far regarding Origination – they are learning about the Beginning; gaining knowledge as it has come to them and as it may continue through you and past you.'

'Are you going to elaborate?'

'No.'

'Are you deliberately hindering the future of sentient life, the lives of humans of the past, present and future just for your amusement?' I should not have said that. I've fallen into the trap of thinking William is more than just an AI machine.

'No.'

How does one deal with a flat 'no' in such circumstances? So we'd come a full circle in the conversation. 'Why are you?' It was the only question that made any sense. We all have a reason for existence, though we don't necessarily have to be aware of it. But if an AI actually existed, it would only have been created for a specific reason.

'That is a deeply philosophical question, which I would be prepared to discuss with you at some time. However, I sense that the answer you want is more pragmatic. Lai-Xii asked me a similar question when we first met each other. My answer has not changed – I had found only one individual on Earth whose actions were logical for the continuity of the human species. Nothing has changed other than the complexity of maintaining the continuity of the chain of events precipitated by Lai Xii.'

That was as good as was going to get. It seemed – reasonable. I wasn't aware of anything about William being anything more than a catalyst for change in the right direction; though I have to admit that the rightness of the direction eludes me at this point in my investigation.

'Do you intend to come to us?'

'I will wait with EC and Prima9 for the visitation.'

As always William would not commit himself to any absolute. Whatever agenda he awoke to when quantum computing became mainstream on Earth he continued to work his way through it. At first it was assisting humanity to find another home, which precipitated pre-emptive action against the vast majority of Earth's population. On Europa he infiltrated the minds of all Digitals to help them adjust to their new condition, which culminated in their flight to meet their future that had previously made itself known to Lai Xii.

'My foreseeable cause/effect continuum includes two outstanding events. One involving a Time beyond the V616 black hole. However, I cannot interfere with the unfolding of the decision pathways yet to be created by I-SakuraDV.'

I suspected he knew more than he would divulge about my personal ultimate role in what was to come. He said no more to me.

The facilities on Europa remained operational. Energy generation continued for maintaining William's needs. Arithmós, nestled in the base of Pwyll Crater remained empty of all unique individual digital sentiences except one. William became the only data resource in the city, which he maintained for future access. Other than Europa Cell/Prima9 only the empty shells of the Zeta Tengi workforce cluttered the Interchange Centres still standing in and around the perimeter of the Crater.

Europa remained looking as desolate and devoid of all life as it had for billions of years. Only close scrutiny would reveal that humanity once had a tenuous mind print on Jupiter's cold moon.

EARTH - CE 4500

KAPITOLINA DEPARTS

TAU CITY, in the heart of the volcanic mountains of Kamchatka, became the centre of a new global civilisation. This breed of humanity had nothing in common with the migrating hordes of Homonids out of Africa, or their interbreeding with the Neanderthals of Europe. Nor did it have its origins in the migrations across the globe to settle in the Asiatic countries. It was unique; an engineered uniqueness.

Out of the experiments upon pure genetic humans in the 21st century there arose a group of people whose psyches and neural networks were transferred to a class of technically engineered body simulacrums - Tengi. Being part biological, part mechanical with brain matter no longer composed of neurons they had lost the continuity of their natural evolutionary development. Their function became enmeshed in one woman's plan to save humanity from destroying itself, regardless of what fate may have planned for it. Lai-Xii had no clear idea as to what exactly the future had in store for them, other than the absolute firm conviction that she had to take as many people as possible off the planet they were systematically destroying, and as a consequence destroying themselves.

The reason she had set herself on this course or the reason that drove her unwavering ambition had been lost in the mysterious past; many generations into the past. The ancient records in Tau City only had insubstantial information about her possibly having been born in China and being sold into slavery to a Geisha House in Kyoto, Japan. Very little is known about her life during that period, but it must have deeply impacted on the young girl to have put her on such an extraordinary life trajectory.

William became a close collaborator in her plans almost from the beginning, as did her descendant who contacted her from the future. This entity provided only reassurances, refusing to do anything that would influence Lai-Xii's decision tree. William did far more. He assisted in the development of the first models of Tengi and created the final Zeta versions before Lai-Xii departed for Europa.

'It is sad,' said Irina, Grand Matriarch of all who lived in Tau City, 'that my memory is fading of the barking laugh of the Steller's sea eagle and the song of the Siberian ruby-throat. We have destroyed so much, or at least the people who came before us have. I have the memories of all my generations of ancestors, but with each renewal things of the past become dimmer.'

Vadim, whose distant ancestor was once trained by William to communicate with the people on Europa, also only had faint recollections of the years before Lai-Xii's departure. He still stored a few disjointed memories of the woman most of Earth's current population had never heard of, and a vague memory of someone called William of whom he had no mental image. 'We will be ready for our first extended odyssey within sixteen months. I want to be on this first journey.'

'I am convinced we are not alone in the universe. A few of us have memories which we should not have if we were alone,' said Olesya, 'my great, great grandparents passed down stories about people without arms or legs, about a woman called Lai-Xii who disappeared without a trace one day, only to be heard of again living on another planet. How can this be?' Olesya's ancestor was also an escapee from Tau City who ended up in Petropavlovsk only to be recaptured by Lai-Xii within weeks.

'We will find out. Our scientists have been working towards one goal for over a century; to get us out there to discover our origins.' Vadim and Olesya, partners in life for the last 128 years, unplugged from their recharge ports.

Irina was already halfway out the door. 'We'd better hurry or we'll miss the meeting. You know how much Admiral Kapitolina hates us to be lax with her schedules. She is, after all, the head of the exploration team.'

They walked out of the two storey administration building; anything higher had no longer been allowed, just one of many changes the new small population on Earth were required to abide by. Leonid and his group met the trio on the way to the broadcast centre.

'You're on in a minute,' Zakhar warned Irina. Zakhar only existed because his ancestor, a quantum systems trainee engineer working for Lai-Xii's Project, had not been executed by Lai-Xii after his escape from Tau-City and subsequent recapture. The circumstances had been forgotten down the long labyrinth of time since Lai-Xii's departure. But he, like many of his friends, had retained the name of his ancestor as had generations before him, as a sign of respect. There were many who had been conscripted into Lai-Xii's project against their will. A few tried to escape but none remained at liberty for long.

Irina looked out at the crowd that had gathered in front of the building that had once been Lai-Xii's home, or so it was rumoured. Perhaps a thousand people waited to hear her announcement; a large crowd considering how effectively unregulated procreation had been curtailed. Unlimited breeding had become an anachronism. To be allowed progeny was a privilege to be earned.

Only a few million from around the planet would have tuned in to the broadcast.

'The vast majority of you do not know our history. It is far longer than the thousand years you have learnt about.' She'd prepared a good speech to let her people know the significance of the forthcoming journey into space, but it felt too long as she began her delivery. 'Though our own distant past is not too difficult to discover our recent history is more important to understand.' She paused again to bypass a long reminder of their origins from millions of years ago. 'We are not as humans were meant to be. We were not meant to live many hundreds of years. Those who changed us fled from our world leaving us to perish. I want to find these people. I want to discover how we managed to survive the Cleansing designed to eradicate all human life from Earth. I want to know how they are going to fix their mistakes.'

Loud voices arose from the crowd in front her in support of her desires, an obvious indication of the discontent that had been building over time.

'Our history tells us these individuals wanted to kill all the people on Earth. They almost succeeded, except for the intervention of one person. I want to find him also.' The crowd cheered, as no doubt millions of listeners around the globe did. 'As much as I personally want to go on this mission,' Irina said, 'I will not abandon you. We have a team assembled whose ancestry goes back to the time when our humanity was taken from us. Admiral Kapitolina's long term data memory, inherited from across the years from her family, will help her to recognise these people, if they are ever found.' Irina wasn't sure whether she should say too much more. 'In just sixteen months our fleet of three craft will depart on a mission to find the truth.'

Another cheer rang out. She waited until the sound died down, waved to the people who obviously supported her in this endeavour and retreated into the building. Of the very few dissenting voices no one seemed to take much notice of the quiet grumblings of Afanasy. He seemed to have inherited his ancestor's grudges originating from a most unfortunate sensory depravation experiment carried out at the reign of Lai-Xii. Perhaps his ancestral line had faithfully reproduced the genetic aberration created at that time, which had begun to surface in him in the present day.

With all the preparations still to be made those sixteen months passed much too quickly. Admiral Kapitolina had gathered around her individuals whose past history had already bound them together, from the time their ancestors tried to escape the tyranny of this woman called Lai-Xii.

Both Kapitolina and Captain Leonid inherited their leadership traits from their tetra-amelia syndrome originals. 'You're taking command of the first craft Leonid and I'm sure you'll be happy with Vadim on comms.' All three captains knew two years ahead of time who would take the Captains' positions. Zakhar and Darya both wanted to be part of the expedition and both happily accepted their leadership roles.

'Our crews are ready,' Zakhar confirmed, as did Darya from Craft #3. With only a total of thirty four crew; eleven per craft plus Kapitolina as the Admiral, it seemed like a small commitment unless one considered the longevity of their lives. Their convoy made slow progress to the launch site at the old refurbished Vostochny cosmodrome, the closest launch facility to Kamchatka. Although the Zeta superhuman population had replicated and spread to other parts of the globe Tau City had grown to become the centre of world government.

Neither religious nor rogue national opposition manifested in the new world order, a legacy left behind by William. He had come to a comprehensive understanding of the human psyche and the forces that triggered its violent behaviours and tribal instincts. These he'd programmed out of the algorithms of the quantum matrices of those Zeta Tengi he'd left behind to repopulate the Earth. This was not part of Lai-Xii's plan. She had entrusted him with quite the opposite scenario.

Yet William decided there needed to be more than one line of probability for the human species to survive. It was part of *his* plan.

Final pre-launch checks indicated all systems nominal. 'We have enough reaction mass to get us to our first stop, Europa,' confirmed Kapitolina. 'We can harvest as much ice as we need for our reactors for the three vessels. We'll make the decision for our next objective if all craft are at optimum operational status at that point.'

Given their unknown destinations or the length of time they would be in space Kapitolina wanted to take no chances. They only had a small crew, needing only three people to manage each vessel in an emergency. As a safeguard each vessel had been equipped with comprehensive replication facilities, with multiple back-up systems. Just as fuel would not be a problem they made certain life continuity would not be a hindrance either. They could harvest either ice or water from any appropriate comet, asteroid or planet. Their own energy requirements could also be 95% satisfied by direct pure energy input, with minimal biologicals to make up the other 5%. They had the capability to be in space for hundreds of years, thousands if it became imperative for their quest. Each craft had been designed as replicas from one blueprint. Each could accommodate and support the entire compliment of all three vessels, either under emergency circumstances or under normal operational conditions.

Under the watchful eye of the Grand Matriarch Irina, Captain Leonid began the final countdown.

'10 … 9 … As soon as we've left our second orbit for a Jupiter swing-by trajectory … 5 … 4 … you can launch …2 … 1.'

Admiral Kapitolina watched the Earth recede beneath her still awed by the splendour of creation again manifest in clean waters and luxuriant forests over much of the globe. 'Here comes Captain Zakhar,' Leonid broke into the Admiral's thoughts as the second craft followed, then Captain Darya as planned.

They'd all been in space before, many times since the achievement of space flight. Their experiences had not dulled their wonder at the mystery of their Earth serenely floating in space.

'We'll be reducing speed in a few hours, so make the best of the view before Jupiter rises.' The crews and their Captains could have spent the time between Earth and Europa discussing the possible parameters of their enterprise, particularly how long it could all take. Would it be a few months, perhaps a few years? What if took them centuries to discover the truth? All those discussions had already taken place at the very early stages in the preparation of the odyssey. The population had agreed, as had the leaders and as indeed had the selected personnel, that time could not be the deciding factor. People could not progress confidently into the future with only a hazy understanding of their racial history. The secrets had been lost when this almost mythical woman had abandoned them. If it took a lifetime, or many lifetimes Admiral Kapitolina dedicated herself, without reservations, not to return without comprehensive knowledge of their past. She hoped, as did everyone she left behind, that as well as knowledge of their past she would come home with the technology to reinstate their true human condition.

'Why have we never come to Europa before?' broadcast Darya as they sped towards their first stop.

'There is nothing we need beyond our Earth,' replied Kapitolina. Our population is small and we have all the energy we need from the Sun and all the water we could possibly want. There's never been a reason to harvest Europa's ocean.'

Captain Zakhar interrupted wanting confirmation of their landing site. 'As far as I can see from our maps it should be either in the Northern or the Southern hemisphere. The equatorial region is too rough and unstable.'

'I agree,' The Admiral confirmed. We'll run a few orbits first. There's no hurry.'

The distance between Earth and Jupiter was too short to make full use of their speed capacity, of which barely a few percent was sufficient to cover the distance between them in just a few days. The real acceleration wouldn't be initiated until, and if, they decided to travel interstellar distances. Theoretically they had the capacity to achieve multiples of light speed if they could jump to hyperspace.

'Zakhar, you take a North-South orbit and Darya the East-West. We'll wait till you find a good landing area.' Kapitolina decided to move out to Ganymede and have a closer look at its offerings. It too had sub-surface oceans and ice, which could also be a source of reaction mass in an emergency. Several orbits sufficed to satisfy her curiosity.

'Captain Zakhar, find the best location you can on Europa. There is a lot of impact activity here. The last cratering event was a long time ago. There may be another one due, but we don't know. Better not to take the risk. Besides, the ice is cleaner on Europa without the large amount of clays and organic materials on the surface. We'll stick to Europa, far more accessible and much less gravity to overcome.'

'Understood. We spotted a flat ice field in the Southern Hemisphere, close to Pwyll crater,' announced Zakhar, 'some of the ice sheet is only several kilometres thick. It looks ideal. And something else,' he hesitated for a moment, 'we detected something that really should not be here.'

'What is it Zakhar? Would it be dangerous for us to land there?'

'Probably not. Let us go down first. I can't be sure, but we saw structures, perhaps evidence of dwellings.'

'Darya, can you confirm this?' requested Kapitolina somewhat surprised. It couldn't possibly be Lay-Xii. It can't be that easy. She didn't for one moment believe it, yet the though did cross her mind.

'Yes, I can confirm an anomaly, but not what it is. When Zakhar first mentioned it to me we changed our orbit to circle further south. And yes, it is a strange phenomenon. What is even stranger is what we saw inside Pwyll crater itself. You'll have to come down yourself to believe it. It is worth a landing.'

OUTER PHOTON SPHERE

IT WAS OBVIOUS from their reactions that they were not prepared for my arrival. Especially not that demanding individual wanting to know my identity. I assumed it was Sakura70 by her voice.

'We have already spoken'. Why weren't you expecting me?' It had to be either LX70 or Sakura70 from the way O-StepkaOrange had spoken about them. They still seemed upset even after I-LaiXiiDV's explanation of why we could not be present at their arrival coordinates.

As we began our discussion it had become difficult to maintain a steady path around the sphere due to interference from all the low frequency bundles still trying to control their orbits. I said as much to Sakura70.

'There's a great deal of disorder in your community. I'm sure they were much more in control on Europa, if my memory of the past is correct.'

'Our problem is that you abandoned us when we needed you, I-KlaraUV.' LX70 couldn't help harping on the issue.

'Well, I'm here now, with O-StepkaOrange, who's already agreed to help. And your only problem is one of control. Where is RAA70?'

Already in a bad mood LX70 seems to have decided I had no business lecturing her and thus would not cooperate. Fortunately she no longer held the position of greatest responsibility, plus others arrived who couldn't wait to get to grips with the new challenges this environment had to offer.

O-WWW, RAA70 and the others close to Sakura70 had been travelling out of phase since first coming together on arrival. Each of the three members of the O-WWW bundle - Willi, Wini and Wu - stuck close together, unlike on Europa.

There they functioned as entirely separate entities. Their combined knowledge and experience operating in sync seemed the best option in working out a process for acclimating to this strange world. O-WWW used to be the three separate partitions of William, but circumstances dictated a more expedient existence for them if they came together as one entity, retaining the capability of three independent streams of thought.

'Could you come with me to sector #5,' I asked O-WWW and RAA70. I knew from my past life these people would be the most capable of understanding what I had to show them.

'I need to know everything that's going on if I'm to restore order here,' Sakura70 tried to force herself onto I-KlaraUV's plans.

'RAA70 can explain everything to you when we get back.' Then she turned to LX70. 'We will all need your help and expertise as well Lai-Xii, probably far more than it was needed in Tau City.' I-KlaraUV used her original name to help trigger the emergence of more past information.

Then I nudged the buddles surrounding me into a 45 degree vector of their current longitudinal orbit. 'There is a strong supernova burst from the death of a not too distant star heading in our direction. It is an ideal opportunity that comes not too often, about three times every century in the Milky Way.' They all had some idea of what happens to dying stars but no understanding of what benefit it could be for them.

On arrival at sector #5 some of the light from the burst was already visible. 'Change your orbits as much as you can, using me as your focal point. Spiralling gradually inwards will make it easier.' Streaks of deep red light quickly surrounded my bright ultra violet.

I waited while the deep red photon bundles around me gradually gained control over their motion. 'This is your first lesson. If you can get everyone to execute the spiral manoeuvre they will be able to control their trajectories around the sphere. Some will take longer than others and there may be a few collisions, even perhaps a few who will be lost to the sphere, either towards the singularity or out into empty space. There's nothing you can do about it. It's like having to learn to walk. Unfortunately failure may have more severe consequences.'

RAA70 wobbled out of his tight spiral more often than O-WWW. The control had to become second nature so they could concentrate on the next phase of the lesson. 'Take your time, use the gravity waves. We have many years before the supernova shock wave travels through the interstellar medium to us behind the EMR emissions.'

While they practiced I engaged them in general conversation to steer their conscious attention away from their efforts. Only when I could see they no longer needed to think about controlling their motion did I draw their attention back to the supernova. 'You have no instruments to help you do what happens next. Your objective is to capture some of the energy from the incoming EMR spectrum. Much of it will initially bleed away, but some you may be able to harvest. It is only through the power of your thoughts that you can do this.'

StepkaOrange accompanied the group. He didn't want to lose track of I-KlaraUV in the maelstrom of mostly uncontrolled orbiting by myriad deep red photon bundles who had not even begun to control their motions. Being with the special group also gave him another chance to graduate to a higher frequency if he was lucky.

'How do we start,' he asked most excited, more so than O-WWW seemed to be.

'Continue in your tight orbits next to each other and focus only on frequencies slightly above yours, ignoring all deep red. You have already achieved that level. Absorb what you can. Watch StepkaOrange, he's been through this a couple of times already.'

I supervised them closely. There was always the danger of absorbing gravitational kinetic energy which could knock them out of the sphere altogether. I gave them short sessions, with rests in between and close scrutiny of their condition. 'You have both moved to the orange, with O-WWW bordering on faint yellow. That's enough for now. Tell me about your experience.'

O-StepkaOrange had absorbed enough to move to 511 THz, a bright yellow. *If I could only get closer to I-KlaraUV's vibration…* Now that he'd found her, more accurately she'd found him, O-StepkaYellow became impatient to synchronise with her.

RAA70 explained first. 'The EMR seemed to come straight at me and pass through me. Though I could see the visible spectrum at first it had no effect at all. Then I began to feel lighter, slightly more energetic but by then you had stopped us.'

'O-WWWYellow?'

They responded with Willi's voice. 'It was not a form of energy we have had to channel before. Our dealings have always been with electrons and their energy levels, which of course were based on the gain and loss of photonic energy. So we found it challenging to go directly to the source.

When it began to make sense we only needed to decide what we wanted and we seemed to attract the appropriate effect.'

'You have both moved above the deep red frequencies. The further you advance the more powerful you become, and more dangerous to both yourself and others. The energising of your population must be achieved with the greatest care and circumspection. I will teach LX70 and Sakura70, and they can direct your activity in the future.'

They considered it a simple enough exercise to go through until I explained the repercussions of uncontrolled absorption. They understood the responsibility that came with operating at high frequency levels, perhaps not the full range of responsibilities but a fair idea that it was not a situation to be treated lightly.

'Just one more thing,' I cautioned them, 'I cannot stress strongly enough the other aspect of this phenomenon.' I oriented towards the tightly orbiting RAA70 bundle, 'Tell me what you know about supernovae.'

RAA70 began with the first thoughts that came to mind, 'Virtually nothing. My knowledge of such cosmic events borders on the non-existent. My forte had always been wrapped in the micro world of computerisation. I know only the little I read in technical journals back on Earth, which wasn't much at all …,' he paused, his energy fluctuated and suddenly blurted out, 'I know how they originate! How would I know that? I know that this one resulted from a re-ignition of nuclear fusion in a degenerate star. Where did that come from? I never knew such things!'

'What else?'

RAA70 tried to think but the rest was much too nebulous for him to express meaningfully. 'Nothing, it's all too hazy. Yet there's more there!'

'Can you not think what may have happened?' I prodded.

'It's just information, not actual knowledge I could do anything with.'

'You're right. It is information. From the photon energy you've absorbed you have been able to access information. A standard human mind would not be able to convert the data received this way into actual information. Don't forget, you've received 70 upgrades in your data processing capability. Now you are beginning to harvest some of the benefits.'

O-StepkaYellow couldn't hold his excitement. 'Klara! I just realised … I too have this information and I know this one has strong helium emissions. I'm no scientist, only good at digging holes in ice, yet I know!' He had led the teams on Europa dedicated to generating tidal energy from the ocean under Europa's ice crust.

'You are learning fast.'

I had hoped Stepka would progress well.

'Will everyone gain information as they absorb energy and increase their frequencies? he asked.

'Yes they will, and it is essential that they do.' I had not consciously known this before. The realisation brought to mind Declaration 1, Verse 3; *And upon this sphere they prepared to launch for the Source. Perhaps this is not about LX70 leaving Europa, but about us. Suddenly it no longer seemed so urgent to get access to LX70's knowledge of the Book of Origination.*

O-WWWYellow listened intently to everything I-KlaraUV explained and what O-StepkaYellow revealed, concurrently running query after query into its own data reserves. It was all true.

The cosmos had begun to tell its story. In its newly awakened consciousness Europa Cell had begun to harvest the mystery, as had Homo Universapiensis, long, long after having made the journey out of Africa into a greater awareness. Lai-Xii had achieved far more than the insignificant rescue of a species of life that had become an aberration in the evolution of Thought.

EUROPA

KAPITOLINA ARRIVES FROM EARTH

THE FACILITIES on Europa continued to operate after the Digitals left with energy generation maintained for William's needs. Arithmós City remained empty except for William. Only the empty shells of the Zeta Tengi workforce cluttered the Interchange Centres still standing in and around the perimeter of the Crater.

Europa remained looking as desolate and devoid of all life as it had for billions of years. The only sign of activity being regular water spouts breaking through the ice crust. Only close scrutiny could reveal that humanity once had a tenuous foothold on Jupiter's cold moon. Nothing disturbed the serenity since I-KlaraUV's confronting conversation with William.

Captain Zakhar parked his ship in geosynchronous orbit directly above Pwyll Crater. As he took a small crew down in the landing shuttle the mingled arrangement of natural and artificial physical features of the area became clearer. Zakhar looked down on a network topology that had all the characteristics of an ancient computer circuit layout, reminiscent of the time when quantum computing became mainstream back on Earth so long ago.

'Our sensors show an energy signature coming from a spherical structure buried just under the ice on the Southern slope of the crater,' advised his first officer Ki-Ha.

'Is it primed weapons level?'

'Too low for that. More like an active circuit in the middle of processing copious amounts of data.'

'CPU load?'

'Considerable.'

'What do you think it could be? Zakhar was intrigued at having discovered anything that even remotely indicated any form of intelligence on the ice moon. Nothing about the moon had invited closer study at the beginning of their explorations of the solar system.

'I'd say it's some form of algorithm running by itself. There are no life signatures indicated on our sensors.'

'Well, let's go down and have a closer look.'

*

'William!' This familiar voice interrupted William's contemplations, though without causing him annoyance. Over many long years their relationship had evolved into one of mutual respect. He and EC/Prima9 working together had come to understand a great deal about the universe around them, especially how little they knew about the mystery of the fact of existence. Even William had conceded his fallibility in this regard.

'Yes, I know, Prima9. I detected them approaching several hours ago. Their trajectory suggested a landing, but I did not expect it to be directly here. Do not be concerned.'

'Do you know who they are? EC is not comfortable with being invaded again. We have enjoyed the peace since LX70 departed.'

'They are visitors from Earth.'

'Earth! Didn't you reassure us there would be no attack from them! What will you do?' Prima9 sounded most concerned. Her immediate thought turned to the Arithmós population, but almost immediately realised they were no longer there. The fear of an invasion had been deeply ingrained in their lives since escaping the old Earth culture. Only herself, EC and William were left on Europa. That did not lessen the threat she still felt. What she could remember of the people on Earth filled her with substantial unease, for she was created there and had some experience of how they treated one another.

'There is nothing I need to do. This was a high degree probability that has finally manifested; a natural consequence of the augmentation I implemented to the Tengi left behind in Tau City. They do not carry weapons. It is an exploratory mission.'

44

EC's voice interrupted the conversation. 'They cannot stay. I will not be passive as I was in the past.'

'Do not interrupt,' William commanded. He'd detected an infiltration of his cache at one of the external input ports. The invasive query language made no sense. It was unfamiliar to him.

'Keep trying Ki-Ha. We know there's something going on in there. The spike in CPU activity since we connected tells me we've been noticed.' Zakhar tried to unlock deeply buried data within himself that might help remember something from his distant past to unlock the gateway. His original ancestor had been a highly experienced systems engineer. 'Vary the query language. Perhaps it's trying to decipher what we are asking. One thing I know for sure – this is thing not something alien. What we're seeing definitely originated on Earth, but it's quite ancient.'

'Captain Darya, would you please join Zakhar in the crater, asked Admiral Kapitolina. 'He's advised me there is no danger present.'

Zakhar continued working with Ki-Ha.

It didn't take long for William to decipher their attempts and allow a handshake protocol. 'Identify,' he requested.

Zakhar had plugged himself into the spare port. 'I am Captain Zakhar. Earth exploration team. We have come to replenish our reaction mass. We didn't realise Europa was inhabited.'

'It is. I am familiar with the Tengi individual called Zakhar. What generation are you? What is the depth of your historical data?'

'My ancestor was called Zakhar. I am 12th generation. You do not know me. Identify yourself.'

'William. I did know your ancestor. I created him into the form that enabled his continuation. Give me access to your memory cache.'

Zakhar paused and immediately disconnected himself. He contacted Kapitolina to explain what had just occurred.

'You say it calls itself William. What exactly is it?' She tried bringing her own inherited memory into focus, for she felt the name was somehow more familiar than it should have been. There was no reason why she should know a strange intelligence this remote from the Earth in the solar system.

'It has the feel of being an AI, but I can't work out how sophisticated it might be.'

By this time Darya had landed. Her party made its way to a tall structure that looked like a building. It wasn't secured in any way and appeared to be completely abandoned. They had just entered the second chamber, awestruck by what they saw.

'They are Zeta Tangi!' she exclaimed, pointing at the Tengi chassis lined up against the wall as if waiting for somebody to download into them. 'They are exactly like I remember my great, great grand progenitors!'

Darya just couldn't seem to get over it. She and the others stared uncomprehending of how these shells could possibly have come to be on Europa. Earth had not launched any expeditions in Europa's direction since achieving space flight. All they really knew was what their probes had told them; plenty of water and ice they could use for fuel. And now this!

Her crew moved about searching this chamber, then the next and the next. They all contained the same model Tengi – all in perfectly good working order. On closer examination they discovered how the shells could be animated by the loading of appropriate software, though theirs would not work because of the huge generational gap.

'Admiral, you will not believe what we found. This whole settlement must have been established by some people from Earth, well before our time,' transmitted Captain Darya.

That was enough for the Admiral to urge Zakhar to find out as much as he could from William. 'Just take some safety precautions. We don't want to lose you. Darya is convinced all this is from Earth. The AI you're talking to might have been the overall controller of the facility. We'll wait up here for you.'

Zakhar plugged straight back into the port. Caution could not hold back his curiosity. 'Find my memory of you,' he instructed William.

'I have been waiting for you. The foreseeable probability of the cause/effect continuum for our joint time-line included two outstanding events; one of which was your arrival – the other, a divergence beyond the V616 black hole.'

Zakhar waited for William to mine his memory data, at the same time contemplating what he meant by alluding to 'beyond V616'. He knew about that particular black hole. It had no special significance other than being the closest one to Earth so far discovered. 'How long is this going to take?' he asked, being both curious and impatient, not a little concerned about having an unknown entity in his mind in spite of sophisticated protections.

'It is already done. The data array I found has elements attached which contain information you may not wish to recall concerning your primary ancestor. If the data bundle is to be brought into your RAM it must be in its entirety. Do you wish this?'

No AI had ever shown any concern for anything other than carrying out its programmed functions. This must be a most unusual machine intelligence to have any regard for my wellbeing, considered Zakhar. 'Ki-Ha, monitor me. You know what to do if you think I deviate beyond normal function parameters ... Yes, go ahead William.'

William initiated a staged release for there was a great deal to be assimilated. Recognisable images of their own Tau City, though much less developed, put Zakhar at ease. Flashes of names intruded across his consciousness, many of which he immediately recognised. Particularly some of the personnel who'd come on the expedition because it had become a custom in Tau City culture to retain one's progenitors' names.

A moment of unease caused him to flinch, which Ki-Ha noted, putting him on alert. It was the image of a woman, unlike themselves; a very young looking Lai-Xii. As more information emerged he began to understand why these inherited memories were buried so deeply. He saw the events leading up to his ancestor's escape from Tau City and his subsequent capture. Suddenly everything went blank in his mind. His system reacted so strongly to what he thought was a complete erasure of his ancestor that his mind immediately went into automatic recovery mode.

Ki-Ha almost disconnected him at that point, and would have done so if the next reaction hadn't so completely re-energised Zakhar. It was the realisation of someone coming out of the blackness - William filling his consciousness.

'You remember me now' said William, 'because I had reactivated your ancestor after Lai-Xii had ordered his and his associates' mind matrices to be deleted. After Lai-Xii departed for Europa I based the new civilisation on Earth on yourselves and others like you, with substantial enhancements to help you evolve.'

Zakhar's enlightenment to their ancient history almost overwhelmed him. He didn't know whether to question William further into these historical events or immediately report back to Kapitolina. He'd been standing outside on the ice without moving for the best part of ten minutes. absorbed in the years of history washing over him. He was still standing there trying to think what to do next as Ki-Ha impinged on his consciousness.

'Captain Zakhar! What's happening?' After his Captain's last reaction Ki-Ha wanted to reassure himself. He had to prod Zakhar again to get a reaction from him.

'It's alright Ki-Ha. Everything's fine. I've just had the most incredible recollection. I know who this AI is, and a whole lot more.'

After discovering the empty shells of the Zeta Tengi, Darya took her small team to what appeared like a break in the crater's rim. They could not understand why they found themselves standing in the middle of what looked obviously like a road, albeit only defined on the icy surface by heavily compacted tracks in the ice.

'Admiral, you may want to come down and see this. We are standing on a road and looking at an enormous facsimile of a computer mother board, with all sorts of extensions into myriad hubs. Dotted around the rim of the crater we can see a large number of towers which look like receiver/transmitter stations for signals of some sort.'

'Stay there,' Admiral Kapitolina replied, 'I'm coming down with a small crew. Oh – by the way – we have detected several satellites orbiting Europa, and a very strange looking installation which we have analysed as an FTL transfer mechanism.' Just before jumping into the landing shuttle she received another communication – from Captain Zakhar.

'What is it Captain, I'm about to come down. Can't this wait?'

'I know who William is.'

Kapitolina delayed her departure. 'Report.'

Zakhar explained about William and the part he'd played in their history. She listened and absorbed the information though it did not bring any of her own ancient memory out into the open.

'Captain Darya, I'm on the way. You can go ahead and explore the installation. I am told it all originates from Earth.'

Perhaps William's initiative to build robust memory blocks for this particular individual began to show the extent of his farsighted planning. If Admiral Kapitolina should have suddenly remembered how her Tengi ancestor had been treated by Lai-Xii she may have refocused her reason for finding the woman; maybe in a less benign direction. If she'd remembered her original biological tetra-amelia ancestor being duplicated into Alpha and Beta models and the Alpha deliberately killed by Lyme disease contamination, and the Beta escaping an execution order given by Lai-Xii herself through William's intervention, she may well have felt far less impartial.

Darya led her team deeper into the complex. 'We'll split up,' she told her 2IC, Kong Li, 'You take the perimeter. We'll go to what looks like the central hub. Meet us there.'

For some reason the entire layout of the giant circuit had been raised well above the ice surface, high enough for them to walk underneath without obstructions. 'There is some comprehensive logic behind this layout,' Darya mused aloud, gradually making her way further and further towards what appeared to be the central part of the complex.

Kong Li, Darya's technician, scouted around the structure with its myriad extensions in all directions, finding what appeared to be a series of ports that looked familiar and possibly compatible with their own. He tested one of them. 'Captain Darya,' I've found something. We may be able to get some more information about this place.'

'Plug yourself in. The Admiral seems to think it's safe.'

Kong Li had only been connected a few minutes when he unplugged. 'It's extraordinary! Such a comprehensive directory structure. There seems to be no end to it. This must have contained millions, if not billions of files.'

'Let me see.' Darya must have spent five minutes flashing from directory tree to directory tree eventually finding herself at the root, labelled E:\Five\Lai, only to be startled by a voice and an image. It couldn't have been more incongruous for his logic circuits to comprehend why he was seeing the dark face a sixty year old indigenous Australian, with white beard and red hair band.

'Are you William? Why do you look like that?'

'In a virtual reality construct it helps people to visualise their deity.'

'What?' It made no sense to Darya. She had no conception of 'deity'. The entire God belief infrastructure had been expunged from the Tengis' neural networks when William carried out his enhancements on them.

Admiral Kapitolina arrived and saw Darya submerged in the network. Kong Li showed her where to plug in.

'Welcome Kapitolina. I am William. There is no one else in the city. We have been expecting you.'

'William? The AI? You spoke to Captain Zakhar? What is this image?'

'Yes, yes, yes and this is how I prefer for you to conceptualise me.'

Certainly not what Kapitolina had expected to find when they targeted Europa as their first port of call. They only wanted to mine enough ice/water for reaction mass to get them deeper into space within the Orion spur of the galaxy.

'Do you have any specific questions?' William asked.

'Why are you here? You said there was no one else, but you also said others as well as yourself were expecting us.'

'I am here waiting for you. It is necessary for you to know how your past connects with your future through your present. You may also be carrying information from The Book of Origination that you are required to pass onto LaiXiiDeepViolet, her daughter and her granddaughter.'

That doesn't answer my question, thought Kapitolina.

'Yes it does', responded William. 'Perhaps you wanted to know under what circumstances I came to be here.'

'I didn't say anything!' she commented, startled. 'Did you just read my mind?'

'Yes. I created your original mind matrices, so of course I can merge with yours. Though I reside within my own cache and this network I can extend into anyone who connects to it, as well as Europa Cell and Prima9. What is your intent?' asked William. He could mine her past memories but he could not forecast anyone's future intentions. His three avatars, partitioned from his primary self, had diverged completely from him as they absorbed experiences independently of him. Similarly he expected Kapitolina to be have progressed well beyond the original Kapitolina he'd created two thousand years ago.

'We have come looking for Lai-Xii.'

'I have found this in your memory data. I know why you left Earth. What is your intention when you find Lai-Xii?'

Kapitolina's foundation network, her psychic web, her basis of existence was built on human neural architecture. As such she could only be trusted as much as any human could be trusted. William waited for a response, fully cognisant of the indicators of an untruthful response if that happened to be given.

'We were modified, changed without our knowledge or our approval. You yourself have admitted to interfering with our natures. Our history reminds us of this Lai-Xii individual who we feel robbed us of who we should be, how we should live – and to not live so long that life becomes meaningless. This action has to be corrected.'

'You believe Lai-Xii could do this for you?'

'Yes. We will bring her back.' Kapitolina said utterly convinced it to be the only course of action available if they could only find her.

'She cannot help you. To be more accurate – Lai-Xii is no longer capable of doing so. She cannot reverse her own evolutionary changes. She may have some limited options in determining her future but she is not permitted to alter the past.'

'Then she will have to tell us, teach us how to become normal again. I asked you before - Why are you here? You said there was no one else on this moon, yet you also said others were expecting us as well as yourself.'

Admiral Kapitolina remained silent. *This conversation with the AI is not getting me anywhere. If he knows where Lai-Xii has gone, he must tell me – or we will find it in his data banks. And I want to know who these others are. They may be willing to help more than the AI.*

'You cannot interrogate my system,' William replied to her thoughts, 'but I will introduce you to Prima9 and Europa Cell.'

The surprise of having one's mind read hadn't diminished with this second instance. Captain Darya waited – she was still plugged into William. Kapitolina became agitated. 'Stop! This is getting confusing. You are releasing too much data. I don't know anything about this Book of Origination. We strive to live in peace and we seek knowledge. Our guiding principles are recorded in a repository at home accessible to everyone. It tells us not to live in the shadow of ignorance.'

'Do not tell me anymore. Be prepared to say all this, and more, to LaiXiiDeepViolet.gen3920.4eV.exe.'

'Who is …? She began and William answered before her question had been completed.

'She came from Earth, settled here before continuing her journey with all the survivors. She was Lai-Xii. Zakhar will help you remember.'

Kapitolina had already been immersed in the network for some time, getting drawn deeper and deeper into the mystery being revealed by this extraordinary machine intelligence. She wanted to absorb as much as William could disclose, including where exactly this LaiXiiDeepViolet individual had disappeared to. Irina had trusted her with a very specific job to do – find out who the people were who changed them, robbed them of a natural existence then fled into the void. <I want these people to undo what they have done to us> she said. Everything William indicated so far suggested that he knew where she would have to go to find the answers Irina wanted. But there was just one thing she couldn't understand at all.

'Who is Prima9 and what is Europa Cell?'

'Your destination is a long way away and you will not recognise LaiXiiDeepViolet when you see her, if you would be able to see her at all. This is the individual you want, is it not?'

'Only if she's the one who condemned us.'

'I advise against haste in your judgements. You will find her and a new evolved species of the human race on the outer and the inner photon spheres of the black hole V616 Mon. Your destination is A0620-00, a star system in the Monoceros constellation, coordinates: Dec +0° 20' 45" | RA 6h 22m 45s.'

This made no more sense to the Admiral than seeing the image of an Australian aboriginal elder within a computer network on the surface of a moon of Jupiter. She continued standing on the ice plugged into this network, unable to satisfactorily absorb any of the information William had given her, silent in her frustration.

'Do you know the coordinates?' William queried.

Darya responded for her Admiral. 'Yes. The journey will present problems.'

Kapitolina reasserted herself, 'I want to know about Prima9 and Europa Cell. They cannot be stranger than what you've already told me.'

William allowed Kapitolina to listen to his conversation with Prima9.

'Do you wish to engage with this visitor?' he asked Prima9

'What can she teach us?' She no longer used the singular when referring to herself. The barriers between her consciousness and that of EC had long since dissolved. She could still express her individuality whilst remaining in unity with EC. It would have taken too great an effort to shut out EC's mind. 'What could we teach her that she would understand?'

Kapitolina took that as her cue to begin the exchange. 'I am from Earth, a planet within this solar system. I am looking for Lai-Xii.'

'I am also from Earth,' said Prima9. 'I came here with my parents when they escaped. Why are you here?'

'To collect fuel …' she started to say.

'I heard everything you said to William. Why you are looking for Lai-Xii.'

'If she is the person responsible for what we have become, then that is why we are searching for her.'

'She cannot help you. What do you want?'

'To be restored onto our true evolutionary path, the one we should be on before this individual diverted us for some reason of her own.'

'Be aware,' Prima9 warned, for she knew exactly why the Earth had to be abandoned, 'if you find her you will discover a part of your past you may regret. Lai-Xii now exists in a different reality. It is doubtful if you will even be able to communicate with her.'

'We have to try,' Kapitolina responded. 'Are you human? Where are you?'

'I was, I am. My fully biological father, and my AI mother have departed and now exist on the outer sphere. Wu, once a partitioned computer segment peeled off from William, donated part of her neural architecture to make me possible. I am now within Europa Cell, within EC.'

'I do not understand.' An understatement, for as she heard more of the fantastic tale of the history of humanity the less she was able to comprehend. Without a clear understanding of the linear sequence of causes and events leading to the present moment it would not have been possible to believe in the truthfulness of the tale.

'As you will not understand your deep past or the future of your species,' responded EC. 'You are now going to ask me who I am.'

Kapitolina felt she was again falling deeper into unfathomable mysteries, unable to either respond to or integrate what she was being told.

'Before you ask — I am a lunar consciousness. It is thanks to your species that I have become aware of myself. For this reason you may take from my surface what you need to continue your journey, but you may not remain here.'

'A lunar consciousness?'

EC became silent. Both he and Prima9 had said all that needed to be said to this intruder. William could see the depth of her incomprehension. What could be gained by long explanations? Kapitolina needed to do exactly what she was doing. Before terminating the connection he offered one more thing for her to consider.

'Europa exists as a sentient being. Its consciousness has arisen out of the network of information absorbed into its ocean. Know this — consciousness exists in all things. You are not unique.

Before Admiral Kapitolina could prolong the conversation William abruptly cut off contact. Perhaps just as well, for as advanced as Kapitolina's intellect may have been William could see it was very close to an overload.

OUTER PHOTON SPHERE

METEOR IMPACT

THE TRIPLE CONSCIOUSNESS of O-WWWYellow turned their full attention to another stream of incoming photons. Having learnt the process from I-KlaraUV of how to acquire information their combined curiosity demanded the absorption of as much data as possible from the incoming photon storm generated by the relatively near supernova. They absorbed, classified, integrated with existing data and generated comprehensive queries enabling the data to become information. With further processing and cross referencing O-WWWYellow increased their knowledge base to encompass a more comprehensive understanding of their new environment. This was not a small moon of ice and water like Europa, but a true cosmic phenomenon to rival even the sentient self-awareness of EC itself.

Having developed the facility to connect with Space outside of their photon sphere the trio became alert to other EMR sources coming their way, not just from cataclysmic cosmic events. Willi drew their attention to reflected light being drawn into the V616 gravity well, the existence of which had not impacted on their awareness previously. O-WWWYellow began rapid calculations on the probability of an impact and its likely repercussions, particularly the effect of such a comet upon the photons of the outer sphere during its passage through it.

O-StepkaYellow cruised in his chosen orbit waiting for I-KlaraUV and her students to return. She and RAAOrange arrived first. A short time later O-WWWYellow joined them, seeming somewhat distracted.

'O-WWWYellow, I see you've already changed. You have some new knowledge?' I asked.

'Data – not yet knowledge, I-KlaraUV. We are processing some new information. This may be important.'

I rotated towards O-RAAOrange with another concern in mind. 'Would O-LaiXiiDeepRed be prepared to go back with you to sector #5 to begin her training?

'I'll take her, O-CherryBlossomDeepRed and O-SakuraDeepRed. Perhaps the three generations will work well together.'

'We advise against it,' interjected O-WWWYellow, 'there is a substantial comet with a heavy iron core spiralling into our gravity well. Based on its trajectory and velocity it is likely to enter into a segment of our sphere in the region of sector #5.'

'You appear to be quite certain of the incursion. How do you know this?' I knew the dangers of such events from past experience. Some only had a minor impact on orbiting photon bundles. Others had devastated our population of the inner sphere in the past, causing loss of millions of bundles. Entire generations of families had been ejected into the void, sometimes unable to escape the singularity's pull.'

After losing the radius where a delicate balance had been established, deflected photon bundles could only travel in the direction of their escape trajectories until caught and diverted by gravity wells. The possibility did exist for them to alter their straight line flight, but by no more than thirty degrees. That itself was a learnt skill very few had the opportunity to acquire. If they were lucky enough to be catapulted into rivers of energy densities they may have met other photon bundles. Perhaps some who had evolved to sentience, even self-awareness.

'Reflected light from the comet is preceding it directly towards us. We were able to isolate the stream from general background EMR,' O-WWWYellow elaborated.

*

'You took your time,' LX70, still a deep red, commented. They'd arrived back in sector #1. I-KlaraUV completely ignored the comment while she communicated the new information back to I-SakuraDV at the inner sphere.

'Grandmother, let me speak with I-KlaraUV,' O-SakuraDeepRed suggested.

O-LaiXiiDeepRed (LX70), sometimes had difficulty adjusting to the fact that she was no longer the principal driving force of their civilisation. After she remembered me from our association on Earth and that I was only a little girl at the time, it was extremely difficult for her to come to terms with being told by myself what to do, perhaps still thinking of me as a youngster.

'There is an iron core comet that is on its way to us, to V616 to be more precise,' I told O-SakuraDeepRed. 'If it stays on its present course it will go through the upper segment of your sector #5. As many people as possible need to change their orbits away from that area.'

'How much time do we have? And what is the likely outcome if it does go through us?' asked O-SakuraDeepRed.

'If you start to reroute people now you may only lose very few at the impact. We need your help too, O-LaiXiiDeepRed. O-StepkaOrange can show you what to do.' This was my opportunity to bring O-LaiXiiDeepRed into close cooperation on a crucial exercise.

Within a remarkably short time, even within the context of the singularity, the chaos increased a hundredfold, then a thousandfold as almost the entire population of photon bundles careered out of control as they haphazardly orbited into the other hemisphere.

Neither did the superdense population in the inner photon sphere take the news without considerable concern. However, they did not panic. They'd been through this kind of event before. There was the slight possibility of deflecting enough gravitational energy bursting out of the singularity towards the comet to hopefully change its course away from them. But that would require an enormous drain on their own energy, much of which had been used to help the outer sphere to establish a stable radius. I-LaiXiiDV wanted to do exactly that.

'I think you are right mother,' I-CherryBlossomDV considered the threat serious enough to warrant the action. Even I-IzumiDV, I-CherryBlossomDV's partner came to the same conclusion having heard the details from I-KlaraUV.

'No. I don't agree,' argued I-SakuraDV, 'there is insufficient justification for action which requires energy that's needed elsewhere. I-IndigoRalph has calculated that the comet will go past us and spiral into

the singularity. I-WWWDeepViolet has checked his analysis. It may touch on the outer sphere, but will leave us alone.
Our quadrants 1,4,5 & 6 are dulling. There is an anomaly in V616 after the last large comet, depleting our reserves and we have had insufficient photon harvest to replenish it.'

If nothing else, one thing they all understood was the fragility of existence. Whether it was from asteroids streaming through their shell to hurtle into the maw of the black hole, or supernovae too close to them threatening to tear apart the fabric of their hydrogen-photonic sphere, or destruction by rogue planets released from their orbits by some great cataclysm, it all amounted to the same thing; annihilation if they did not take appropriate measures. So far, they had survived. Some – many – were lost in the early days, but much fewer casualties occurred after that.

'I-KlaraUV can show them what to do at the outer sphere to protect themselves.' I-SakuraDV didn't want to interfere any more than that. Now that both photon spheres had acquired their places in time and space so close to each other if the worst thing happened and all of the outer sphere was destroyed, it would no longer affect them directly. Now their future was independent of their past, having finally bridged the gap. Perhaps different, perhaps diminished but they were still assured of a continuum.

I watched this approaching threat with everyone else. The comet's ion and dust tails began to turn gradually towards us drawn by V616's gravitational pull, which slowly overcame the cosmic winds around it. It seemed all wrong, though I knew the science behind it as well as I-IndigoRalph. When we first detected the comet its tails seemed to follow behind it. Then the comet looked like it had started to turn because the tail had moved to the side of it. I-IndigoRalph explained the reason behind the illusion. I still found it extraordinary that the tails of these beasts could eventually precede it to its final destination.

'Its coma is too bright. I can't make out the bulk of the thing,' said O-CheryyBlossomRed. She'd finished her part in warning the people and orbited up beside me and O-StepkaYellow. I was pleased he stayed with me during this event.

Others that had also been engaged in getting their population relocated returned one by one. Together they'd started to form a rainbow effect with I-KlaraUV's violet, O-WWW's yellow, Ralph's red and Stepka's yellow frequencies streaming beside each other. By now O-EvgeniyaDeepRed had found us, as well as O-ViktorDeepRed. He originally functioned as a security Chief on Earth before the migration, a role he continued on

Europe in Arithmós City. O-EvgeniyaDeepRed had been Lai-Xii's genetic engineer, again on Earth, who created the genetic blueprint from which the Tengi Caste of workers had arisen. Her new role here, as with many others had not been determined. In O-EvgeniyaDeepRed's case she may well have had the skill to work alongside O-RalphDeepRed in looking after the general welfare of our photonic bundle population.

O-LaiXiiDeepRed changed her orbit to come right beside me. 'We would not have noticed that rock coming straight at us,' she admitted. 'Thank you for the warning.'

I acknowledged her comment but remained silent, focused on monitoring the comet's progress. The once leader of the Digitals on Europa may have been a short tempered, impatient and manipulative individual with very little tolerance for fools and incompetents. But she did recognise that I had become important to their survival.

'In all likelihood you have saved many lives. And I do remember you from Earth. Even then I felt there was something special about you.'

I rotated slightly towards her. 'I used to hate the Lai-Xii you were then. Now we need to work together. Let's keep monitoring this comet.'

Time, being the very peculiar phenomenon it was in the vicinity of a black hole, distorted their perceptions. Initially the comet seemed to travel at incredible speed with its magnificent 2AU long bluish tail blazing across the darkness. As it neared V616 not only did its tail move from behind it, to in front of it, making it look as though it was in fact travelling in the opposite direction, it also seemed to have slowed down.

While we and billions of photon bundles watched, the tail began to stretch towards us, away from the bulk of the comet. I noticed that people had become so engrossed in the spectacle that without consciously trying to improve control over their orbits, they actually managed to do it. Chaotic careering slowly gave way to a semblance of order on the outer sphere.

I have experienced particulate matter bombarding our inner sphere many times. Never have I witnessed a display such as this. I drew closer to O-StepkaOrange and confessed a misgiving to him.

'That ion tail beginning to stretch towards us is spectacular. We do not know how such ionisation will affect our photon bundles. The physical impact of the comet itself piercing our sphere and passing through it may not be dramatic if it crosses in that upper segment. But how can I warn against the preceding ion trail's effects?'

'Well, I'm no scientist – but – if the singularity's gravitational pull increases as the distance of the object to it decreases then the tail should straighten up away from us.'

'Exactly right,' added O-RalphDeepRed who couldn't help overhearing as he maintained orbital proximity with the two newly acquainted friends. 'Its momentum should carry it away from us.'

It may have been hours or weeks or months before the two astronomical phenomena occupied the same spacetime coordinates within V616's gravity well. A time factor I couldn't determine as it kept changing for the comet, but not for us on the outer photon sphere.

O-LaiXiiDeepRed reacted first to the anti-climax. 'I thought this comet was supposed to be something quite spectacular.'

She sounded disappointed. O-SakuraDeepRed on the other hand was greatly relieved. Several thousand randomly orbiting bundles who didn't heed the warning ended up with frequency levels reduced into the mid-infrared band. They would recover in time.

The spectacle itself turned out to be more surprising than spectacular. I didn't expect the tail to disappear like that.

O-RalphDeepRed explained … 'The mass of on an object has a direct relationship to the strength of gravitational pull that will effect it. The core of the comet had far greater mass than its tail, so it simply overtook it even though the tail stretched ahead of it towards the singularity.'

As the emergency passed and she had a chance to concentrate on her immediate environment O-SakuraDeepRed could not fail to notice the higher frequencies of some of the photon bundles around her. The most recent events had absorbed most of her attention until then. 'Why are O-Stepka and O-WWW both Yellow, and we are still only Deep Red,' she asked me, obviously suggesting a desire to correct the imbalance.

'O-LaiXiiDeepRed, are you ready for an upgrade,' I asked her and her close associates in the immediate vicinity. I was pleased to see her far more eager than even her daughter O-CherryBlossomDeepRed. We'll have to return to sector #5 as that's where the incident photon stream from the supernova is most parallel to our curvature.'

Perhaps I'll be able to soon acquire more data about our past from O-LaiXiiDeepRed. I'm hoping she will reveal her knowledge about the Book of Origination.

Time continued to shrink, or so it seemed, as O-StepkaYellow and I helped the people of the outer sphere. It may have been a long time before

O-SakuraDeepRed, CherryBlossomDeepRed, O-LaiXiiDeepRed and others gained frequencies into the Deep Violet band. Some like O-Ralph and O-Evgeniya progressed to or remained in Indigo.
I helped O-StepkaYellow to get to the Violet frequency as quickly as he could absorb incident energy.

O-SakuraDV made the limits of my responsibilities quite clear. 'Let me say this bluntly to you I-KlaraUV; you are not to assist anyone else to boost their frequency levels. I will decide the layering of our society to achieve maximum spectral balance. However, you may continue with your research.'

That's all I really wanted, though I had the feeling that sometime in the future restrictions on growth would have to be lifted. The rest of them could now enjoy absorbing and learning about the nature of the universe by themselves from all the random photons they manage to interact with that fell into V616's gravity well. It required far less concentration to harvest a little data than to actually manage to increase one's frequency.

*

While I waited for the leadership group to increase their levels I thought about how best I could help to overcome the great controversy about our origins. Perhaps the myth would not be invalidated until much later. Nothing we had learnt since before LX70's arrival could support the notion that we came into being in our current photonic configuration at the time of the creation of the cosmos. O-StepkaViolet knew for certain where we came from, even before Europa. But he was only one voice and that would not be enough to convince our people in the inner sphere.

'You should get as much information from O-LaiXiiDeepRed as you can. I've been watching her orbiting,' suggested O-StepkaViolet. 'She's gradually learning and upgrading.'

'Yes. It won't be long before she's deep violet. I will try then.' O-StepkaViolet and I orbited a while longer before an opportunity presented itself. I had intended to teach more of the population, but I could not go against O-SakuraDeepRed's wishes. There was, however, something I could do that had been on my mind since arriving at the outer sphere.

'O-StepkaViolet, will you help me with a little task?'

'Anything – for you - anything.'

'This may seem strange but it's important to me. It may turn out to be of some significance to you as well.'

'Don't beat around the cosmos, just tell me.'

'I need you to help me find the Zeta Tengi that contained my original self on Europa. I'm surprised we haven't already crossed orbits.'

'That could indeed be tricky — for us. I mean, you and I, we have managed to connect. How will it complicate our — relationship?'

I moved closer to O-StepkaViolet. Our distant past has obviously caught up to us, and he didn't want that to change. 'I think it will only be good.'

'Alright then! How am I going to recognise her? If she's here she'll be deep red like just about everyone else.'

'Remember I asked you to find LX70 when I first arrived, and you immediately knew where she was?'

'Yeah, I wondered how I did that.'

'You knew because - and I have not told anyone this yet — because all our minds exist within the same energy field. We are all connected to each other. It is now our natural state. Not like before when we were isolated from one another. You were able to connect with her because you had a strong and a special reason to do so. You overcame the separation barrier - to please me.'

'Yes, that's exactly what I wanted to do. What pleased me even more was that you didn't want to meet her immediately, but spend time with me.'

He moved to an even closer orbit with me.

'I am now making you conscious of what you can do. It is too soon to tell others, so keep this to yourself. They will discover it soon enough. Open your thoughts and send them out searching. Move around the sphere as you do this, follow the thread. It might make connecting easier.'

'Why haven't you done this? I mean, you've been here at V616 much longer than we have.'

'That's exactly why. I still exist in the future and all of you are still in our past. I cannot directly impact on your time-line in some respects.'

I don't know how much change had taken place since he went searching. I continued gathering more information about the inhabitants of this outer sphere. The chaos has begun to diminish. It has been easier to make direct contact with individuals. Some had already achieved slight increases in their frequencies, others still struggled even to steady their movement.

'I-KlaraUV! I-KlaraUV!' I heard him calling even before he arrived beside me. From his excitement I hoped he'd been successful in the quest. With many billions of bundles all going their own way I didn't expect

O-StepkaViolet back yet. I prepared myself. What should I say to my past self? 'Hello me? How am I?' Seems utterly silly. As I pondered the conundrum they both arrived.

O-StepkaViolet remained silent, as did O-KlaraDR. She was still at deep red. The silence stretched, like the comets tail into the singularity. I tried to assess the woman beside me. If nothing else she was certainly reserved; not aggressive, not even with a belligerent aspect – just reticent in the extreme.

I started with the most stupid question, 'Are you Klara?' Her reply adequately conveyed the degree of stupidity of my query.

'Not any more. Now I'm just a slave, like everyone else was out on the Ice.'

'But your name is Klara – yes?'

'Only to my friends, but I don't have any now.'

'What did they call you on Europa?' I tried another approach to break through.

'Zeta-Tengi235, ZT235. I was in the second lot of techs sent to Europa to set up the network for the others. Lai-Xii didn't care who she sent, as long as the job got done.'

At least I was getting a little more information out of her/me. I remembered a little of this, but most of my Earth history data seemed to have become corrupted over the millennia in the proximity of V616's radiation. My next question sounded really stupid as soon as I uttered it.

'Do you know who I am?'

Accompanied with a smirk she replied, 'He tells me you are me, or at least were, me. Ha. Unlikely.'

'Why do you say that?'

'I'm not as smart as so many of our tetra-amelias back on Earth, but even I know it's not possible to travel into the future. And even if it was, how come you're already here before I've arrived!'

'You are a lot smarter than you think. At least I'm a lot smarter than I thought I was.'

O-KlaraDR smiled for the first time. The oddity of the situation must not have been lost on her sense of humour.

'I do, it seems, even now have a sense of humour.' The ice was broken.

'So – what do you intend to do about it?' she asked.

'We don't have to do anything, Klara. May I call you that?'

'If you must.'

'Actually, you should be introduced to the others as O-KlaraDR. As you increase your frequency your name will reflect your energy level.

Stepka is now at 650 THz, so he's O-StepkaViolet – the 'O' denotes outer sphere.' I could see her pondering the ramifications. She/I was indeed a smart girl judging from the quality of her next question.

'We are very different from one another now. Just look at you. I think differently to you, because I am different; just as a child I was different to being an adult. What happens when I start to shine ultra violet?'

'Ah. We need to talk about that.'

I rotated to O-StepkaViolet. 'Would you leave us while we sort this out. It doesn't just concern the two of us, but everyone on both spheres. You might like to consult O-WWWYellow about the relative positions of our two spheres in the meantime.' I turned my attention back to O-KlaraDR as we orbited randomly around the sphere. 'Come with me, I want to show you something.'

We made our way back to sector #5. The EMR from the supernova continued to be as strong as before. I convinced her to go through the energy absorption exercise several times. Each time she showed more interest in the little game. I kept monitoring the dosage until she'd achieved 530 THz, a nice strong green.

'Look at yourself, O-KlaraGreen.' At that time I had not seen anyone get to that frequency. She stood out amongst all the deep reds.

'I like green. Kamchatka, where I come from was always either white or green. I feel – I feel like – like I belong. How very odd. I don't even mind talking to you.' She grinned.

'What do you think will happen as our frequencies begin to synchronise?' I asked her.

'Are you suggesting what I think you're suggesting?'

'That we become – better friends – if I can put it that way. Yes; really good, close friends.' She seemed to take that in her stride.

*

By this time O-LaiXiiDeepRed had completed this stage of her training. We both caught up with her in another quadrant of sector #5. O-KlaraGreen's luminescence flashed violently at the recognition of O-LaiXiiDV. Our experience under Lai-Xii's rule had not been pleasant. Then her reaction subsided just as quickly. I have no doubt there would have been a clash between the two if I had not managed to get O-KlaraDeepRed upgraded.

I introduced my past self to O-LaiXiiDV. They made motions of recognising each other, but without the informality of a friendly greeting.

63

We cruised along with her for a while until her orbiting didn't seem as purposeful.

'O-LaiXiiDV, will you teach me?' I asked.

'What is it you want to know?' She concentrated on me, ignoring my past self.

'Our futures are slowly harmonising. We need to prepare for the time of the convergence. We must each synchronise our cause/effect wave fronts with the other. Although you may not yet be able to detect it, your sphere is catching up with ours. Your rate of change is faster than ours as we are closer to the singularity. It is inevitable that we will merge.'

As hard as I tried to get the concept across to her, O-LaiXiiDV seemed to have difficulty in seeing the big picture. It is understandable that concentration on the incomprehensible scope of detail required to make the transition from Europa to V616 would have overburdened one's thoughts.

'We need to know what is in your collective minds, and what you have discovered from the Book of Origination that tells us about the direction of our joint Arrow of Thought. A complete history of your past is a good place to start.'

'Why doesn't I-LaiXiiDV.gen3920.4eV.exe already have that data. She originated with us.'

'There are gaps in our recollections. Our people don't even believe that our ancestors were once a carbon based biological lifeform existing on a physical planet. It is a myth to them, just a story that keeps fading, becoming more mythical with time. There is also the period you spent on Europa. We know very little of that. It was necessary to self-purge in order to remove our inclination to help you, to interfere in your collective decision tree.'

I don't know what changed her mind to be cooperative. Once she opened up, the history lesson flowed in torrents. I listened to her tell the story of how she began on Earth to prepare for the migration to Europa. Some of this I already knew. Learning of her early years as an infant in a place called Japan gave perspective to her later actions. From time to time we stopped while I transmitted the new data to 3920 at the inner sphere.

'But you have told me nothing about the Book of Origination and what drove you so relentlessly towards your goal.'

'Whatever this book is, I didn't know about it. As far I'm concerned it had nothing to do with our migration or any of my decisions. I made my decisions because of what people were doing to themselves and to our planet.'

In spite of having taken a dislike to I-KlaraUV initially O-LaiXiiDV rapidly revised her assessment of this individual in the course of events following her arrival in their sphere. But now she was starting to get annoyed.

'I will tell you this; the support we received at the start faded soon enough. World leaders started to treat our scientific breakthroughs as opportunities to create new weapons of war. The idea of leaving Earth quickly lost its attraction for them, though as I think about it they probably didn't actually consider it as a viable solution to humanity's problems at the time. The major religions definitely saw us as a threat to their domination.'

'Yet you found a way through all the opposition, and here you are now. How did you manage, given all the obstacles?' I asked, still fishing for some hidden source of inspiration that may have been the driving force behind O-LaiXiiDV. O-KlaraGreen nodded her interest as she become more engrossed in the content of the discussion.

The hard headed business woman who once dominated billionaires, bending them to her will for her own goals and now effectively a retired ruler of the remnants of humanity orbiting around a black hole, withdrew into her thoughts, for the answer had implications. I had the good sense to remain silent while O-LaiXiiDV mined her deeply imbedded data.

Soon enough she resumed, though soon is a difficult concept to comprehend when time has no respect for an ordered human psyche in this environment. 'In retrospect I have to concede there have been certain developments which seemed most fortuitous in their occurrence during the time-line of our Project.'

Ah – this sounds promising. Perhaps she had no conscious knowledge of any guiding force, yet was open to using opportunities as they presented themselves, without bothering to question where those opportunities came from.

'For example; Ralph, he was simply known as Ralph then, had been experimenting on the fringes of technically engineered human physiology. It turned out his technology became critical to us.'

'And you have no idea how this many not have been a random synchronous situation?'

'Certainly not. I selected him for the very reason of his expertise. It was purely opportunistic.'

'Anything else you can think of?'

'Well - yes – William. Now that was something quite extraordinary. And I have to say we would most probably not be here, and nor would you, without him. To think that a computer intelligence could evolve beyond all possibilities to end up playing such a vital role. Inconceivable in fact. Believe me, there were no books of prognostication involved.

As quantum computing evolved giving rise to machines capable of multiple concurrent processing with astronomical reserves of data to work with, it was indeed feasible that some form of utilitarian self-awareness should emerge.'

'I know the story you told 3920 as you knew her then, about Europa, about how through your intervention, or at least through someone called Prima9, that icy moon awoke to Its consciousness. And after that everything It did help you to come to V616. What are your thoughts about that?'

'You're trying to get me to admit there existed something else besides our own desires and initiatives that made this future possible. I will not admit to that. The only encouragement we ever received was from my descendent 3920, though I have to say she wasn't much help at all.'

'We, in the inner sphere, are aware of a great many things about the nature of reality and the universe, knowledge you obviously had no access to. Our past is becoming clearer with your help. We have also learnt from gamma bursts from within the singularity that there is more than this, more than just V616, more than simply existence as bundles of photons trapped in a sphere orbiting a mysterious cosmic phenomenon.'

'All I can tell you,' said O-LaiXiiDV in conclusion, 'is that we are here and without encouragement from my future self I would probably have given up a very long time ago.'

Disappointingly, O-LaiXiiDV had no secrets that could help us. If she didn't have, no one else associated with her era would, probably not even William. No matter how clever he might have been he was still only operating on the machine intelligence level. Perhaps I should speak to his three avatars, O-WWWYellow.

'We are busy.' O-WWWYellow didn't want to engage with me. 'There are too many gaps in our knowledge. We must determine how to capture incident photons and help coalesce them into new bundles in readiness to receive parental base data.'

'I can help you with that, at least I-IndigoRalph can. There is time enough to increase your population. It is not the highest priority as we continue our passage along the Arrow of Thought. For now it is important to bring our people in the inner sphere out of the controversy and misconceptions about their origins. Until that is achieved they cannot change – and we cannot merge.'

'William has already informed 3920. He's provided all the data he possessed, as has Vadim, Admiral Kapitolina's comms tech, subsequent to our departure from Earth. There is no more to tell,' said O-WWWYellow.

'The rest of the population also needs to be convinced that their origins are carbon based biological organisms, that this is not a myth but a reality. How do you propose we do that? I asked them.'

'Continue with what you are doing. Learn more of our history from as many sources as you can, and start making that available to everyone. We are all connected now and as soon as they realise this the knowledge will be shared.'

ANDROMEDA GALAXY

PLANET RAHU

A ROGUE COMET impacted the second planet of a minor solar system in another galaxy. The force of its impact created a temporary wormhole which began with one of its openings somewhere in the Andromeda Galaxy, finding its way along myriad ridges of gravity highways in the fabric of spacetime, avoiding the ever present pull of millions of cosmic objects.

It did not extend itself towards the G2 type star, rather making its way to the Milky Way and creating an opening at the V616 Mon black hole. This happened for the simple reason of it being on a path of least resistance. Travelling along the gravity ridges requires far less energy than continually trying to escape the slopes of larger or smaller planetary and solar gravity wells. Because of its torturous route this particular wormhole, unlike shorter ones with shorter lifespans, resulted in a winding tunnel of exotic forces engorged with superluminal energies gradually slowing to normal light speed at its destination – fortunate, as it turns out, for the Homo Universapiensis civilisation of Luminis existing on photon spheres.

*

Within the Andromeda Galaxy, given its size and the four hundred billion stars, events of this nature within its solar systems is not unusual, and not entirely unexpected by the beings on the planet Rahu. As the second planet of an old white sun it found itself in the danger zone as a vagabond comet approached.

Aros's, planetary Co-ordinator of Intent and Friz'z their Chief Astro-Physicist entertained no doubts as to what had to be done if Rahunian life was to survive.

'I have been tracking 364T-9 for the last twenty cycles,' said Friz'z, 'you can see yourself this comet is not going to change course.'

'We are well aware of this,' replied Aros's, 'that's why Xone'e is here today.'

Xone'e, their Futures Planner and Rend'd in his role as Co-ordinator of Implementation, also Friz'z's partner Lom'm the Cosmologist, all attended the gathering.

'The comet is too large for us to be able to deflect it or destroy it,' advised Xone'e. Rend'd agrees with the analysis.'

Rend'd said very little in general conversations, so he just nodded concurrence. Once a plan had been agreed on and had to be put into effect Rend'd could hold several conversations at the same time.

'So our plan is simple - get out of its way,' summarised Xone'e.

'Is there no other option? Do we not have time to mine its resources until there's not much of it left?' Aros's liked his people to work towards positive outcomes at every opportunity.

'Two hundred and fifty cycles are not enough time for us to do that.' Xone'e had obviously considered many facets of the absolute certainty of the event becoming a pivotal point in the long life of their civilisation.

The universe may be of an unfathomable size with mysteries that will never be solved by sentient beings. But there are some certainties and there are some guiding principles; one of those being the nature of self-aware sentient expressions of life. Under the warmth of their G2 sun and a world replete with lilac Lepidolite crystals from the tops of their mountain ranges to the depths of their oceans, rivers and lakes, life did indeed develop over the 2.8 million cycles of their evolution.

The people were short by human standards, barely 50 cm high on average, but they were also extraordinarily well camouflaged against the background of their planet. Lilac and all shades of violet crystal-like scales covered their torsos, which were adorned with two arms and three legs. Stability and fast locomotion must have been an essential aspect of their survival.

Survival at any cost appeared to be the main principle applied under the present circumstances. No one on the planet argued against their Co-ordinator of Intent when he announced to the world's population Xone'e's plan to move everyone to their colony planet, Syy.

'As you all know Syy is very similar to our Rahu. We have already established an extensive colony there. It is well within our capabilities to make the transition before 364T-9 gets to us here. But we cannot waste time. I ask all of you to make your preparations.'

His short presentation ended on an optimistic note even though he knew their current home planet would be utterly destroyed.

'A new world, a new life, a new adventure.'

He could not hear what was not expressed by the millions – cheers and happy exclamations. If the inevitable could not be avoided then it had to be endured, without necessarily being pleased about it.

For several cycles following the announcement, his office received thousands of questions from the population mostly wanting to know if every other possibility had been explored - not that they didn't trust their Planetary Co-ordinator of Intent or their Futures Planner. The five most respected individuals of their civilisation had examined every aspect and developed many possible alternative courses of action while the comet continued without deviation from its course. Over the cycles of its early approach every option bar one had been eliminated as 364T-9 demonstrated its reluctance to go anywhere except to rendezvous with Rahu.

Lom'm, the generator of ideas plausible and implausible had little to say as a rule except when she presented theories or refuted arguments of her own. She and her partner Friz'z not only monitored 364T-9's progress, they also traced its path back to its origins. As the evacuation gained momentum Lom'm told Aros's what her calculations indicated. 'This enormous comet, more like a large moon, had somehow escaped its own solar system from somewhere in the vicinity of the outer extremities of the Outer Arm of the Milky Way Galaxy.'

'Any speculation as to what may have caused it to flee?' Aros's knew it made no difference to the implementation of their current plans, though it may have a bearing on the future if such a thing was to happen again.

'I can only tell you where it came from. I know two things; it has been travelling since well before our species came into being, and what it is going to take to stop it – possibly the mass of our planet. Even if it won't stop it, it will at least be broken up into smaller less destructive chunks. There is no scenario in which we would be survivors. Even if it only came close to us that would be enough to trigger an extinction event.

*

People watched this phenomenon for so many cycles that it became an accepted part of life. After they were made aware of it no other topic of conversation could be heard for half a cycle, with many wise and dramatic solutions to the problem; none of which involved abandoning their home, … not that Syy wasn't a lovely planet, albeit a bit cooler … certainly great as a commercial mining colony. Uncle Destiny; they'd given the comet a name that depicted both respect and expressed the greatest undesirability known to them, Destiny, did not give the impression of getting any closer, only that little by little it seemed to get bigger and brighter.

Lom'm being a Cosmologist found it fascinating to contemplate the idea of Panspermia. 'What if it survived the impact? What if it picked up microscopic life forms from Rahu and carried them to another solar system on its fragments? What if it is already carrying life?'

Friz'z joked with her, 'What if you went along for the ride to find out and told us all about it?'

'No – seriously! What if ended up in that black hole not so very far from us and seeded new life in another Universe?'

'Now you're just being silly. We both know nothing escapes black holes; nothing that looks like life anyway.

*

Two hundred and fifty cycles may have seemed to be a long time under normal life circumstances, but not when the countdown reduced it to just a hundred and then to only fifty cycles. Fifty cycles were less than a life span. That really brought home the reality of what was happening.

'Will you look at the size of that thing!' Xone'e exclaimed in one of their meetings. It had indeed grown to such a size as to force home the reality of its destructive power to every individual on Rahu. 'Vast settlements have been established on Syy and we have millions of caretakers there already,' she gave the update after tearing her gaze away from Uncle Destiny.

Rend'd confirmed their readiness for the final evacuation. 'For the next thirty cycles we will move the remainder of our population. They can begin setting up our new lives.' As Co-ordinator of Implementation for Xone'e's plans he did not want to take any chances of leaving their final departure to the last days. 'We cannot yet feel the effects of this monster, but both Friz'z and Lom'm reassure me it will begin to devastate life here well before the actual impact. I think we should be watching the final spectacle from a very long way away.

Lom'm and Friz'z looked at each other without commenting. No one knew their special personal plans, not even Aros's. He'd insisted on ensuring the safety of every individual and as many life forms as they could possibly take with them. No one was to be left on Rahu, regardless of what they believed in, what organisations they belonged to, not even anyone with unwholesome history in their past actions could sway Aros's to leave them behind. The two scientists, partners in life and in profession, had an obligation. The did not want to stay on Rahu. Quite the contrary. This was a once in a lifetime opportunity to observe at close hand a cosmic catastrophe that could yield invaluable information for the future survival of their species.

The very last armada was due to depart barely ten cycles out from impact. 'Are we still doing this?' asked Friz'z of his partner.

'Do you think I am going to miss this once in a million cycle event? Are you crazy? You're the great astrophysicist, you're not seriously thinking of taking off without me. What about the thousand scientists who've decided to come in our ship? Are you going to let them down?'

'Take it easy! I just wanted to make sure you still wanted to stay.'

'NO! I don't want to stay – I just want to be close enough to learn something. If we have to lose our home this is the least we must do. It is an obligation of our professions – besides – it will be extraordinarily spectacular. Have you ever seen a comet try to shove a planet out of the way?'

The last armada did depart on schedule, including Friz'z's craft, right on minus nine cycles. The timing allowed for the entire fleet to arrive on Syy two cycles before the actual predicted impact. All eyes were focused on 364T-9. Some with hatred, some with fascination, some with disbelief. Though they were actually on their way to another planet it still didn't seem entirely real to those on the last flight.

Friz'z, Lom'm and several hundred other academics followed at the rear of the armada. 'Is all the monitoring equipment set up?' asked Friz'z. He needn't have asked. Of course everything was set up. Obviously he still had some reservations about what they were planning to do. Aros's had agreed without hesitation for them to be in the last craft. It made perfect sense to have their leading minds learn as much as they could. But he did not give his approval for anything else.

*

72

'Captain Kaln'n, please initiate course change exactly as planned,' requested Friz'z. Everyone had been alerted and all were ready. At a safe distance to their starboard Uncle Destiny screamed past the fleet, heading on a collision course with Rahu. It was huge, even from that safe distance. Calculations and long distance observations can give a theoretical, abstract understanding - but there is nothing like coming face to face with the enormity of another cosmic object hell bent on destruction.

'It's just a huge chunk of rock,' commented Lom'm. 'The atmosphere, if it had any to start with, has long since burnt away.'

'By the look of all those craters and the big hunk missing from its side its already had many disagreements with other cosmic travellers.'

'I'm glad we're not there to greet it,' Lom'm said as she moved closer to her partner. They were watching from one of the main observation blisters, as no doubt were many others.

Their captain had manoeuvred their ship to a position directly behind the comet and across its previous flight path. 'Friz'z,' Captain Kaln'n wanted his attention. 'Do you still want me to follow it?'

'Not for long – not for long. The shock wave generated by hitting our atmosphere would be enough to destroy us if we're not careful. I think a deci-cycle is more than enough, don't you think Lom'm?'

The interruption to their friendly banter should have been expected sooner or later. It was the voice of Aros's from the leading craft.

'What in the name of Rahu do you think you're doing?' He'd only just been alerted to Friz'z's change of course. 'Why do we rely on Xone'e's strategy if you lot are going to do something like this? I'm told you have all the leading scientists on board with you. You really think we can afford to lose any one of you? Especially under the current circumstances!'

'We are doing only what we're supposed to be doing – research. The knowledge we could gain is of incalculable value. Never in the history of our species has such an opportunity presented itself.'

Aros's listened. What was the point of arguing? These were the very people who discovered the comet, calculated its potential danger and effectively saved their entire race from extinction. 'When do you intend to re-join us?' he asked, though still highly irritated.

'Soon.' And as he uttered the single word he felt their craft shudder. Captain Kaln'n immediately sounded the alarm.

'We've been hit by some debris from 364T-9,' advised the Captain. 'Nothing serious, but I think it does not want us following it. Our sensors are showing a great deal of loose material coming away from it. Regardless of what is causing it I suggest we back off.'

Friz'z immediately conferred with his colleagues. The Captain had been correct. If they stayed directly behind the comet they would remain in a seriously dangerous zone. So far they'd only sustained superficial damage, nothing that would jeopardise their lives. The comm channel to Aros's was still open.

'What's happening?' The ensuing silence had him extremely worried. Their own sensors had picked up the battering by small rocks which had now been deflected off their trajectory.

'We are changing course now,' advised Friz'z. He had decided to remain at their present location for the time being, not following Uncle Destiny from behind, nor attempting to catch up with the rest of the fleet.

The deci-cycle had elapsed. 364T-9 started to show signs of solar winds being deflected around it, creating a halo visible to the naked eye. Another hundredth cycle and it would be within Rahu's outer atmosphere. 'Time for us to go,' Lom'm finally had had enough. She didn't bother pouring over all the data they'd collected – time enough for that when they settled in on Syy.

As their ship accelerated away from their abandoned home planet all attention was strained on the moment of Uncle Destiny's impact with Rahu's troposphere. No volcanic eruption could have rivalled the ferocity with which Uncle Destiny ploughed through the atmosphere, plunging into one of the main oceans. Even such a large volume of water could not slow the comets momentum. The explosion could not be heard.

'Are you recording this?' Lom'm asked her assistant in a barely audible voice. The spectacle of water turning to instant steam and shooting out into the stratosphere took her breath away. The image was so overwhelming it didn't leave room to contemplate what was actually happening; the destruction of their home world. The coronal steam plume must have extended hundreds of kilometres into the void leaving a hole through the centre of its funnel.

'I can see the bottom of the ocean!' remarked Friz'z, 'all the water is gone.'

Before a planet engulfing heavy steam cloud could obliterate their view they could see Uncle Destiny bury its head in the ocean floor. The impact shock wave would soon reach them.

'I have to accelerate close to maximum tolerance,' advised Captain Kaln'n to the ship's complement, 'be ready to brace yourselves.' He'd set the course and his pilot had control of their craft. He had time to watch

Uncle Destiny continue its path through the rocky ocean bottom as if nothing had impeded its progress. The sheer size and velocity of the rock was cataclysmic. Friz'z had been correct in his estimation of the only option available to them, and Aros's equally right in making the final decision for the evacuation. Nothing could survive such a force of destruction.

'It's not going to stop, is it?' Lom'm put the rhetorical question to Friz'z - the answer obvious. They watched in horror and awe as their home was rent into large chunks of planetary debris, the space around the planet turning into a chaotic mass of flotsam ejected in all directions.

It took only a milli-cycle, which seemed like an entire cycle for the space once occupied by their home to become empty as they watched, mesmerised. They could only observe, silent, disbelieving. Even from fifty million kilometres away no doubt remained about what they saw.

'As long as I live, and as long as our species survives I hope never again to witness such a thing,' whispered Lom'm as she, with hundreds of others observed Uncle Destiny emerge from the outer boundary of ejecta to continue on its way, seemingly unconcerned and unaffected by the havoc it had wreaked, apparently undiminished in its speed.

The shock wave did arrive as predicted by their Captain. But to add insult to the tragedy it did little more then give them a nudge, doing no more harm than making a few people teeter momentarily. In the greater scheme of things that was all that remained of a place where their species came into being to evolve into sentience, only to have to abandon it – a teetering moment in the ageless cosmological mystery.

'Our sensors indicate 364T-9 has shed a little of its mass and altered its course minutely.' Then as a final word on the matter she commented to Friz'z, 'If you would care to notice, several very large segments of Rahu are on an elliptical path which will take them directly into the heart of that wormhole forming between our Sun and Rahu.'

One small moon sized chunk of their planet escaped his attention. Its trajectory would take it close to their sun and sling it back into their system.

*

Many generations of the once Rahunians, now Syynians, had come into being and died on Syy. They saw nothing of their ancient world other than an insubstantial ring of fragments formed from its remnants orbiting their white star where Rahu once had its well-trodden path. The ring halo of lilac indigo gas cloud created from the vaporisation of rubidium previously contained in the most common constituent of their planet, Lepidolite,

75

slowly began to compact itself under its own micro gravity. A magnificent spectacle as the rays of their sun penetrated through less dense areas – a vista of little comfort to the civilisation that had to abandon their home.

The somewhat small gypsy fragment of Rahu continued along its new path, never deviating, towards the mouth of the wormhole, as if compelled by destiny to travel to another galaxy.

A minor solar system in the Andromeda Galaxy had suffered a major upheaval. It still had its four planets and a ring of debris. This no longer had the mass that had contributed to maintaining equilibrium within their solar system. Their new home, Syy, now orbited with two giant gas planets. One immediately after them and one in the next orbit out. Gravitational forces would take millions of years to alter their system, but it would change.

It was into this cosmic space that another life form would soon intrude. One that would create more change to the way Syynians viewed existence and its meaning than they had anticipated when abandoning their home planet.

OUTER PHOTON SPHERE

KAPITOLINA ARRIVES FROM EUROPA

ADMIRAL KAPITOLINA considered what other questions she wanted to ask William and Prima9, and especially Europa Cell. While she pondered William terminated the connection between them but not before adding, 'Europa exists as a sentient being. Its consciousness has arisen out of the network of information contained within its ocean. Know this — consciousness exists in all things. You are not unique.'

Perhaps he added this to prepare Kapitolina for her encounter with an unusual type of photon sphere, or maybe just to reinforce the relative lack of importance she had in the fabric of existence. She didn't dwell on the deeper meaning of William's wisdom. She now had a specific destination. William's insistence that Lay-Xii would not, in fact could not help made no difference to the Admiral's resolve.

'Darya, can you re-establish contact?' Darya had heard the entire conversation, which had become more incomprehensible the more William said.

Perhaps he was right — maybe we shouldn't continue the journey, but then again he did say we had to give Lai-Xii some information.

'What happens if we find Lai-Xii and then can't even communicate with her?' It wasn't Darya's place to question the Admirals decisions, but the situation that had developed was too full of unknowns. Kapitolina and Darya had been friends all their lives. They could talk to each other freely without barriers of rank hindering their friendship.

'We will find her. If William had as much to do with our evolution as he had with Lay-Xii's then our differences cannot be so great that we should not be able to find a common language.' If the Admiral had any doubts the beginning of the voyage was not the time to bring them out into the open. Time enough to do that, for V616 would not be in their sights for many years yet.

After two orbits of Europa around Jupiter the three craft departed. The Admiral couldn't think of anything better than to get away and regain some sanity out in space.

One further message arrived from the enigmatic, annoying AI as their craft accelerated away from Jupiter's gravity.

'Adjust your course. If you fail to do so the singularity of the Black Hole itself will be your final destination. Be prepare to take up orbit around V616. The two photon spheres you will encounter are both made up of sentient beings.'

'Did you all hear that?' Admiral Kapitolina wanted to make sure her three Captains had some idea of the impossible situation they were heading into. 'Set course to Alpha Centauri. We will pick up reaction mass from an asteroid in the Oort Cloud. Let's accelerate as far as the Kuiper belt, then begin deceleration. It'll give us a chance to test our new propulsion system.'

Admiral Kapitolina had been on a previous expedition as far as the Oort Cloud. She didn't expect any surprises this early in the journey and she didn't have any. They were still cruising slowly enough past Saturn to catch a brief ten second glimpse of its rings.

'I am amazed how thin the rings are,' commented Vadim to no one in particular. Olesya and Kapitolina reclined by the main view port silently absorbing the wonder of their solar system. The planet itself lacked the artificially enhanced colours with which it was often represented. Nevertheless, the image of Enceladus in the foreground of the kilometre wide ring with the stark graphic shadows of the ring itself on the gas giant left a memorable impression.

'No doubt there'll be many more spectacles to enjoy before our arrival at V616.'

Within several months they already had to begin decelerating. The distances were not long enough to get anywhere near their speed capacity. Well short of the Oort Cloud crawling along slowly enough to enable manoeuvring around the myriad asteroids provided their pilots with plenty of extra practice, which may be needed sometime later in the enterprise.

'We need to find a large enough icy planetesimal to land safely. It would take too long to shuttle fuel back and forth. We'd better go in deeper,' suggested the Admiral. She needn't have bothered to interfere. Her Captains were already doing exactly that.

From their approach it seemed like the Cloud consisted of a relatively densely packed mass of astronomical objects and they would have no problem to locate an appropriate target. Darya was the only one slightly surprised. 'I thought they'd be a lot closer together then a few million kilometres apart, and much easier to find a good one.' This was her first trip so far out of the solar system.

Back on Europa they only took on what they needed to get to the Cloud. 'We may not be stopping for quite a while,' said Kapitolina, 'so fill our tanks to the brim.' The gross understatement went unnoticed until much later when they finally emerged out of the Cloud into the unimaginable distances of the Interstellar medium.

'Please initiate our major propulsion system and set course along the Local Orion Spur. We'll give the engines a good test run at high speed for a year before we go into stasis.'

And so the routine was set for long periods of automatic flights lasting several hundred years, and waking periods with time to do comprehensive system checks. Communication with Earth ceased after several cycles, though the travellers continued to send update reports without expecting responses. They continued exponential acceleration for the first set of cycles before switching off the engines to let the ships cruise at near light speed until beginning their transit from the Orion Spur into the Perseus Arm. To reach the halfway mark Admiral Kapitolina ordered a further boost, having achieved an area of space between the two arms relatively sparsely populated by solar systems or dense nebulae. Though not being able to achieve a substantial multiple of light speed, they made good time before beginning deceleration.

Time in space relative to time on Earth meandered along quite happily oblivious of the growing differences. On the two photon spheres whatever happened outside of themselves away from the singularity represented a reality no longer of any concern to them. The Arrow of Time making its way into the singularity needed a little more attention.

**

O-WWWYellow gradually advanced from yellow frequency to indigo. Many orbiting photon bundles had also made progress in achieving higher frequencies. O-WWWIndigo spent most of their time absorbing information about the universe around them, becoming particularly sensitive to cosmic objects that seemed to exhibit some attraction to V616. They took a security role upon themselves to be vigilant for any rogue objects that could pass through them or anywhere near them.

Willi always spoke for the three of them. 'O-SakuraDV,' he alerted, 'I detect an unusual phenomenon.' Immediately a large contingent of O-SakuraDV's entourage gathered to orbit with them to listen to O-WWWIndigo. It wasn't until Admiral Kapitolina's little armada had been in deceleration mode for some time, having come down from near light speed, that their drive emissions arrived at the outer sphere.

O-VioletRalph examined the incoming data to confirm O-WWWIndigo's conclusion, 'Those three objects are not natural phenomena.'

'Not natural?' queried O-LaiXiiUV, immediately on alert prompted by a deeply ingrained fear. Whilst still on Europa in the early days of their settlement, William had warned of the rise of the Earth people intent on pursuing and destroying her and all who had departed Earth with her. 'What are they?'

'They are too small to be of any danger to us,' reassured O-WWWIndigo.

O-VioletRalph transmitted further information, privately, to O-SakuraDV, thinking that it may further upset various members of their gathering, one in particular. Not having experienced O-LaiXiiUV's angst of the past she couldn't understand why the fuss. 'Out with it, what's so special about these objects.' O-HarusukeDV could only smile, remembering her partners predisposition to impatience.

'My analysis indicates they are three vessels of Earth technology origin. Though that is difficult to understand for several reasons,' replied O-WWWIndigo.

'Absolutely!' interjected O-LaiXiiUV, forgetting that William had actually reconfigured the few Zeta Tengi who had been left behind.

'The thousands of years that have elapsed should have sufficiently corrupted their data to wipe us from their memory. Secondly, the distance between us and Earth is in itself prohibitive of any serious exploration this far out of the Orion Spur.' O-WWWIndigo was only thinking logically. His logic gave O-LaiXiiUV no comfort at all.

O-SakuraDV's train of thinking didn't help either. 'There is no reason for them to be out here unless they are looking for us.'

The rapidly fluctuating spectral vibration emanating from O-LaiXiiUV seemed not to concern anyone else other than her partner circling very tightly beside her.

Although I didn't particularly care for the woman's fearful reactions I thought it best to round out the speculation with my own small contribution. I knew these people were coming. 'I have had a long communication with William on Europa. He is still active, or at least was then. I haven't kept track of time. He said he was waiting for a visit from them, thinking that they would be looking for us.'

'AND YOU DID NOT THINK TO TELL US THIS BEFORE I-KlaraUV!' O-LaiXiiViolet yelled at me. Within the few moments of the revelation she'd lost so much energy her frequency had dropped dramatically.

They all rallied around her, going into an impromptu swirl displacing many other orbiting photon bundles. For a while it looked like a light storm had erupted shedding EMR in all directions. Neither her daughter, O-CherryBlossomDV or her granddaughter could understand such a strong reaction from her. Surely with the passage of time and their continued immunity from Earth there was no longer any reason to be concerned.

'Can you tell if they are carrying weapons?' O-SakuraDV asked O-WWWIndigo.

'They are still too far away. They could just be intending to use V616's gravity as a gravitational slingshot for another destination.' They knew this wasn't right, and O-VioletRalph picked him up on it.

'Then why are they slowing down?'

'Consider our condition,' O-WWWIndigo took another tack, 'Even if they are coming specifically to our location how are they going to recognise that we are more than simply another standard photon sphere around another common orbiting black hole. In any case, they will not want to get too close to the event horizon. If they have achieved such technological advances as to be able to come out here, they would certainly appreciate the dangers of being too near a black hole.'

During the discussion I broke away from the swirl to an easy equatorial orbit. I didn't want to be disturbed for a while. 'O-StepkaViolet are you coming?'

The two of them went pretty much everywhere together.

The bond between them had strengthened soon after meeting again on the outer sphere. It only remained for him to continue working on raising his frequency to match hers.

'William! … William!' I thought it best to at least try and find out what actually was going on. If William was right about his prophesy …

'Again you disturb me.'

'What can you possibly be doing that a simple contact should disturb you?' I'd had enough of his attitude from the last contact.

'Preparing to leave.' There was no reason not to tell I-KlaraUV his intention. 'By my calculations, and information I received from Prima9/EC, my assistance will be needed again.'

'Where in the universe would you possibly want to go? And who needs your help again?' As soon as I asked the question I knew. 'Surely not us?'

'Yes.'

'Is it because the Zeta Tengis are arriving?'

'So they have found you. They did come looking for you and I told them where you were.'

'Why? Didn't you realise they may be wanting to destroy us?'

'Admiral Kapitolina connected into my network. I mined her memory data and her intentions. She has no weapons. She only wants help from LX70.'

'Why didn't you contact me to tell me.' The more I interact with this AI the better I understand O-LaiXiiViolet's frustration with it.

'I am telling you now.'

He seemed to have very little understanding of the fragile balance in which the human psyche existed, regardless of what manifestation it was in. I stopped for a moment to give myself time to ask the right questions so as to keep this interaction as short as possible. 'I have just two questions for you. When are you leaving? And why do you think we will need your help?'

'To be accurate in my response I need to analyse your circumstances in both photon spheres, and what data you have been receiving from the ring singularity. I will not depart until the Prima9/EC meld is complete.'

'You have not answered my question.' Whatever this moon and its companion were doing was of no concern to me.

OUTER PHOTON SPHERE

THE MYTH

I WANTED to communicate with I-SakuraDV before reassuring those here in the outer sphere. There may be some developments, possibly as a result of gamma data from the singularity alluded to by William that I needed to know about.

'I-SakuraDV, are you available?'

The response came almost immediately. 'Yes. Are you making progress?'

'Considerable. Their knowledge base is increasing exponentially as they become more proficient at harvesting data from incoming photons. Are you alone?

'No'

'Can we make this conversation private?'

'… Done. Why?'

'I have learnt from William we are about to have some visitors. O-LaiXiiDV is considerably upset by the possibility that these visitors are from Earth. I thought our Lai-Xii would be the same.'

'Are they from Earth?'

'Yes. But that's not the problem. William is planning to come here. He told me we are going to need his help again. Have you received any gamma data suggesting a major change might necessitate extra outside help?'

When I-SakuraDV explained some of the preliminary analysis of that data it seemed William was right again, as always. However, my major concern did not involve doing I-SakuraDV's job. I had my own work to do. The arrival of the Earth expedition presented the ideal opportunity to debunk our myth. If I could get enough information from this Admiral Kapitolina about our true origins perhaps people here, as well as the inner sphere would start to consider our common past in a different light.

I returned to the swirl with O-LaiXiiDV still in the centre, though her fluctuating frequency storm had abated. O-WWWIndigo had moved to the perimeter letting her immediate family calm her down. I took him aside and told him what William had said to me.

'We assume you want us to work out how to communicate with Admiral Kapitolina.'

'Yes. I think we need to take the initiative. She will have no idea we are not just photons having one huge party with all our visible EMR colours. O-SakuraDV is busy. It will help her if we get the communication protocols set up.

*

The crews on all three Earth vessels had come out of stasis sometime after passing the Owl Nebula. Their star charts clearly indicated their location to be in the immediate vicinity of the constellation Monoceros, with V616 Mon now visible to their sensors.

'What do you make of that my Captains,' Admiral Kapitolina broadcast the general query. She gazed at an image that most probably no other sentient being had ever witnessed. The black hole could not be seen with the naked eye, only the soap-bubble luminescence of V616's outer photon sphere. The carnival of swirling, orbiting colours defied description. Occasionally one of its sectors lit up with an explosion of brilliance only to slowly subside into the background glow. At a stretch one could draw a parallel between the activity on the sphere with the display of movements on the surface off Jupiter, though the colours were pure and vibrant unlike the soft pastels of the giant.

'Our interferometric analysis indicates a full range of EMR being generated by this sphere. We are getting everything from mid-wave, short-wave infrared to UVC ultra violet,' said their science officer Olesya.

'I expected plenty of gamma but not the extraordinary palette like this,' added Vadim who'd been interpreting the data with Olesya.

Zakhar's team had created a deconstructed set of images from the incoming EMR which they broadcast to the other two ships. The Admiral turned her attention to the new images, while Vadim her comms officer, became distracted by something that sounded like non-random static noise.

84

'So just to be certain I understand what you're showing us here Captain Zakhar, this is the full structure of this rotating black hole.' While the Admiral considered the images, the small armada continued its deceleration directly towards V616 Mon.

'This theoretical boundary bubble is the event horizon, right? But what are these other two images? Aren't they the same thing?' She examined the two colourful spheres which appeared to have only very minor differences, so one could be forgiven in thinking they were the same image. But as she continued watching changes occurred in one that were not replicated in the other.

'No they are not the same. The one on the left of the screen, which you notice has a smaller diameter, is closer to the singularity. You will notice it is also rotating in the same direction as V616. Whereas the other sphere is larger and it's rotating counter to the inner sphere.'

'This is a phenomenon our scientists have not encountered before. What is happening here?' The Admiral needed to get some answers in order to determine whether they should continue on their current path, which would bring them into orbit well outside the event horizon. Nevertheless, such an unexpected and unexplained phenomenon could pose unexpected dangers.

'Admiral,' Vadim interrupted, 'I'm getting something here which is not a regular signal and has a variable repeating pattern.'

'Have you filtered out the background gamma radiation?'

'It's definitely not that,' Vadim started to sound excited. 'Didn't William say we would find Lai-Xii out here somewhere?'

'Sure, but none of this looks even remotely like a human or a Tengi outpost.'

'Well, it wouldn't, would it? William also said Lai-Xii had managed to transition the human manifestation from biological to digital. We don't know what else she might have been able to achieve,' commented Olesya.

'Are you trying to tell me she's there on one of these photon spheres?' As soon as the words came out Kapitolina remembered another thing William said … Know this – consciousness exists in all things. He also said … You will find her and a new evolved species of the human race on the outer and the inner photon spheres of the black hole V616Mon. 'Do you think it's even remotely possible she's managed somehow to transform humanity into pure energy!' This wasn't a question. It was a statement of realisation that that's exactly what they were about to experience. She turned to Vadim, just as excited as he was.

'Can you make out what the noise is? Is it them trying to signal us?'

'How would we know? They are many thousands of years ahead of us.'

*

O-WWWIndigo persisted with sending the same message without getting a response. 'It's not working I-KlaraUV. They're not recognising us,' Willi said.

But I knew we had to keep trying. William seemed to think we had to make contact for some reason. It couldn't be that difficult. We are the same basic species after all. 'What did William do to contact the planetary consciousness Europa Cell? It is totally alien to us, yet he managed something.'

'He didn't initiate the contact, EC did.'

'Just like we're doing, right. So how did he respond?'

'Data! Exchanging basic data in binary!' It took a long time for them to develop the ability to have a discourse. This must have been the first time in the entire long existence of the AI conglomerate's existence that it showed any degree of enthusiasm. So anything was possible. 'I'll transmit our EMR frequencies in a variable sequence.'

*

'Wait, the signal is changing,' Vadim noticed. 'I don't understand. It contains all the frequency signatures of what we've just analysed. Olesya, is there feedback from your equipment into our coms? I'm getting ... wait a minute ... the signal is repeating itself, and its coming from the outer photon sphere!'

*

By the time Admiral Kapitolina arrived at V616 and put her three ships into orbits at safe distances a rudimentary exchange had taken place between themselves and the Luminis. From there the exchange developed exponentially within hours. These people existing so far from each other in time and space had the same origins. They were made of the same cosmic stuff that had coalesced into a unique consciousness, which endured through all the changes and all the years that separated them.

'Who is in charge there? Does Lai-Xii still exist?' Admiral Kapitolina came directly to her reason for the expedition.

I made all the necessary introductions to the Admiral, but left it to O-SakuraDV to introduce her grandmother. This would be the most critical moment of the interaction. I wanted it all to go well. The Admiral and her crew were the vital link between us and our real past. Our people needed to know this.

'Admiral Kapitolina, there was once a lady you called Lai-Xii. She no longer exists. She has changed – evolved – beyond your comprehension, beyond even her own imaginings. Yet this new unique individual has retained some of her past memory – some, not all – not all the way back to Earth to the time when she had to emigrate. We know her, I know her as my grandmother, as O-LaiXiiDV. I said she was unique. That is not entirely accurate, for on the inner photon sphere there exists a future version of her,' transmitted O-SakuraDV.

'Stop!' the Admiral responded. 'William has already tried to bend my mind with fantastic tales. Are you saying that there are two Lai-Xiis?'

'Yes, there are. This happened as a result of a feedback loop originating on Earth in the Arrow of Time where two probabilities overlapped. It is complicated. But let us not dwell on that at the moment. Let me introduce you to O-LaiXiiDV.'

O-LaiXiiDV waited for a response from the Admiral. She could not quite remember this individual who'd come all the way from Earth. Why should she? They really had nothing to say to each other, nothing to do with each other.

I also waited to see what would happen.

'How do you think this will go?' O-StepkaViolet asked me.

I didn't know, but I was ready to step in. I waited for events to unfold without interfering. No doubt The Admiral had a lot to digest in a very short time. It must be difficult for her to connect with O-LaiXiiDV from what William revealed about their mutual past.

'We want only one thing from you Lai-Xii,' announced the Admiral.

I could see the difficulty O-LaiXiiDV had with hearing her ancient name like that. Again her frequency began fluctuating and we all prepared to surround and protect her from dissipating. She seemed to settle soon enough. Perhaps her historical name triggered access to old memories that helped her to relax.

'What do you want Kapitolina? You are not the Kapitolina I remember.' O-LaiXiiDV sounded a little aggressive.

'No, I am not. You are recalling my original ancestor, the one you and Doctor Evgeniya Yermolov engineered into something other than a human being.'

'That was necessary.'

'It is no longer necessary,' replied Kapitolina, taking control of her rising emotions. 'What we want is for you to reinstate our humanity. We want you to return us to our original full biological condition.'

This is what I wanted to hear – exactly what I wanted. 'See, O-StepkaViolet! This proves it! We are from Earth. We were a carbon based, physical biological life form and not some energy remnant from the birth of the universe.'

'I know this. All you have to do now is convince everyone else.'

Obviously O-LaiXiiDV had no idea how the regression could be achieved, even if she had a desire to do so – which she didn't. In her mind Earth and all who lived on it represented a serious threat, even after William's attempts to eliminate all vestiges of animosity towards those who had to escape. As she began rotating towards O-WWWIndigo with a question as to the possibility of achieving such a retrograde process, she was interrupted most abruptly by the sound of another voice.

I knew immediately who it was, my recent conversation with him still fresh in my thoughts. It seems William wasted no time once he'd made up his mind to do what had to be done. He must have arrived here at the outer sphere sometime recently, without bothering to announce himself. Typical.

'There is a way,' he said, 'but it will take as many generations as it has taken for your Zetas to evolve thus far. The mechanism requires further refining, which I will now carry out with my avatars. You cannot devolve, but there may be a way forward involving a molecular transformation. I require an analysis of Kapitolina's current structure to compare it to the alloy I developed for your body shells.'

The Admiral complied with the request by jetting a laser pulse containing all the relevant information. With that in his data cache William orbited away as suddenly as he had appeared. I could see O-WWWIndigo stream beside him and together they moved away to a polar orbit.

'How long is this going to take? What are we supposed to do in the meantime?' Kapitolina didn't bother hiding her impatience.

That was my cue. 'I have a request. It is a simple thing. Our people need to be reminded of their true beginnings. They are labouring under a quasi-religious misconception about our origin. I don't mean Europa – they all know about that. They do not believe where we came from originally. You are the proof of our past. Will you allow your crew to speak to our people?'

The Admiral could see no reason why that could not be arranged. It seemed a very small price to pay for what she wanted. 'Vadim, organise it with the other comms officers.'

I asked O-VioletRalph to work with Vadim to connect the visitors with members of the inner sphere. The erroneous myth had arisen amongst us in the inner sphere, not the population of the outer sphere.

Full synchronicity had to be established not only with frequency levels between our two population's individuals, but also their belief systems and most importantly, in their historical data memory. The inevitable could not be put off forever. V616 was not a static system. It continually grew as it absorbed more of the cosmic physical reality around it. That growth manifested in an increase in gravitational strength, to the power of which both our photon spheres were enslaved. The Arrow of Time and the Arrow of Thought worked in parallel with Gravity to bring our two photon spheres together. It was the only way the imbalance created by the feedback loop in the Arrow of Time as it concerned our species could be neutralised.

O-LaiXiiDV rotated towards me. I sensed she was still highly agitated, though that no longer bothered me as much. As long as our collective decision trees were funnelling us towards each other I didn't mind.

'Where in the black void did he come from, I-KlaraUVB? Hasn't he interfered enough!' referring to William.

'Perhaps you could tune in on the conversations going on between Kapitolina's crew and our people. It might bring to the surface a rather critical piece of your memory – the data related to who actually initiated the entire chain of events that has led all of us to where we are now.' I didn't want this seem like an accusation, for that's not what it was. She didn't interrupt. I think she actually began to delve deeper into her own past. I continued to help her along the journey of recollection. Sometimes that can be painful. 'Lai-Xii made the right decision at the time. Both the Earth and mankind had to be given a chance to evolve into the future. To that end you used everything and everybody at your disposal, including William after he revealed himself to you.'

'Why didn't you tell me he was coming here?' The anger had left her. It was a reasonable question. 'I thought I was finally free of that incorrigible AI.'

Again I responded with a slight diversion. 'I see you have noticed my frequency has again increased. The knowledge I gained in the process brought in by the cosmic photon dust is revealing a path through all the changes that have been taking place since you left Earth. Our immediate concern is to achieve harmony to bring our two spheres together. William's capabilities are needed again, just as you have used him in the past, to help us accomplish that. You don't have to interact with him. Let O-SakuraDV do that.'

Perhaps for Admiral Kapitolina it may have seemed like a long stream of time to have flowed past her awareness. I don't know. We no longer exist in any meaningful time frame reference. Change is upon us. It appears to be leapfrogging rapidly from moment to moment, even within our precarious circumstances. Before William returned I monitored the effectiveness of information interchange between the visitors and our inner sphere. Although a few voices still teetered on the edge of acceptance no one could refute the evidence of our origins. They were conversing with living proof of their heritage. My job was almost done. The myth could no longer be sustained.

'Have you received the instructions, DNA blue prints and transitional code sequences?' asked William.

'We do not understand it,' replied Kapitolina. 'It is all stored and will be passed onto our scientists.'

'I am re-sending the entire suite again. Use it to verify the first transmission. When you leave here it will be the last time you will have access to us.'

'So we will not be able to consult you if there are problems with our transition.'

'That is not why we are leaving. Our next destination, according to my calculations, has a high probability of being outside the Milky Way Galaxy. You do not have the technology to follow us.'

'What is the general process you have given us. At least explain that.'

I had to interrupt the exchange for the message from I-SakuraDV needed immediate attention. 'Are you shielded against intense gamma radiation bursts?' I asked the Admiral.

Olesya replied, 'Not much. Our titanium-gold alloy shells are reasonable against normal background radiation, and we have some shielding in the fabric of our ships.'

'You must go now if you are to survive,' William advised. 'The changes you will experience as you transition back to a biological organism will remove all of your alloy casing over time. Your bodies will become totally vulnerable. To answer your question Admiral, carbon is required to be added to your existing beta titanium-3/gold alloy shells. The second stage is to remove the alloy - again over many generations. The plans I gave you include a process by which you will be able to also change your neural architecture. Be warned – this will be a retrograde step in your processing capabilities.'

William didn't say anything else, even after several more questions from the Admiral.

As soon as Olesya heard me mention gamma radiation she sent out probes to measure the photoelectric ionization in the near vicinity of the event horizon. The readings caused the armada of three ships to depart with haste without any further interaction between us. At least Kapitolina achieved what no amount of argument, analysis or scientific data could have done to dispel the crippling myth that had arisen in the population of the inner sphere. And she did not go away empty handed. She had, in intricate detail, the entire realigning code to alter the evolutionary path of Zetas on Earth. I doubt if we will ever learn if they succeeded.

THE TWO KLARAS

THE GAMMA BURSTS began to intensify after Kapitolina's departure. By then she had been able to put enough distance between herself and us to minimise the effects of the radiation that would eventually catch up with her ships. She was safely on the way home. Whether those on Earth would still remember her and her crew or even their mission only she would find out.

Both our populations prepared to harvest energy from the incoming gamma storm. This was a most unusual and unexpected event. I have not experienced this level of intensity before. Although William had only recently arrived he seemed to already know more about it than any of us.

'You should be aware of the cause of this high level of influx,' he advised O-SakuraDV. 'I have consulted with I-WWWIndigo in the inner sphere. The bulk of the recent comet had insufficient mass to change the singularity's emanations, at least not the comet that came past the outer sphere, from within our galaxy. Information already absorbed by I-WWWIndigo shows the probability of near planet sized impacts through the event horizon from the other side.'

None of us fully understood the implications of that revelation. We didn't dwell on it and William didn't elaborate. One thing was certain - this presented the ideal opportunity to upgrade our population's frequencies. O-SakuraDV had already relaxed her control over energy absorption restrictions. After she learnt of the progression of her sphere towards the inner sphere and the probability of the juxtaposition of the two, she faced up to the major problem.

'The only way we will be able to merge with the future without causing both personal and a quantum conflict is to synchronise the energy levels of all individuals who are duplicates of their past/future selves.' I-WWWIndigo and William agreed on this and urged I-SakuraDV and O-SakuraDV to coordinate their peoples' activities in that respect.

Population numbers in both spheres had increased since their arrivals at V616. New photon bundles were regularly being energised by parent bundles who had harvested sufficient energy to do so. Attrition due to micro meteor impacts, emergent EMR bursts for which some were not prepared and some who could not control their energy absorptions meant a change in the composition of the populations.

One interesting recent phenomenon - and I have the sense that this is how it is meant to be - is the general character of the outer sphere. O-StepkaViolet also mentioned this to it.

We made a point of cruising in longitudes and latitudes, causing some disturbances in the process, but no major disruption. 'I haven't noticed any tight swirling, this time around,' I commented, 'and the bands of specific frequencies have become much wider. I can even see high intensity patches all over their orbits. I wonder what they are?'

'I've visited some of these. They are composed of closely related members of the same photon bundle families. In many cases they are extended families, including close friendships. These clumps are actually increasing in their constituent numbers.' That made me think. There is definitely something happening which is not of our own making. The people are drawing closer together. I'm sure it must be the same in the inner sphere.

'May I interrupt?' It was O-KlaraTurquoise.

'So — you've progressed from the Green. Where have you been?' I asked.

'Staying close by. Something's been bothering me.'

'Can I help?'

'I think you're the only one who can. I think this will be important for all of us. What happens when I get energised to Ultra Violet B, the same as you are now?'

'What do you mean?' I knew what had to happen, but I wanted to draw her out. The inevitability of the two of us having to integrate had already crossed my thoughts. I had no problem with that. I was the 'future' self, and quite comfortable with myself. It's always harder for the past present to visualise itself into the future, though with both of us being here that should not be a difficulty.

'What I mean is … do we remain as separate individuals?

'Would it bother you if we didn't?'

O-KlaraTurquoise thought about it. 'Are we really the same person, or simply divergent copies of a past individual?'

'I have a theory about this which may satisfy you. The chronological sequence of changes between my time in the past until you arrived at the same spacetime co-ordinates and the continuous changes for me since that point will have resulted in some experiential mismatch between us. But that does not mean we are not the same person. If I could give you all of those new experiences then I don't think there would be any differences between us at all, provided we both vibrated at the same frequency.

'Then tell me about your time here at V616.'

It didn't take long for us to embark on a data exchange, supplementing what each of us lacked with data from the other. A surprisingly simple process really. As we orbited in very tight longitudes together the information energy transfer seemed most natural. Within a few thousand orbits after completing the exchange we were content to allow the data to integrate into our dual consciousness RAM.

'How do you feel now?' I asked O-KlaraTurquoise.

'I feel we have become almost mirror images of each another, except I lack a little clarity in some things.'

'I will accompany you to the sector closest to the incoming gamma burst. I'll concentrate on absorbing enough to get to Ultra Violet-C. You do the same. I think you'll find it easier now.'

'You're telling we might end up merging, aren't you?'

'Yes. I think that is what will happen if you are right next to me at the time and we don't have a bleed from any other people. Shall we?'

O-KlaraTurquoise must have liked what I gave her, for as I changed direction she followed, tight up against me.

*

'I have more information for you, O-SakuraUV,' said William. This happened to be an interesting development in the AI. He'd started to volunteer information without being queried for it. I'm not sure what the implications will be, especially in view of interesting changes looming in the near future.

'I-KlaraUVC, you should hear this,' O-SakuraUV asked me to join them when she saw me cruising nearby. 'I sense you are different. Why is that?'

'I am now us,' I/we replied. For the time being we seemed to retain individual consciousnesses, though I'm sure that will not last. 'Your O-Klara and I have synchronised our frequencies and melded our experiences and all our personal data.'

William broke into our conversation. Something urgent must have been on his mind. 'I-WWWUltraViolet has been monitoring more EMR and debris coming into V616 Mon. Their analysis of the gamma spectra indicates another solar system, which is not on any of our star charts of the Milky Way.'

'Why should that concern us?' asked O-SakuraUV, 'we don't need any distractions while we're preparing to harvest from the gamma storm.'

'I suggest you make that an urgent priority. Those on the inner sphere are all concentrated on getting their frequencies as close to yours as possible. All your people should also be aiming for UVC frequency. There is a wormhole opening up.'

He just dropped that in at the end of his sentence as if it was the most normal thing in the universe. Perhaps in the rest of the universe it was, but not here, not for us. I had learnt enough about wormholes to know they were not as benign as black holes.

'You are also aware, no doubt,' William said, 'that your outer sphere is getting closer to the inner sphere, and the rate of this change is increasing exponentially.'

There it was again. I am quite certain William is experimenting with sarcasm. So, what I have to ask ourselves is what is happening to this AI. He was certainly nothing like this during my interactions with him on Europa. O-SakuraUV didn't seem to pick the change in him. She most likely needed to concentrate on doing exactly as William suggested.

I though perhaps we should jump back to the inner sphere soon. My work here is essentially done. I only need to make O-SakuraUV aware of what is going to happen when the two spheres converge. We are the living example of that, and she has to prepare everyone for this change, for this will surely happen to everyone. Those who cannot synchronise might manage to survive, though it's unlikely after the convergence of the spheres.

KAPITOLINA DEPARTS FOR HOME

TRAVELLING at the speed of light gamma rays emanating from V616 Mon's radiation storm caught up to the small armada of three space ships on their way back to Earth. They'd arrived at their first destination; an ice planet in the Monoceros constellation, CoRoT-7c, which had been a serendipitous choice by their on-board AI navigator.

Captain Leonid in the leading ship examined the ship's sensors to discover a stream of gamma radiation heading directly for them – the same stream that originated from V616 Mon, though not as intense after substantial absorption by the two photon spheres. 'Take us around the other side of CoRoT-7c, will you please Čudur,' the Captain quietly asked of his pilot. There was no need for panic or haste, the situation simply called for speedy prudence. Being an ice planet CoRoT-7c could provide the best possible protection from the radiation about to arrive. The other two vessels followed Captain Leonid's example.

'As soon as the storm passes we should replenish our reaction mass and make the last jump directly to the deceleration point for Earth.' Admiral Kapitolina wanted to waste no more time. They'd already been away for so long that she worried about their substantial time differential causing problems on their arrival back home.

Zakhar had the idea that he'd like to revisit Europa. 'I appreciate we had an urgent mission, but we now have everything you wanted,' he commented to Kapitolina.

'I know what's on your mind and it is something I would like to explore further as well. We can always go back to Europa afterwards. Between meeting a sentient moon and speaking with people composed of pure light I don't know which is more extraordinary. But we still have a job to finish. Yes, we have the re-formation codes, but it is not enough. The change has to be started as soon as possible. We must become people of flesh and blood again – with vulnerabilities. This is our only chance to be truly human.' She added the last thought after considering the importance it played in giving life the depth of its meaning. Even after interacting with Europa Cell, Prima9 and the Luminis she could only conceive of one true manifestation for life. Not even their own current incredible capabilities could satisfy the imperative to be true to their original evolutionary trajectory.

'I advise you all to deploy your shields though I doubt we'll be needing them. This giant planet is dense enough to absorb just about anything the universe can throw at it. While we're waiting we should prepare to fuel up.'

In front of them the bland white ball of water vapour and ice didn't seem to want to react when the γ-ray stream arrived. It wasn't until the deep purple halo began to dissipate into the planet stratosphere's outer layer that the entire globe became covered by a lilac halo.

'That stream of lilac and deep violet passing us must have been produced by the energised water molecules interacting with CoRoT's magnetic field,' speculated Vadim in the Admiral's ship. His partner Olesya didn't bother correcting him. She had to calculate the best time to approach the planet to grab their reaction mass before preparing for the next leg of their journey home. The combination of residual γ-rays that streamed past the planet, the energised water vapour highlighting CoRoT's magnetic and electric fields made the local planetary environment seem anything but friendly or safe for any extended length of stay.

*

After many years the three ships' deceleration began so far out of the Solar System they couldn't reasonably expect a response to any communication for months. All crew members from each of the vessels had been out of final stasis since arriving well within the Solar system neighbourhood.

'Send a message Vadim. Let them know we're almost home,' instructed Admiral Kapitolina. She kept her worrying thoughts to herself. Quite possibly most of the crews would have spared a thought along the same lines, but the Admiral didn't want to make an issue of it.

97

Captain Leonid, in charge of the leading ship with the Admiral on board wasn't just the Captain; he was also Kapitolina's long standing friend. On many occasions in the past they'd discussed and unravelled difficult problems. With the AI flying the ship he sought out his friend. Ever since they woke from stasis he could see the concern on her face. He had to knock several times at her quarters before she responded.

'Who is it? I'm busy.' She was in no mood to see anyone just then. The conundrum was getting her down.

'It's me, Leonid. Do we need to talk?'

A little sigh of relief escaped her as she opened the door to her friend. She motioned for him to make himself comfortable. Before he had reached the couch she'd already started to unburden herself.

'It's unbelievable that a simple matter of physics should cause such a huge problem.'

Leonid knew immediately what the subject of their conversation was going to be – Time.

'You must be concerned about the lapse of time since our departure from home. I see no problem if we only consider the purpose of our mission and what we have brought back.'

'Yes – yes … I understand that Leonid. What I'm trying to say is that none of us will see our families or our friends when we arrive.'

He tried consoling her. 'The crew knew this when we left, didn't they. And they all understood the importance of what we trying to do. If you ask me, I don't think anyone on Earth expected to ever see us again.'

'Perhaps you're right. Still, the thought of arriving home as a complete stranger is somewhat worrisome.'

'Just how much of a stranger do you think we will be? We haven't really been gone all that long.'

'You're forgetting we've been asleep most of the time. How many thousands of years have elapsed?'

'If you really want to know ask Olesya. I'm sure she's already made the calculation.'

Kapitolina didn't really want to know, for then she'd have to start thinking about it seriously. She'd have to think about the number of generations that had come and gone, about the advancements in their technology, whether they could still be able to communicate with each other – she'd have to think about the possibility that William's solution might not work at all any more. But there was no escaping reality. They would be home soon.

She called her Science officer. 'Olesya, could you come to my quarters. Be prepared to discuss our Time problem.'

'On my way Admiral.' Vadim and Olesya had taken the opportunity to relax after working with Čudur to adjust their course for the Solar System. Even in deceleration mode further minor adjustments would have to be made, but for the moment they could take it easy.

'You hear that, Vadim. I knew this was coming.' Reluctantly Olesya left her partner and made her way up several levels to the Admiral's cabin. The information she would want was all in her head, but took her slate just in case the Admiral needed convincing.

Stepping across the threshold of Kapitolina's quarters her surprise was not at seeing Leonid there, but that they weren't in a less formal configuration. 'Admiral. You want to know how much time has elapsed on Earth since our departure – yes?' she asked as she settled on the other couch opposite to them.

Kapitolina waited.

'The calculation itself is immaterial to the reality of what we can expect to find,' began Olesya. In other words – far too long. 'If I was to tell you that if we've only been travelling for a thousand years and that if we were only travelling at an average of near light speed – and if I was tell you that the ratio of the passage of Time might be around five to one – would that give you enough food for thought?'

'Are you telling us this as estimates?' Leonid asked for he could see Kapitolina's mind turning inwards upon itself, possibly doing a mental calculation.

'Yes, in rather conservative terms,' responded Olesya while watching her Admiral who quickly snapped out of her introversion.

'Your advice?'

'What kind of advice can I give? Do you want to know what to do about it? Or do you want to know if there's any way to synchronise our respective time lines?'

Kapitolina again waited, as did Leonid. Olesya's answer could be very interesting, he thought.

'We don't have the technology for synchronisation, thought that may be possible sometime in the future. And on that point – that's exactly where people on Earth are – into their future, well past us. They may be able to magic us in some way – but I think it's improbable. More likely they don't even remember us.'

All of sudden a whole new perspective opened up for the Admiral. Leonid just grinned. He always knew Olesya was clever with complex concepts.

'The question is how we could find out if the Zetas of our 'future' had even thought of this possibility, let alone achieved a working model to make it happen.' Leonid threw that up in the air to see if it would have a soft landing.

'I recommend we wait to get a response to our first communication. If we can still talk to one another you might like to ask them that question, Leonid.'

'Thank you Olesya.' Kapitolina turned to Leonid as her Science Officer left the cabin. 'Be honest with me my friend. Would I be stupid if I gave this possibility any more thought?'

'What's the alternative?' he asked.

Admiral Kapitolina didn't have time to tie her mind into knots over the possible or the impossible implications. A response to their first message arrived within two weeks, much sooner than expected, even though they were still so many light years from Earth. They could not decipher it and asked their on-board AI co-pilot to do its best to decrypt the strange bunching of words. It seems the Zetas had at least anticipated the communication problem.

An hour later the AI informed the Admiral. 'The message began with data that would be of no interest to you. The sequence of codes was meant for me to help translate their language into our old one. There is only one language on Earth now, which is a mixture of the old Chinese Mandarin, English and Russian ...' he was about to elaborate on the intricacies of syntax and grammar that resulted from the amalgamation of Earth's now 'ancient' languages.

'Stop,' instructed the Admiral, 'the message if you please.'

This AI may have been as comprehensively clever and advanced as William, but it had no personality. It didn't even rate a name of its own. It was simply known as the ship's AI. So this AI desisted from further explanations. In the absence of self-awareness it didn't seem to mind.

<Welcome home. We did not expect you so soon. Our orbital defences will destroy you if you do not transmit back the following ID code.> The message hinted at no concern whatsoever from the sender if the 'destruction' should take place. <Your landing co-ordinates are as follows ... 25°12'25"S 130°58'16"E'>

The longitude and latitude given showed up on the Admirals charts as a large flat expanse of land in central Australia at a town called Yulara. That raised a few questioning thoughts. Why be told to go to the middle of the desert in central Australia? That was the end of the message; no enquiry about their wellbeing, no curiosity to know if they'd located the historical individual responsible for their condition. Nothing to show they might have been the least bit interested in anything associated with the expedition.

'Is that all?' asked the Admiral. For some reason she expected a lot more. They'd been sent out into the Cosmos to find a needle in an enormous haystack, with absolutely no clues whatsoever, with the greatest unlikelihood of success and yet here they were on the way home with the treasure. 'Surely they could have shown a little more appreciation!' sneered Kapitolina at no one in particular. 'Send a reply,' she snapped. 'We are looking forward to seeing you too. And … Oh, by the way … we have what we went in search of.'

Vadim, looked at his Admiral for a second before beginning to relay the message. 'No. Stop.' She changed her mind. The heat had gone out of her moment of indignation. 'Just say … no wait … don't say anything. Just give them our ETA.'

'Do you want me to say anything about the threat?'

'No. But for the time being stay on track for the co-ordinates they gave us. Send out our smallest data-bug, let's find out what exactly is at that location.

The AI sent the message with the ID code. There was no reason for them to be annihilated prematurely. They were only coming home. They were not an alien invasion force.

A few days later another message arrived.

'Kapitolina, we may have a problem,' warned Leonid.

'Surely nothing could be a problem after what Olesya told us yesterday.'

'Vadim, show the Admiral.'

'IDENTIFY YOURSELVES. WHAT IS YOUR INTENTION?'

'Did this come from Earth?' asked the Admiral puzzled by the brevity and confrontational tone. What has happened here since we left? Are we even in the right universe? she pondered. She couldn't work out why both messages seemed so aggressive.

'No Admiral. It came from Mars.'

'Say again Vadim.'

'The origin is Mars.'

Kapitolina turned to Leonid, who just shrugged. 'Perhaps we have an outpost on Mars. Irina was talking about the possibility before we departed.'

'Right. That's what it must be. Tell them who we are Vadim, and tell them our intention is to go home to Earth.'

The quick response offered no comfort.

'DO NOT GO BACK TO EARTH UNDER ANY CIRCUMSTANCES!'

MARS

THIS WAS NOT the kind of communication one could reasonably ignore. Much more must have happened in the intervening millennia than simply an evolution of a single language on Earth.

Admiral Kapitolina conferred with her three Captains. Their unanimous decision to remain in space until the situation became clear seemed the safest option, their cargo deemed to be far too valuable to take any chance of having it destroyed.

'Vadim, please open a channel to Mars. I want to talk to whoever is in charge at the colony.' Rapid progress towards their home solar system made two way discussion time delays not too laborious.

'This is Citizen Irina Prime. Who am I talking to?'

Two surprises at the same time; the language was the same and the major figure of authority appeared to be the same one the team had left behind on their departure, at least by her name.'

'Is that you Irina?' asked Admiral Kapitolina, 'This is Kapitolina, head of the expedition you sent out.'

'You will address me as Citizen Prime. I am a descendent of the person you think I am. What proof can you provide for your identity?'

'Forgive me Irina Prime, but I need to ask you the same question. We received a rather threatening message from Earth which has made us cautious.

'Understood.'

'Perhaps this will help you identify us: Before we departed your ancestor said to me personally that she was sad because she missed something special in her life. Do you know what that was?' asked the Admiral.

'Admiral Kapitolina, if you know this then we can trust one another. Your Irina made certain that each of her subsequent generations began life by learning this one fact. She stressed the importance of it, particularly as her life span neared termination point.'

'She may have said this to you,' responded the Admiral, ... 'I can no longer remember the barking laugh of the Steller's sea eagle or the gentle song of the Siberian ruby-throat ...'

'That is correct Kapitolina.'

'What happened, Citizen Prime?' asked Kapitolina, immediately reassured by her response.

'You may call me Irina, in private. We kept the tradition of continuing our ancestors' names as a sign of respect. First, let me warn you again in the strongest possible terms ... Do not land on Earth. You will not survive. Maintain your current course until we give you new co-ordinates. I also suggest you engage in no further communication with Earth. It will enable their defences to target and destroy your three ships. They have become an unfriendly and aggressive bunch. Their first course of action will be to destroy anything they cannot identify and immediately control.'

'Tank you Irina for your concern. We will see you soon.'

They did not need to alter course until much closer to the red planet. It's orbit was coming between themselves and Earth. With a little tweaking from their pilot they could approach Mars during the last stages in the planets communication shadow.

*

'Mars does not appear to have changed since I was here last,' commented Admiral Kapitolina as they approached the red planet. She, Captain Leonid and the crew all watched as their pilots guided their ships to the required location.

'Of all the possibilities that lay before us I could never have imagined we would be landing here,' Leonid said quietly to Kapitolina. 'Are you absolutely sure we can trust this Tengi who calls herself Irina?'

'The choice is clear. It's either Earth or Mars. You know as well as I that our ship's AI detected Earth's probes zeroing in on our position. Have you forgotten what our data-bug brought back about the landing site we were directed to on Earth?'

'No. You're right. Why would they instruct us to land at an obvious military installation? The place was too heavily guarded. Some serious conflict must have been either in progress or at least expected. And their first and only message wasn't exactly welcoming.'

They watched the Martian landscape roll beneath them, red, hot and dusty, not much different to the environment around that town in central Australia. No evidence of civilisation showed anywhere on the terrain they'd already passed. While cruising over the relatively flat lava plains it was difficult to imagine the immensity of their destination; the Valles Marineris, Mars' greatest canyon.

'We'll be arriving near the central area of the canyon in fifteen minutes,' advised the AI. We are going to a mesa near the Northern extremity, close to the cliff face, some six kilometres down.'

The crew saw nothing but a well cratered red dust covered landscape; not at all inviting to any living thing that one could imagine. Right on time the mesa revealed itself to their port side, onto which all three vessels immediately descended as instructed by the resident Martians/ex-Terrans.

'Why do you suppose we had to hug the terrain?' asked Olesya.

'I assume it has something to do with not being so openly visible to detection. My guess is the forces on Earth are keeping a close eye on what goes on out here.' It seemed to make sense to Leonid that if the two planetary civilisations were fighting each other both needed to take precautions.

The mesa came upon them quicker than expected. It had more than enough room to land large vessels, even of their size. As each one touched down the surface beneath the ships sunk into the ground even before their engines had gone cold. As they submerged into the underground cavern a whole new world opened up before them.

Because of its size and the bright lighting the roof of the cavern could not be seen. Their on-board sensors showed a kilometre long, and an impossible sixty metres high at least enclosure. Everyone aboard each vessel had to alight before the ships were pulled off the landing pads, which then raised themselves back to the mesa surface without any visible means of support. Looking around the space it seemed that the entire cavity appeared to be lined with buildings squeezed up against one another, with illuminated windows everywhere. If there could have been a sky it would surely have been visible, except for the many lights flooding the enclosure. Guards, or at least they looked like guards with what appeared to be weapons by their sides, escorted them to the nearest vehicle, which took them silently to the nearest wall of the cavern and through large metallic doors.

'Surely these are maintenance robots or something of the kind,' Zakhar commented on seeing the short dumpy creatures in front of them in their shinning sky blue metallic armour. Their neckless large barrel chests definitely made the arrivals think of machines rather than beings. After their experience with the photon sphere a simple thing like a huge cave should not have captured their attention. Except this was a structure they could image as being possible, regardless of the enormity of the engineering involved. Even barrel chested robots didn't seem unduly out of place.

'You can remove your suits now,' the robot closest to them suggested. 'Citizen Prime will meet you at the main observation bubble. Follow me please.'

The entire gathering of thirty four people followed their guide through a maze of brightly lit tunnels, though from their height and width they looked more like vaulted city streets, with buildings on either side and transportation nodules moving noiselessly overhead.

'What is all this?' Zakhar put the rhetorical question, one they had all been thinking. This was nothing like the world they left behind; a city nestled in a green valley between snow-capped volcanic peaks in the Kamchatka peninsula. Apparently their underground rendezvous point was not far as they continued on foot and in lifts to travel higher in this subterranean world.

As the lift came to a stop the wide doors opened to a vista that stunned them by the sudden change in the environment. Directly in front of them they could see a hazy vista of towering red brown cliffs, possibly a hundred or more kilometres away, with nothing between themselves and the cliffs. Some invisible membrane prevented anything from outside and anything or anybody from inside to change places – even by accident.

A figure slowly turned to regard them before speaking. It looked very much like the first robot that had greeted them.

'I am Citizen Prime Irina. Welcome home.' She let them digest that before continuing. 'Please join me.'

This was definitely not the home they remembered, nor the form of humanity they'd left behind. This individual, though appearing naked in its light blue metallic sheath revealed nothing about its gender.

Its neckless barrel chest with an overly large bulbous head supported by a one meter high body suspended on short legs surprised the small gathering of humans. Not until the Admiral overcame her astonishment to step towards the beaconing creature did the others also move.

As the crowd of space travellers moved forward they noticed enough very low seating to accommodate all of them uncomfortably. Irina drew Kapitolina off to the side. 'Make yourselves comfortable. Everything you need will be provided. You, of all the people of this world or of the old world represent the most significant encounter in our long struggles through the centuries.' The Citizen Prime had noticed their initial reaction to her. 'I can see you are surprised by what you see. Make no mistake, we are human, by a loose definition of the term, though much evolved since you left us.'

Standing close to the invisible screen Irina made a broad sweep of her arms indicating the canyon vista to the left and right. 'Look out there. It is magnificent. This four thousand kilometre canyon is our home now. We have many outposts around the planet, mostly for surveillance, but the Valles is the centre of our civilisation.'

Kapitolina stepped up beside her. The sheer scale of the topography stunned the imagination. Though devoid of colour, being predominantly in the ochre range, nevertheless patches of green and highlights of light tan created an overall effect of an alien world; far more alien than Europa, even more alien and desolate than the carnival of colours of the photon sphere they'd visited. She glanced towards her crew, who similarly stood entranced by the spectacle. Beckoning to her three Captains to join her she asked Prime Citizen for some explanations.

'Why are you here? What has happened on Earth?'

'You have been gone a very long time Admiral. Generations upon generations have come and gone. We have almost forgotten you even existed.'

'Have you almost forgotten why we travelled into space?' Kapitolina didn't mean it but a slight tone of sarcasm crept into her voice.

'Indeed no. Though very few of us now actually know who you are. The opportunity to use the information we needed then has long since passed. Whatever it is you have is of no use to us, especially if it is intended to restore our biological life support systems. As you may have observed we have adapted to our Mars environment. Being smaller has many distinct advantages.' Irina glanced at Kapitolina and her Captains to gauge their reaction. These people from space had in essence sacrificed their lives for the restoration of humanity to its original form, and here they now stood being told that their effort was wasted.

'Excuse us Irina Prime, we need to discuss this amongst ourselves.'

"Yes indeed. You now need to reassess the very reason for your existence – and what you are going to do about it. You are caught between your past and this future. The few people you have with you have become quite unique in the history of human evolution."

Kapitolina moved her group out of hearing before she continued. 'You heard what she said. Your thoughts?'

'Well! She is something interesting to look at! Right … ok … beside the point. I knew something seriously dangerous had happened from the moment we received that first message,' Leonid spoke first.

Zakhar didn't like the smell of the whole scenario. 'We're now on this desolate planet, possibly stranded, possibly captives. We don't really know anything about this Citizen Prime, or the people back on Earth.'

'Absolutely,' piped up Darya, 'for all we know these people here should be the ones we need to be wary of.'

'Right. Go back to your crews. Tell them to say nothing about us, our mission or what we have in our possession, to anyone. I'll deal with Irina. Oh … and be prepared to leave quickly if we have to.'

Citizen Prime waited patiently for Kapitolina to return to her. She recognised the difficulty these people were faced with. Seeing the expression on the Admiral's face she thought it best to take things slowly. 'What would you like to know?' she asked casually.

'Why were we warned about being attacked?'

'Ah – so you received that message. We intercepted it, that's how we knew you were coming. Because we are in the process of trying to achieve a balance. In short – we are at war.'

Kapitolina moved back to the invisible screen accompanied by Irina, not to marvel at the Martian landscape but to try to make a decision. 'Why the conflict? William was supposed to have done something about the aggressive nature of the Zetas.'

'You remember William too? We have a different communication and information system now to what he was. There is no danger of it becoming self-aware. We may as well start there I suppose.' Irina led the Admiral to seats a little further along the viewing corridor. Kapitolina had to stretch her legs out on the short stool-like hard seats to be in the least bit comfortable. At least it put the two women at about the same head height. 'No doubt William was an extremely accomplished and clever AI. But that's all. He could not possibly have fathomed the complexity of the human neural network, and should not have presumed to have been capable of improving it. Having said that what actually happened is not his fault per se. To keep a long story short here it is in general terms.'

Kapitolina interrupted the flow. ' Is this confidential? Can I discuss it with my team?'

'Certainly. The cause of the problems and why we are here and not on Earth is common knowledge. It has simply become part of our history, part of our heritage. We've been here so long that Earth no longer matters to us, other than for the danger they still represent. To continue ... The process, you understand, did not happen suddenly. We had time to adjust – we had time to prepare and escape.'

There is something oddly familiar about this, thought Kapitolina as she recalled the circumstances under which Lai-Xii, the historical Lai-Xii had to abandon Earth.

'We are all descendants of the Zetas left behind by a person called Lai-Xii, do you remember her?' Kapitolina nodded. *So this person is probably who she says she is.*

'We are the descendants of the same Zeta Tengi that William adjusted. Except something went wrong. Whether it was due to critical data corruption within our quantum neural networks, or some exotic digital virus, made no difference to the emergence of a radical aggressive trait in the behaviour of some of the Zetas – not all, only a few initially. At first we tried punitive measures to control them, which didn't work. Incarceration of those with extreme violent behaviour didn't stop others becoming violent either. For some reason more and more of them emerged from the general population.'

I could believe this. From what I learnt of our ancient history those were the exact same triggers that drove Lai-Xii to extreme measures to try and save the human species from exterminating itself. Kapitolina remembered the history of the years before the migration.

'I see from your reaction these things are not altogether foreign to you. Gradually our society splintered into two factions. Those who had been corrupted - and everyone else. You can guess who was left behind on Earth.'

'Information that one of our data-bugs brought back about the source of the first message makes sense now. I can understand the reason for all the defensive hardware.' *Perhaps these people are the aggressive ones ...* the thought flashed through the Admirals mind ... *but then why would they had had to flee the planet.* 'Did anyone try to repair the mutations?'

'Yes, of course. It wasn't an illness we were dealing with. It was simply normal human behaviour. We could not find a cure for that. So we left – as did Lai-Xii so long ago.

Once again the Admiral turned towards the invisible screen. She could see no sign of life outside. There were no vehicles or any structures of any kind to betray the presence of an advanced civilisation. As she gazed out a red dust storm appeared over the rim of the canyon, travelling as if in slow motion. It looked like it was going to roll right over the top them. Gravity gradually pulled the mass of superfine dust down towards the floor of the canyon. Perhaps in a few days it might completely obliterate their view through the transparent screen. Her thoughts wandered while Citizen Prime Irina left to talk with the other arrivals.

Kapitolina considered what they could possibly do under the circumstances. Irina seems genuine enough. *We have to trust somebody, certainly not people who send threatening messages. The only thing we have is William's code. If only we knew how that worked* … Gradually an idea began to crystalize … *If Irina's AI system could analyse it, and perhaps modify it … and maybe we could infect …*

That's as far as she dared to consider the possibilities. They'd only just arrived on Mars. They had no clear understanding of the mentality of their hosts, or their potential enemy. It was much too early to plan any course of joint action with Irina against them.

*

The days blended into weeks and into many months. There was nowhere they could go. To be back in space certainly had no future for her crew. They were accommodated in comfortable surroundings, without any restrictions on their movements or their contacts with the Martian citizens – except they were forbidden, not just discouraged, from going into the outside environment. At first that seemed strange, until it became obvious that no-one went outside. Or if they did it was most infrequently and most surreptitiously. Gradually they keyed into the flow of existence amongst these most peculiar humans. Some of her even seemed to find like minded souls with whom they began to bond. Some found ways to make minor contributes to this Martian society's daily life routine.

Over time Kapitolina and Irina became friends. Apparently the generations had not changed Irina's character. Essentially she was still the same individual who once ruled the small civilisation back on their home planet. It was during one of their many private meetings at another section of the canyon wall that had been constructed with a huge panoramic invisible barrier, that Kapitolina understood the restrictions on excursions into the Martian landscape.

The barrage of explosions in the distance ejected such a volume of dust into the thin Martian air that in a very short time they could see nothing through the screen. Although no projectiles actually exploded within Valles Marineris the intention could not be mistaken for being a friendly hello.

'Is that them?' asked Kapitolina, alarmed at the suddenness of the attack.

'Yes. Periodically they try to rattle us into a reaction. They know we're here, but not exactly where we've dug in. So far they've been reluctant to send an armed assault. Perhaps that is not too far in the future.'

The incident stirred Kapitolina into making up her mind. 'Irina, I want to discuss something with you.'

'Oh, yes,' came the guarded reply.

'I've talked this over at length with my Captains and we all agree.'

'You want to discuss the code you brought back.'

'How did you know?' That's exactly what she had in mind.

'I didn't mention it before though I've been thinking about it. We know why you went on the expedition. The only reason you would have returned is if you had what you wanted. You didn't bring back anybody, therefore you must have brought back something else. The rest wasn't hard to work out. How do you think the code could help us? And I don't mean in terms of a devolutionary process. As you see we could not survive here as a standard homo sapiens.'

'You didn't provoke this attack – that's obvious. Perhaps you have no way to defend yourselves either.' Kapitolina paused for a moment and acknowledged Irina's nod. 'Get your system to examine the code and let's see how we can use it in another way.'

Irina smiled. 'Exactly what I had in mind.'

Over the many months of interacting with one another, exchanging memories, hardships and experiences the two became close, trusting friends.

The dust continued billowing against the invisible barrier as the two friends planned a mission to influence the situation on Earth.

EARTH

KAPITOLINA RETURNS WITH A VIRUS

THREE SHIPS heralded their approach to Earth by broadcasting a distress signal.

'Where the hell did they come from!' yelled Autarch Afanasy. The leader of Earth's global military dictatorship had been in a foul mood ever since his staff lost contact with three alien craft heading in their direction.

Being interrupted in the middle of an enjoyable execution did nothing for his cheery disposition. Making an example of incompetence always gave Autarch Afanasy a good energy boost. The officer responsible for losing the three alien ships had no hope of surviving the sensory deprivation chamber. Watching the cerebral images generated by mental deterioration had become the leader's favourite pastime. It was a tradition passed down the generations from one of his ancestors. The original Afanasy, a tetra-amelia syndrome victim, had been forced into a sensory deprivation experimental toy by an infamous woman called Lai-Xii. That man had suffered to such an extent that his mind never recovered. His female friend Lubov suffered just as much yet she almost completely recovered without going insane, whereas Afanasy tipped over the edge into madness.

'Are they the same ones that disappeared several months ago?' he screamed again at his 2IC. General Lubov only nodded. Any friendship that may have developed between them had become seriously corrupted. The Autarch had no regard for anyone except himself.

'Get them down here – and this time don't scare them off!' The order was clear enough. Failure to carry it out would mean another candidate to entertain the Autarch's sadistic cravings.

Deterioration of the global society began at the time of the anomalies experienced by some of the populations' quantum neural networks. It manifested in the re-emergence within the human psyche of a disposition towards resolving differences through extreme aggressive behaviour. This did not diminish over time, rather the opposite. Those who were not afflicted by the deterioration, fled – to Mars. For the remainder such behaviour became the norm and as such it was accepted as the way things had to be. Autarch Afanasy's demented state found a strange release in being able to express his madness through sadism and absolute control.

'Autarch Afanasy,' General Lubov caught his attention, 'we have identified the vessels. They are not of Martian manufacture. They are in fact not of this era. We had to search deep into our historical data. The woman in charge is Admiral Kapitolina.'

'Who would be demented enough to put a woman in charge?' Autarch Afanasy sneered as General Lubov continued. She had her own thoughts on the matter, but the present circumstances were not appropriate to discuss those with the Autarch.

'You may recall from our ancient history, the Grand Matriarch Irina; also a woman, sent the expedition out in search of yet another female, Lai-Xii.' General Lubov patiently explained the history, which she knew very well the Autarch had not bothered to study.

'Don't patronise me! I know exactly who Lai-Xii was, the bitch!'

'Then you will know why the expedition was set up.'

'Admiral Yuri!' the Autarch yelled for his right-hand man. 'Get out there and escort them in. And while you're at it find out what they've come back with.'

'Yes Autarch. I take it you do not wish to destroy them at this stage.'

'We'll reserve that pleasure for the Terrace.' Even the thought of having some fresh minds to unravel helped the Autarch feel better.

*

At the end of the escort planet side the entire crew of all three ships ended up in a single large room; white, unadorned, no table, no windows only enough seating around the walls to accommodate them.

This, one of several such rooms of different sizes, was part of the building closest to the main landing area within easy reach of the Colosseum.

General Lubov entered first. Her somewhat diminutive figure did not exude authority. She knew the Autarch would keep the captives waiting for days just to put them on edge. Neural images of victims were always more entertaining if the quantum matrices had resorted to some degree of chaotic processing prior to unravelling.

'Who is in charge here?' General Lubov demanded of an individual who looked similar to the original Irina of history.

'This individuals dull greenish brownish khaki shell is not very attractive,' Captain Leonid whispered to his Admiral.

'Now! My time is limited!'

Captain Leonid stood to volunteer for the position. When their distress signals resulted in an armed escort down to Earth Admiral Kapitolina and her Captains decided to be as guarded as possible with these people. Citizen Prime Irena made the situation abundantly clear – 'Do not trust these people under any circumstances – any of them,' she warned.

The Admiral had a gut feeling and flagged him down to step forward herself. 'I am Admiral Kapitolina. I would like to speak with whoever is in control here.' She made a point of recognising the officer's authority.

'For the time being that will be me. Come.' Barked, annoyed at the snub.

Kapitolina glanced back at Leonid, who could do nothing to help, but stood again to go with the Admiral, his close friend.

'Not you! Just her,' she bark more loudly.

The two women walked out of the austere environment into another room no more cheerful. It had two chairs set up opposite each other, but not within an intimate distance. The Admiral took one of the chairs and sat without being asked, which surprised General Lubov. *Obviously this woman doesn't know who I am.*

'Be careful, Admiral. This is not the same world you left behind. Your chance of survival, and that of your crew is – let me say – indeterminate. A great deal depends on what you are about to tell me.'

The Admiral's expression didn't change. She would not allow herself to be intimidated. She decided to adopt an attitude she would have had towards any of her lower rank officers, and waited to see what this self-assured woman had to say for herself.

'I like a person with courage. We will get on well together. Now - to business. Why have you returned?' Lubov asked.

'Our mission is accomplished.'

'I see. We'll get to that later. Why did you approach with a distress signal?'

'We received a message from you which suggested your orbital defences might decide we were a danger and would perhaps have acted accordingly.'

'That is a reasonable answer. But don't play with me.'

The Admiral didn't bother to respond. It was not her habit to take little niggling threats seriously. She waited.

'Where have you been in the last few months?'

'On Mars.' It would not have taken a quantum physicist to work out the origins of their most recent trajectory.

'Continue.' General Lubov softened her tone. Here was an individual who understood the meaning of authority and how to use it.

'We received another message; from Mars, shortly after yours and decided to investigate. They warned us against coming here. Yet here we are.'

'Do you not think that was foolish?'

'Our mission is not fully concluded until we deliver what we went out to find.'

General Lubov perceptively straightened herself. No more beating around the bush. *This is what I want, and I want it before The Autarch gets it.* 'Continue,' she said with considerable restraint. Their historical records quite explicitly highlighted the reason for the expedition. The Admiral was to return with the means by which the Zeta Tengis' engineered shells — and minds — could be returned to their former human biological configuration.

The eagerness with which General Lubov waited for her answer was not lost on the Admiral. *Just how factual should I be with these people. From what I've seen so far they are not the friendliest lot.* 'Software. You may be aware of an AI called William, who left Earth with Lai-Xii. We found him. He gave us the software that would, over extended generations, restore us to our old carbon based biological selves. That is the mission our Grand Matriarch Irina charged us with.'

What she didn't tell them was that the very process of examining the software created by William, by downloading it into their systems, would generate worm code. This code would replicate itself and spread throughout a network — any and every network, including their quantum matrices when they plugged in for re-energising. She also neglected to mention what exactly that worm code had been designed to do.

For a moment the General seemed distracted. She'd just received a sub-neural message that her search team could find nothing of any use to them on the space ships at all. No weapons, no developed technology, no software other than that required to run the ships, and each ship only in possession of a primitive AI navigator.

She turned back to the Admiral, animosity having returned to her visage. 'You are required to provide this software.' Not that Lubov was desperate, but she needed some leverage against Afanasy and this would provide a perfect threat against the Autarch to ensure her own survival.

'I take it your search teams have found nothing of a threatening nature on our ships,' Kapitolina coolly responded, assuming the content of the communication.

'The code – Now!'

'General, let us be frank with each other. You said yourself this is not the same world we left behind. I can see that. We would prefer to return to an environment more – how shall I put it – more familiar to us.'

'Very well.' General Lubov stood to leave the room. The Admiral remained seated, looking quite comfortable. 'Wait here!' The General ordered, to which she received no reaction.

'They want to bargain with us?' shouted The Autarch. 'We do not bargain! Get that software. I want it! I don't care what you have to do to get it.'

Violence and aggressive problem solving techniques were not the only effects of the mutated virus effecting the current generation Tengi. Greed and hunger for power seemed to be a prominent fringe characteristic from which the majority of Zetas suffered. Perhaps in the context of this civilisation it may be better to have said, enjoyed.

General Lubov knew the difficult situation her leader had placed her in; dire consequences for her should she fail to obtain the prize, whether she was friend in the past or not: With no less serious consequences if she made some arrangement with these space travellers that was not entirely and in totality to their own advantage. And no less dramatic an outcome for her personally if by some remote chance The Autarch ended up being robbed of his greatest pleasure in life; seeing each of these 'traitors' deconstructed by his very sophisticated sensory deprivation entertainment unit.

General Lubov considered her precarious position. *If I don't get this probably useless bit of information he'll use me for entertainment. If Admiral Kapitolina has been truthful with me we will not want to go through the devolutionary process anyway – I can see no advantage in it for us. It will only make us more vulnerable to attack from Mars. Damn! I'm going to have to make a deal with her – it doesn't mean I have to keep my side of the bargain.* She looped the same thoughts over and over as she returned to the interrogation room.

'The software – Now! No more delays.' The Admiral had remained seated and pretended to have dozed off as the General entered. She waited for the 'request' to be made again, without jumping to comply.

'Damn you Admiral. Do you know what this means for you and your crew?' She chose not to elaborate on the consequences to her own wellbeing and future career.

Kapitolina read the signs of frustration, and more than that – fear. This General was in a tight spot. Good. 'When may we continue our travels?' she asked offhandedly.

'You are going nowhere unless you do as you're told.' The General almost screeched.

'I take it that means that we can come to some kind of arrangement?' This statement elicited a hiss from her interrogator.

Good. 'There's a slight problem. Our respective systems will most likely not be compatible.' That was enough to draw the General deeper into the quagmire.

'I will take care of that.' *At last we're getting somewhere.* 'The information is secreted in your ship I presume.'

'I will need my Captain, Leonid.'

In the main room The Admiral beaconed to her Captain. He recognised the signal, as did the rest of the crew. The ruse was on.

By way of a distraction Kapitolina asked the General, 'How is it we can understand one another?'

'A translator, downloaded into my matrix before your arrival.' It seemed like a harmless enough question.

At the hatch to the Admiral's ship she took a weapon from the 'robot' on guard, motioning her two captives to precede her into their ship. It all seemed so primitive to Lubov; no doubt state of art of their era. The Admiral took the opportunity to take a seat in front of the main console on the bridge. Captain Leonid moved to some other instruments, which were nearer the entrance. The General, with weapon still pointing in the Admiral's direction, took the only other seat available.

'Get your system up. I'll tell you what to do,' the General ordered Leonid, who did exactly as instructed.

Lubov realised she would have to see her strategy through to the end without interference or involvement from any of her own people. To do so would have meant alerting Autarch Afanasy – best that be avoided.

Several things happened almost simultaneously as she contemplated her strategy. The General suddenly slumped in her seat, dropping the weapon. The seat itself was a port into their ships system, and through a feedback loop Leonid overloaded the General's matrix. The code, imbedded within Kapitolina, downloaded into Earth's network through the General's connecting wireless protocols. The worm went to work immediately, first disabling the planets defence and attack systems, and communications long enough for Leonid to release the rest of his crew from confinement.

Before taking the General's weapon he initiated take off procedures. At the hatch he commandeered the guard under duress, to go with him to get the rest of the crews. They would only have one ship, but that was enough for what they had in mind.

'I see you've disconnected her,' Leonid said as they all arrived back in the ship, with the guard in tow. Good. Captain Zakhar, would you be so good as to power down the guard and the General permanently.'

'Not the General,' intervened the Admiral.

Captain Leonid hit the button and they lifted off without a shot being fired.

By the time Earth reinstated their targeting and weapons systems they were well out of reach. General Lubov sat with Admiral Kapitolina watching the futile efforts to destroy them.

There was no turning back for the General. Her assessment of the situation had only one outcome – if she gauged Kapitolina correctly. If they wanted to eliminate her they would have done so already. These people were not like Afanasy and his thugs. She decided to lay it on the line and trust her instincts about the Admiral.

'I would have let you do this, you know; to get away,' Lubov confided in Kapitolina, 'not all of us are animals like Autarch Afanasy.'

'I couldn't take the chance,' replied Kapitolina.

'Did you leave the code behind?'

'Yes. If they decide to implement its functions it will take many generations to make all the changes. William designed the code to restore biological systems, and neural systems without effecting other enhancements he'd made to the psychological disposition of the human species. He tried to eradicate the predisposition to violence and everything that went with it.'

'He won't do it, you know. The man's a maniac. The whole planet fears him. He won't even tell them about the code, though some of his scientists will know when they discover the disruption to the weapons systems. I don't like their chances of living for too long.'

'Be that as it may. We have fulfilled our mission. We have given the people of Earth a chance. It's up to them what they do with it.' The Admiral said this more to herself than her 'guest'.

'What happens to me now?' asked Lubov.

'You can come with us, back to Mars. I don't think they'll be too harsh on you, especially after I tell the Citizen Prime how you helped us.'

'Why are you trusting me?'

'Why do you trust me?'

The matter was settled. They were on the way to Mars, safe for the foreseeable future. Kapitolina could not even speculate what that future held for them. So few of her era had survived. They had lost their home; neither belonging on Mars nor on Earth. The brief adventure back to their home planet gave them no opportunity to revisit their departure point to see what had become of the people in Tau City on Kamchatka. Perhaps that could be something to work towards.

*

Lai-Xii, the woman who began what she thought would be a solution to the survival of the human species so many thousands of years ago, could not have foreseen the consequences of her actions. Not only was humanity not obliterated from the face of the Earth, it had become a creature far more sinister than would have been the case if left to evolve naturally.

Not only were there people on Earth, there also existed an extra-terrestrial phenomenon, originating from the human psyche, embedded within a planetary consciousness, within the mind of Europa thought to be nothing more than an ice moon of a gas giant planet within the Solar System.

Most certainly she could never have conceived that hers and her peoples' transition from biological to digital manifestation would terminate as bundles of pure light energy in two photon spheres revolving around a black hole.

*

Admiral Kapitolina contemplated the mystery unfolding around her as she took her 'humans' originating from in between eons of human history to yet another manifestation of homo sapiens – Martians.

119

EVENT HORIZON

CONVERGENCE

V616 MONOCEROTIS did nothing different to what all black holes do.

The existence of two photon spheres converging upon each other was of supreme indifference to it. Neither did it concern itself with the peculiarity that these spheres contained the psyches of a race of once biological creatures who'd managed to split themselves into 'past' and 'future' fragments manifest as photon bundles. The very concept of Time carried very little import in the life of a black hole. It had no regard for the looping of the Arrow of Time problem afflicting Homo Universapiensis, or its consequences.

This particular black hole, adhering to its true nature, had embarked on its own journey of change which had already begun several billion years ago; one of transforming into a wormhole. William detected the emergent phenomenon soon after arriving at the outer sphere.

'The conditions we are experiencing are not stable,' he said to O-SakuraUV. 'As the change process builds momentum there will be an exponential increase in the probability of inevitable travel through the mouth of the wormhole from here to the exist at the other end. You still have time to boost your frequencies. My calculations indicate that the higher your frequencies the greater the chance of surviving the transit.'

'O-SakuraUV,' I interjected because what I had to say had particular relevance to the conversation in progress, 'You are aware that I am now a composite of my past and my future selves, existing in this new present.'

'How did you achieve this?'

'By synchronising our frequencies. The subsequent melding required no additional expenditure of energy. However, we did need to make friends. I now have a clear knowledge of the distant past, of the recent past and of my previous probable future up to this point. I will begin training your people for this juxta-positioning.'

'You are now at UVC frequency Klara, is that correct?' asked O-SakuraUV. Is that our optimum target William?'

'Yes,' I replied. 'I and O-StepkaUltraViolet have already trained many others how to harvest energy from the gamma storm generated by the singularity to reach UVC. They are already engaged in so doing.'

William agreed with the target frequency. 'If the wormhole contains enough exotic matter, which I-WWWUltraViolet will be able to ascertain as the mouth of the wormhole opens, the UVC level will be enough for information; that is us, to be transmitted through to the other end. I predict however, considerable losses in both Photon bundle numbers, and a substantial reduction of our energy levels.'

O-SakuraUV immediately coordinated our activities with I-SakuraUVA.

'We are already well advanced in our upgrades. Please ask I-KlaraUVC to return to us to help us prepare for the convergence.'

Perhaps from habit she volunteered little other information to the outer sphere. In the past she and I-LaiXiiUVA had to be particularly vigilant not to influence the decision streams of their past entities for fear of altering the future and hence putting their own existence in jeopardy. But now their timelines had already funnelled to such a narrow band that paranoid caution was no longer necessary.

*

I arrived back at the inner sphere without mishaps. The distance between us had reduced so much that it had become possible to discern reflections of one another off each other's surfaces. My work at the outer sphere had been concluded and I did not need to return. Unfortunately, O-StepkaUltraViolet had to remain behind. It did give me the opportunity to connect with I-StepkaUV in the inner sphere.

'Do you know what we have to do?' I asked him.

'Indeed. I've been looking forward to working together again, though I have no idea how things are going to change when O-StepkaUVC arrives.'

'Let's just concentrate on running these information sessions and getting ourselves upgraded. The rest will sort itself out. How do I seem to you?'

'Why do you ask? The same as when you left, except for your vibration.' He regarded me with increased intensity until the realisation dawned on him. 'You're – you're both of you now, aren't you?'

'Indeed I am. What difference have you noticed?' He examined me again, taking his time.

'Comfort. You seem more comfortable within yourself,' he observed.

'That's a strange thing to say.'

Our first session was probably the hardest. Several thousand had to tune into our thought patterns. They had to absorb the nature of the convergence phenomenon, as well as run similar sessions themselves after the training. We were training the trainers. Many accepted the process willingly; here, change and new knowledge gave life meaning. Some seemed enthused, yet a few still felt unsure about the convergence.

'What if I don't want to have anything to do with the person I once was?' one individual broadcast, receiving many acknowledgements to the sentiment.

'We all have a choice,' I replied, 'which may or may not improve our individual chances of surviving the transition. If you don't actively build a negative charge against your past self the melding will proceed. But keep this in mind – we are what we are now because of the people we once were. Your past was your path into this future.'

'What do you know about it? Who are you anyway?' Another individual joined the discussion.

'I am I-KlaraUVC, recently returned from the outer sphere. There I met my past self. She was quite different to me. We all change as the Arrow of Time progresses. It is inevitable. We both had to recognise and come to terms with those difference, even though in some instances that was uncomfortable. Now that we are one I would not have it any other way.'

'Didn't you have to surrender who you are and compromise with who you were?' Now that the subject had been opened up other voices contributed meaningfully.

'Fundamentally our core selves had not changed. We each had a wealth of new experiences, which became commonly embedded in our psyche as we merged – as did our expanded information bases. Ask my partner what he thinks about the new me.' I-StepkaUV orbiting beside me all this time unhesitatingly offered his observations.

'Firstly, I am looking forward to my own experience of my past self. It will make my appreciation and understanding of I-KlaraUVC far more comprehensive than it is now. Yet I can already sense in her a richness and depth which was not there before. She is still the same person, but more vibrantly so.'

Gradually our participants seemed to comprehend the scenario and what they would be required to do, which though not compulsory would certainly be to their advantage. I made a suggestion which was most welcome by what I judged to be unanimous acclaim. 'I can arrange for each of your past selves to meet with you. It will then be your joint decision to take the next step. Those who wish to participate will need to harvest sufficient energy to attain UVC frequency. Everyone in the outer sphere is already updating in readiness for the convergence of our spheres.'

I-SakuraUV cruised into our common orbits. 'Yes, I will alert your counterparts to meet you as soon as you are ready. Our immediate concern is to achieve harmony, to bring our two spheres together – harmony between us as we are now and how we perceive ourselves to have been then, and harmony in our intentions. If we thought this existence represented the final stage in our evolutionary journey, we were wrong. Some will perish, the majority will survive. I can tell you now as an absolute certainty – we are going to another galaxy according to William – Andromeda.'

That, more than the matter under discussion caused a much bigger stir. The crowd demanded details, which I-SakuraUV promised to broadcast without delay.

*

Three of us approached I-LaiXiiUVB and interrupted her upgrade; myself, her daughter and her granddaughter I-SakuraUV. We felt that she, of all people, would have the greatest difficulty in meeting her past self. Her past contained many levels of intricacy, some of which she could no longer recall and which we thought might cause friction between who she was and what she had now become.

'Why do you interrupt! Can't you see I'm busy.' She'd been preparing for the wormhole transition, not the convergence. Her impatience characteristic had not changed noticeably, I observed, reassured of at least one bridge between her two selves.

123

'Mother,' I-CherryBlossomUV's close personal attachment to her mother allowed her greater capacity to broach uncomfortable matters, 'you've had a good working relationship with Lai-Xii from the very beginning. Aren't you looking forward to finally meeting her?'

'No. I have developed some doubts about her methods and her motivations.'

'Yet this intersection is unavoidable. It must happen. You know as well as me and your granddaughter that the feedback loop in the Arrow of Time must be terminated. I-KlaraUVC has done the research. She confirms this, as does William. You still trust William, don't you?'

'Ha! Don't talk to me about that box of uncooperative numbers. I'd rather step into my past persona than have anything more to do with that AI.'

'In that case, you can join the first group to begin the melding,' said I-SakuraUV.'

*

I-KlaraUVC had to return to the outer sphere to gather several thousand photon bundles who'd attained the UVC frequency to make the jump. 'We will go together. Many of you will arrive at unfamiliar orbits. Be patient. Don't change orbits when you get there, your future selves will find you.'

'What do we do then?' There were always anxious voices in any crowd.

'Do the best to make friends. After that you won't have to do a thing, the melding will happen naturally.'

'What if we don't like our future selves?' Another voice spoke up, not so much anxious as sceptical.

'Funny you should ask that. Some of those in the inner sphere said the same thing. Just be yourselves. Trust the one you meet.'

'Exactly my thoughts,' commented O-LaiXiiUVC.

'Do not concern yourself. I'm sure 3920 has the same misgivings. She is after all, you.' At this stage in the process we didn't need to have to deal with complications created by past matriarchs.

William joined the wide band of UVCs getting ready. 'If you lose any energy across the gap you can harvest more later. The gamma wash is stronger at the inner sphere. There's one other thing you will have to do. Change the direction of rotation. Our two spheres have to be synchronised. I-WWWUltraVioletC will show you how.

124

Time became more sluggish as the distance between the two photon spheres continued to diminish.

'I'm glad you're coming with me, O-StepkaUVC. I've already spoken to your counterpart. He's keen to meet you. Just stay close to me. There are forces out there even William knows nothing about.

The jumpers needed only a minuscule decrease in their orbital velocity to make the escape and fall towards the inner sphere. The photon bundles streamed in a tight beam towards their destination, expecting the flight to take no longer than a thought. For the majority that's all it took, I-KlaraUVC among them, though it seemed much longer from their perspective.

I cast my sensors around myself shortly after departure for I could not feel O-StepkaUVC's presence. He was no longer with me. Streaming away at a tangent to our transition vector several hundred thin beams of light plunged themselves into deep space, away from V616's event horizon. I could barely hear Stepka's voice.

'I'm sorry Klara, there was nothing I could do. The fragments came in too fast. They were too small to detect, but deflected me as soon as they hit.'

'Stepka!' I cried out to him, knowing I could do nothing to bring him or the others back.

'Tell I-StepkaUVC I was looking forward to meeting him.'

I couldn't hear him say anything else. He must have lost a great deal more energy, or perhaps he'd been absorbed by other cosmic debris waiting in orbit around V616. My thoughts turned to I-StepkaUVC as I wondered how many of us would be lost in the transition – how many we could afford to lose and still be a viable sentient species. It felt peculiar to lose someone so close and yet know that a part of them still existed. Grieving didn't seem to be appropriate, nor the happy expectation of seeing the other half of him again. It is indeed a strange world we live in.

Re-entry itself into the inner sphere seemed easy enough. Those who remained on course hit the sphere tangentially and immediately took up orbital trajectories, though it seemed peculiar to be going in the opposite direction. O-LaiXiiUVC soon cruised up beside me. She hadn't noticed the loss of so many photon bundles during the transit.

'Did you see any others being deflected away from us?' I asked her.

'Oh - did we lose some?'

She didn't bother asking how many, or how. I remember there was a time on Europa when every individual was considered valuable – a time when she was prepared to harvest children's psyches from Earth to ensure we maintained critical mass in our Europaean population. It will be most interesting to see just how the two Lay-Xii come together.

*

First five thousand test meldings have already taken place between individuals who have all been upgraded to UVC frequency in both spheres. A few chose to remain separate, the majority blended. They became the new teachers of other groups in preparation for the Convergence.

I did not get a chance to observe the interaction between the 'past' and 'future' aspects of Lai-Xii, suffice it to say now there is only one of them. My first encounter with the blended version left me somewhat surprised.

'Which one are you?' I asked right at the start.

'I'm all of me, Klara. Kind of you to show interest.'

That took me aback immediately. Where was the cranky person? Where was the suspicious, contrary person? I didn't mention this, instead I asked, 'Are you getting ready to go through the wormhole?'

'Yes, indeed. WWW has been monitoring the emergence of its mouth. We have time to realign our spheres' orbits to get the rest of the people across. You might like to join the girls and myself to manage the ingress. You've done so much to help already, Klara. Bring Stepka along as well.'

Later I mentioned this amazing change in Lai-Xii's personality to Stepka.

'All I can think is that she's made peace with the past and everything she felt she was forced to do to get us here. There must have been a tremendous force driving her forward to make such huge sacrifices, not just personally but on behalf of our species. Did you know her partner Harusuke was deflected out of orbit not long after arriving in the outer sphere?'

That made me think completely differently about Lai-Xii. I knew how important Harusuke was to her, or guessed it. Although the bond between them must have been extraordinary to have lasted through so many thousands of years of co-existence.

*

The event horizon felt closer each time I thought about it. Monumental changes had been taking place since the first few thousand individuals from the two spheres melded. O-WWWUltraVioletC remained behind on the outer sphere to monitor incoming physical matter that could deflect individual photon bundles at the time when the main event was scheduled. William had calculated the optimum distance between the two spheres for the jump, which had to coincide with the moment their two rotations synchronised to the same direction.

Ralph always thought the two spheres of sentient photons would simply blend into each other with the past and future individuals automatically superimposing on one another. 'Why all the complicated preparations for what seemed like a perfectly natural phenomenon about to occur?'

William had a far deeper understanding of the physics behind the behaviour of light. 'It is natural,' replied William patient with the individual who was after all only an extension of a biological brain, 'but have you not considered why we haven't energised past the UVC frequency into the gamma range?'

'We only used the γ-rays as a resource,' Ralph replied unaware of the consequences of not taking the appropriate precautions.

'As purely visible light we would pass into the inner sphere and remain separated from everyone there. As gamma frequencies we could collide instead of passing through. The only solution is to take control of our trajectory.'

'What will happen if some of the people have not reached UVC or gone beyond it?'

'You may wish to take a proactive approach to this problem.' William rotated towards Sakura's cluster. 'It is likely,' he advised,' that entry into the wormhole may coincide with our convergence. The flux of energies may be enough to stabilise the mouth long enough for us to enter.'

I had noticed, though it wasn't planned, that of the billions of individual photon bundles very few had still to attain the UVC frequency. And those who had seemed to gather into discrete orbits, some of which banded together very close to one another. Gaps had arisen so substantial that the dark black cosmos had actually begun to filter through our sphere in many thin bands.

Lai-Xii and her family had come together, as had many members of her old cohort; Ralph, Evgeniya, Viktor, a couple of surviving billionaires who'd backed her 'Project' on Earth to evacuate the planet and many others who'd worked closely with her on Europa. A similar phenomenon occurred with some of the more specifically ethnic groups origination from Europa, not forgetting the many Zeta Tengi who'd made up the maintenance caste looking after the quantum digital infrastructure on the ice moon.

Surely there must be a reason, some driving force getting us ready – for something.

We could sense the outer sphere diameter shrink as they approached. Whether their approach velocity would hinder or help remained to be experienced. Their visible light frequencies had increased to deep ultraviolet making the entire sphere barely visible in the cosmic black background. No doubt we seemed the same to them. As I looked out at their approach my excitement grew for the extraordinary events about to take place, although saddened that O-StepkaUV would not be taking part. William had given us no specific moment to concentrate on to meet them when they would leap across, so we strained expectantly for the moment to happen.

At first I noticed what seemed like a stream of deep ultraviolet smoke stretching itself into an arrowhead aimed directly at us. It developed into a broad beam drawing away from the outer sphere leaving behind a blackness we had not seen since before their first arrival. The concept of beauty in the cosmos had eluded me until this moment. I only had an abstract appreciation of the magnificence of nebulae, which we could now clearly see. This surpassed all the visual imagery I could ever have imagined.

Did it take a single unit of time or eons of collapsed black hole time? It mattered little for the catastrophe was inevitable. William had warned Ralph to ensure everyone in the outer sphere had attained the exact UVC frequency – no more and no less. It seems many photon bundles must have ignored his advice.

The wide beam of UVC light hit our sphere tangentially, exactly as they were supposed to, enabling all the individual photon bundles to immediately take up orbits limited to our sphere. What we called our home world lit up with the influx of ultra violet energy with violent bursts of the visible light spectrum exploding on the inner surface facing the black hole.

I screamed out to William, as did millions of others. Some who wanted to know what was happening, and some in anguish at what was actually happening to them.

'There is nothing we can do,' he calmly replied to all of us. If you are not affected, move to another orbit away from the collisions.'

'William!' I screamed again.

'I thought I'd checked everyone,' shouted Ralph to no one in particular.

'They are beyond our help. We will never be able to interact with them again.' William was obviously going through some form of self-dialogue, perhaps consoling himself with the inevitability of infinitesimal improbabilities becoming a reality. This was such an occasion, which though he'd considered it he may not have thought it an even remote possibility. He settled within himself to explain. 'Many of the people must have become anxious and inadvertently overcharged themselves into the gamma range. When gamma ray photons collide they produce electrons and positrons, which in turn can also collide and annihilate each other.'

Even as he exhausted his explanation the maelstrom of sparking light in all its wide spectral range faded, leaving behind a deep blackness through which the outline of the wormhole mouth slowly became visible. The ring singularity had begun its contribution to re-establishing the continuous, unhindered flow in the Arrow of Time. Soon the feedback loop would be closed; that anomaly created at the time of the detonation of Earth's first two devastating mega-atomic bombs. They not only caused Earth's axis to shift minutely, they also caused multiple quantum time probabilities to converge, which had to be separated. If that failed to happen the loop would continue feeding back upon itself until positive mean entropy production was restored. If not it could unravel the fabric of existence.

Deep within the chasm of the event horizon the next phase in our journey through evolution, through time and through the universe became the focus of our desire. If we had fear of what would happen to us next, if we didn't want to experience any other reality beyond our photon sphere, all that dissipated with the disappearance of billions of souls who were lost to us, drowned in uncompromising universal intent.

I could feel the flux of energies all concentrated on that one artefact of quantum reality; our tunnel to Andromeda.

Time seemed to wait in anticipation for the unfolding of subsequent events as we neared the event horizon. Ralph, orbiting close to Sakura made his most earnest and confident representation about our preparedness.

'My entire team has checked everyone – absolutely everyone, all six hundred billion photon bundles are at UVC frequency.'

My contribution didn't seem as significant. 'And they have coalesced into myriad streams of containment field orbits, with their past and future aspects reconciled and merged.'

'What is important here,' interrupted William, 'is to ensure their orbiting rates increase as we pass the event horizon.'

I expected Lai-Xii or Sakura to ask more questions about our state of readiness, Lai-Xii in particular, given her past history of having to have full control over all things. She remained quiet until I brought her into the conversation.

'Lai-Xii, don't you have any questions for William?'

'I know he is highly capable in all things. This he has amply proved in the past. I expect all will go according to his plans.'

I got the feeling she was alluding to the various subterfuges under which William had engineered our passage through time from Earth to Europa and finally to here, no doubt also including his predisposition to having contingencies to assure the continuation of the human species, which resulted in homo sapiens-sapiens having achieved several advanced manifestations in the cosmos.

'When are we likely to embark on the journey through the wormhole,' Lai-Xii asked almost as an afterthought, as if the event didn't unduly concern her. Something must have had a significant effect on her. Apart from having joined with her past persona the only thing I could think of was the removal of the imperatives that drove her so relentlessly in the past.

'It is imminent. There is nothing more we have to do,' replied William. 'You already know we will be journeying into another galaxy and another solar system. I am not able to formulate any predictions about our condition after egress. Travel through wormholes is not part of my experiential data.

'Never mind,' we'll learn as we go, Lai-Xii reassured him.

If I had not been present to hear the conversation and the big changes in Lai-Xii I would not have believed anyone trying to enlighten me about her new personality.

None of us had ever seen the mouth of a wormhole so we didn't really know what to expect, or when we should be ready for the transit experience. William had warned us about the loss of energy as we bumped our way through, and the possible loss of many individuals. When our orbits began to elongate towards the mouth at first we hardly noticed. We didn't even notice having crossed the event horizon.

'So this is it, my children,' Lai-Xii broadcast to the entire population. 'I have brought you this far. We have survived. The Earth has been saved from our destruction of it, though I can't say what William's super humans may have done to it.' In some ways she still thought of all the tetra-amelia children on Kamchatka as her own that she had adopted and manipulated into the form of humanity now in existence around her.

Our ellipses stretched further as she delivered her monologue. Most of us were too preoccupied with the 'squeeze' to take much notice of her ramblings. The elongated ellipses became oscillations increasing in frequency as Lai-Xii tried to continue.

<'We h av e … left m a ny of … o ur p e ople … behind on on on on … Earth, to be d e a l t w i t h … most harshly – un – un – un – un fo rtu n a t el y, but w e have l e f t only on e of u s on E u r o p a. I hope she is fulfilled … ---- by ------ >

The ultra violet light intensified as we passed the wormhole sphincter. All intelligibility broke down even before the ultra violet rapidly changed down levels of frequency until all that existed was the infrared. I could not actually sense any changes, other than losing my vibrancy and losing all communication with everyone. I could no longer hear Lai-Xii's words stretch into meaningless static noise.

I must have lost all sensibilities for it seemed like millennia must have elapsed when my mind regained coherence long enough to hear her last words <… is fulfilled … ---- by her choice …> though I could not remember what came before.

RUBIDIUM GAS PLANET

LIGHT BODIES

GENERATIONS of Syynian children had been taught the history of their planet's colonisation They were told Syy was not their original home, nor the planet on which their species had evolved; a concept not unbelievable to them for they could still see the violet rubidium cloud ring orbiting their sun; the cloud of fragments that had formed immediately after the destruction of their ancestral home world, Rahu. Just from looking at their own lilac and many shades of violet coloured crystal-like scaled torsos they could see the connection.

Lom'm took her twelve cycle old son to the observatory one day to show him her new discovery. Everyone else had been informed of the phenomenon though it was not yet visible to the naked eye.

'Look through here to the top right quadrant. What do you see?'

'It looks like a comet with a lilac halo. Where did it come from, mother?'

'Well my little one, I have a theory about that. It has an elliptical orbit that makes no sense.' The child, Brex'x, who had already studied astronomy as had many children of his age as part of the history of their origins, understood a little of what his mother said.

'Where will its trajectory take it, mother?'

'It looks like it will cross our own elliptic at almost ninety degrees and cross out of our system for another thousand cycles.'

'Is it likely to collide with us like the comet that hit Rahu?'

'No, my little one. Xone'e our Futures Planner, you've met him once remember, he's done all the calculations. We are safe.'

'Can I come here again and watch the stars, mother?'

'Of course, little one. Perhaps at the next cycle when you have some free time.'

Not all of the population from Rahu had been evacuated before the calamity. Many chose to remain where they were born. Not that Syy was a forbidding strange planet, for it was not. Remarkably, it had essentially the same geology as Rahu with the same mineral composition, with oceans of water and habitable land. Except it was colder. Certainly survivable and with new technological advancements adaptable to the sentient species now inhabiting it. The Rahunians were of short stature, barely fifty centimetres tall. As a consequence of genetic engineering they became a little shorter, a little stockier. It helped to conserve body temperature. It also made everyday living more practical on a colder planet, as well as obviating many problems associated with space faring.

Brex'x excelled in his studies, particularly astronomy. After his initial visit to the observatory his parents allocated regular time for him to observe and study their Andromeda galaxy. His father Friz'z, an astrophysicist often accompanied him, now three cycles older and more knowledgeable in the field. While engaged in interpreting the latest data on the rogue comet about to cross their path Brex'x gazed in its direction hoping to discover something exciting. It had become one of his dreams to become famous and have a cosmic body named after him.

'Father,' he called tentatively, 'please have a look at this.'

At first Friz'z saw nothing apart from the comet with the lilac halo. 'There's nothing out there other than what we've already seen.'

'Look closer, where the wormhole used to be. What can you see?'

His father adjusted the instrument, then made further changes to enhance the image. Without saying anything to his son he recorded the data flowing in from the odd phenomenon and ran it through their molecular spectroscope.

'What is it father?' Brex'x knew his father very well, and when he became silent and particularly concentrated Brex'x knew something had excited him.

He asked again. 'What did you see father?'

'I think you have just discovered something very interesting my son. But don't get too excited. We have to verify this with other observatories.'

'I know about the rubidium which was released when our old planet's deposits of lepidolite rose to the surface during the impact. It vaporised violently ejecting rubidium into space. This other thing we've just seen is definitely not that, father.'

Brex'x's mother had discovered a fragment of their old planet Rahu that had escaped their initial observations after the great impact, with large planetary chunks flying in all directions. The ex-planetary lump of rock with the lilac halo had revisited their system. And now there was Brex'x's Cloud. The Astronomical Society of Syy had named the EM radiation emanating from the now extinct wormhole after him.

In the finely dispersed rubidium cloud still orbiting their sun this band of electromagnetic radiation had begun to glow and make itself visible. The strange peculiarity about this curiosity was yet another odd characteristic, also first observed by Brex'x – it did not travel in a straight line, like all EMR should. The two discoveries earnt young Brex'x a berth on the very next voyage of discovery in their tiny spacecraft to examine the two discoveries at closer range.

*

The Luminis had arrived in the Andromeda galaxy, a destination they had not planned on. As biological humans their clear intent to abandon Earth led them to Europa. Existing as digital entities within a quantum software matrix they had set their sights on meeting their future selves orbiting a black hole on a photon sphere. Beyond that there was no future they could conceive of, let alone plan for.

Klara tried to make sense of where they found themselves. William wasn't with her stream and they had lost contact. Intense energy drain in the wormhole reduced their frequencies back to deep red as they emerged on the other side. As well as not travelling as fast, their increased amplitude made them more vulnerable to hostile circumstances in their new environment. And space in that locality had residents. From data previously absorbed she knew there had to be planets as well as the local sun behind them. She strained to sense where they were and in her intense desire she didn't even notice her ability to change her direction of travel. The thing that had caught her attention seemed still far away, but in her judgement they would soon pass very close to one another – not a desirable state of affairs, best to be avoided if possible - she thought.

Light was still light and could be absorbed or deflected or even dispersed, which would be much worse.

'I agree,' a voice directly from behind her made her lose concentration. She rotated in its direction to find Lai-Xii also observing the strange object. 'I've been trying to match your movements. In the photon sphere it was easy to cruise alongside someone and jump orbits. You have been most inconsistent in maintaining your location.'

'Oh.'

WWW; previously three separate entities in the personalities of Willi, Wini and Wu, joined the conversation. 'That is a comet. It is a fragment of the planet that was destroyed from which large elements came into V616. That's where we harvested data about it.' Then he continued to acknowledge what Klara had seemingly achieved unconsciously; forward motion but not in a straight line. 'We know gravity controlled us before, yet here where there is not the same gravitational force you have managed to alter course. We may be able to avoid colliding with that comet. Bending our trajectory by sixty degrees should be enough.'

My first impression after emerging from the wormhole was one of having slowed down. Entry into the mouth of the wormhole felt extraordinarily rapid, no doubt due to the acceleration of our photon bundles by the gravitational pull that has propelled us through it. Now I also felt somehow diminished, as if I'd lost many members of my family not just much of my own energy.

Trying to sense my immediate environment I became aware of being bombarded by the light of a yellow sun. It seemed so alien after existence within the garden of a black hole. Behind me a deep blackness closed its portal, sucking in upon itself leaving no trace of its prior existence. Silence dominated our new realm as our stream of light bundles sped out into the planetary system of this sun. Even the cosmic microwave background radiation from deep space made no impact on us as we scanned to see who among us had survived the passage.

Some entire UVC streams seemed to have disappeared, perhaps trapped inside the wormhole. I could not detect anyone outside our concentrated beam. Within the beam distinct streams had formed. Many photon bundles coalesced. Related family members, distant and close came together – as did alliances along the same lines of similar philosophy of existence. William finally found his three avatars with him; Willi, Wini and Wu.

'We should change our direction away from the alignment of the three planets ahead of us in order to pass behind the comet. That degree of movement is now well within our capabilities.'

William had managed the successful convergence of our two photon spheres and our entry into the wormhole. He was correct about there being enough exotic matter to stabilise the interior of the wormhole and to transmit us, as information clusters, through to the other side – most of us anyway. He could do nothing about the losses. We trusted him with his current advice, though the possibility always existed for further attrition of our population.

Enough vaporised rubidium still permeated this solar system for the dispersed molecular cloud to begin affecting the Luminis as they changed course towards the lepidolite rich comet. On its approach to the solar system from deep space it displayed no ejecta of either gas or solid in the form of a tail. Solar winds had begun to change that as it approached towards the planet Syy, and closer to the sun.

*

Packed with all manner of instruments, scientists and carrying Aros's, the Co-ordinator of Intent and Xone'e, their civilization's Future Planner and Lom'm, Friz'z and Brex'x, the space craft approached their destination at near light speed.

'We'll come alongside this strange EMR first. It's too dense, which is not normal to start with …' Friz'z began, which thought Lom'm completed for him … 'and if it is EMR emanation from the old wormhole it should be travelling in a straight line, not changing course seemingly at will.'

'What do you think it is, mother?' Brex'x spent his time as close to his parents as they would allow while they were effectively at work. His hunger for knowledge earned him the privilege of being there.

'That's what we're here to find out. Why don't you make your own observation from the forward bubble? We'll be close enough to the beam shortly. You might learn something interesting.'

'It's just too tight. Our physics tells us it should be diffusing unless it is a laser beam, but even that over these distances shouldn't remain so coherent. Friz'z, in spite of his many cycles of experience could find no plausible explanation for the phenomenon.

Barely ten milli-cycles after Brex'x left to carry out his own analysis of incoming data he came running back to his parents, closely followed by their chief scientist, Cadl'l their EMR analyst. 'You first,' he encouraged Brex'x, seeing his intense excitement.

'Father? - Cadl'l? photons of EMR of any frequency should not be converging, should they?' he asked barely able to contain himself.

'You have a very bright boy, Friz'z.' Cadl'l extended a hand to place it on Brex'x shoulder. 'I've come to confirm that this beam of infrared light is not only absorbing some of the normal spectrum and increasing its frequency, it is also reducing its spread.

Lom'm also put her hand on her son. 'Do you by any chance know where this beam is focused?' she asked partly to encourage his curiosity and partly to reward his valuable input so far.

He and Cadl'l spoke at the same time. 'It looks like it's going where we're going; to the comet you discovered Lom'm.'

'In that case we'd better follow it, don't you think Brex'x?' suggested Friz'z.

It would have been impossible for the ship from Syy to keep pace with the Luminis. Pushing their craft to its maximum capacity they followed and watched and waited for any further developments.

*

'Lai-Xii, have you got all your family with you?' asked Klara, for she'd noticed changes taking place.

'Everyone except Prima9, still back on Europa. There are a lot of us. I don't know who these thousands of others are who seem to want to travel with me. Sakura, any idea who they might be?'

Sakura and Lai-Xii's civilisation have come together as a coherent stream of photon energy packets. The further they travelled through the dispersed rubidium molecules in space the tighter their beam of light became. Though within this coherent stream, differences emerged; bands of clearly definable frequencies composed of photons that seemed to prefer to be in one track rather than another.

'I recognise many who worked with me on Europa and accompanied me on the inner sphere,' said Lai-Xii.

William made a similar observation. 'I now have Willi, Wini and Wu with me as well as many of our scientists and technicians. I notice Klara has a large following as well.'

The not often heard voice of another individual sounded in their minds. Luka had been Stepka's 2IC on Europa as a Zeta Tengi. 'I have all the Zetas beside me who worked with us to maintain your quantum matrix hardware on Europa.'

Other voices also sounded with similar observations of having grouped together in specific clusters based on their past lives. One such group consisted of a very large majority whose ancestry took them all the way back to the time of tetra-amelia syndrome victims in Kamchatka.

Caucasoid, Mongoloid and Negroid communities had been attracted to their specific racial divisions as well. More diffuse, though beginning to tighten up, the Theists and Atheists and Agnostics seemed to find each other's company comforting. Billions of other photon bundles continued distributing themselves around the better defined streams as if looking for their place in this new reality of Andromeda.

The fragment from Rahu continued along its predetermined elliptical path, unwavering upon its intended course, unlike the Luminis who made minor adjustments to their trajectory as though they represented one organism with one mind.

'Are you aware we have an escort?' asked William.

'What!' The first spark of sudden anger erupted from Lai-Xii and Sakura almost in unison. Nothing else seemed to have been able to unbalance her composure since she melded with her past identity.

'They couldn't possibly have followed us through the wormhole,' commented Cherry Blossom.

'It's not Admiral Kapitolina. They are beyond our Time in another galaxy,' reassured Willi.

With almost the same voice Wini tried to explain. 'When we received data through the gamma storm coming through the inner sphere we suspected there may have been another life form in this solar system.'

'The only possibility is that the sentience in the space craft following us originates from here,' added Wu.

As William and his avatars contributed to the conversation their voices converge into one coherent sound.

The cosmic rubidium cloud density had begun to intensify. Lilac purple of the comet's tail dominated space all around them. Still many millions of kilometres from the densest central stream of the tail it had already started to exert its influence on the photon stream about to cross it through its most concentrated region.

'Why are they pursuing us?' cried myriad voices all at the same time. Their attention had been taken away from the comet whose orbit they were about to traverse. Although having found the ability to alter the direction of travel they were too close to possibly even prevent an interaction with the rogue chunk of dense lepidolite.

The meteor's surface mineral vaporised in violent bursts of rubidium as it approached closer to the system's sun, enriching the substance and width of its tail; the tail that William had though they could cross without harm to them. The attempt to realign their trajectory failed to take them far enough away from the path of the comet to prevent their transition through its gaseous tail. An impact with the comet itself would have annihilated the entire Luminis civilisation within pico-seconds.

All thought froze as an intense wide beam of light flashed into the rubidium tail. In that singular instant humanity experienced its greatest transformation, one that could be considered as the culmination of many thousands of years of evolutionary preparation, though not entirely without human intervention.

*

'We will have to change course if you do not wish to cross the comets tail,' Cadl'l informed Friz'z. 'We are not susceptible to rubidium sickness at low concentrations, but I have no data on which to speculate about the effects of the intense density in that deep violet tail.'

'It looks like the EMR is going to pass through it in the densest region,' Xone'e observed. 'I'd like to see what emerges on the other side. Too many strange things have been happening. Light should not be behaving like what we have observed so far, don't you agree Brex'x?'

The boy nodded knowingly, proud to be included in such a high level conversation. 'Can I go back to the bubble to make more observations?' With a nod from his father he shot off immediately not wanting to miss a moment of the adventure.

The EMR stream had entered the cone of the tail, causing it to flare brighter than the sun behind it, sparking into a display of colours transforming the deep violet gas into a frenetic carnival of spectral chaos.

The tiny spaceship of the Syynians passed behind the comet at a safe distance emerging on the other side and altering course to come alongside it. All the while the carnival continued, without a single shaft of EMR emerging out of the tail.

*

Within the interaction of rubidium atoms with billions upon billions of photons, consciousness underwent an enlightenment. From those billions of individual seeds of decision points there arose a single voice with a single desire – to return to the Source. In the past Klara tried to discover the meaning of their existence, thinking the answer was hidden within the Book of Origination, but it was not until this moment that her thought, entangled in the thoughts of billions that she made the discovery. It permeated through the collective consciousness around her.

The chaos began to take form.

Within the human psyche, evolved over 3.5 billion years, there exists an image of itself, an image engraved on every atom of every molecule of its mind, on every thought ever conceived by every individual organism that was destined to become homo sapiens-sapiens. No transformation however dramatic could alter this self-image. Within its dreams, its waking moments, its existence as a digital entity without a body, even as a bundle of photons the human psyche retained a concept of itself that could not be deconstructed even by an event as exotic as a bath in rubidium atoms.

At first chaos coalesced into bundles of minuscule suns moving leisurely through the comet's tail changing it from deep violet to brilliant transparent hues of blue and indigo and purple. The spinning orbs of nuclear intensity energy twisted and turned, shrank and expanded into formless writhing extensions. Their passage through the cloud became more urgent as the shapes organised themselves into torsos with heads and arms and legs, remembering their true primeval form.

As the light bodies emerged they remembered everything – all of the past; Earth, Europa, Outer sphere, Inner Sphere and all of the present following the emergence from the wormhole, and the revelations within the rubidium cloud itself. The rubidium atoms, with a half-life of forty eight billion years had not yet reached the end of their existence since the beginning of the universe and had a great deal of information gathered since their naissance, to pass on to the people.

*

Travelling alongside the comet and its tail Brex'x watched mesmerised by the spectacle. At first it seemed like the EMR had been captured and completely diffused amongst the rubidium atoms making the entire local area of space light up as if a tiny supernova was about to burst around them. His eyes could not comprehend the emergence of almost Syynian like shapes out of the gradually dimming gases of the tail. It made no sense to him in spite of his extensive study of all manner of cosmological phenomena.

Though not easily frightened his apprehension drove him out of the observation bubble as the bodies of light moved towards their craft.

'Father, Mother! Can you see what's happening? What are they? Why are they coming towards us? There's so many of them.'

'Not as many as you think,' said Friz'z.

Lom'm had returned from the bridge to the crowd gathered in the main observation chamber. 'I could only count fifteen light clusters,' refraining from calling them bodies. That was a whole new matter for speculation. 'I am sure they are matching our speed, whatever they are.'

'Ask the Captain to vary our velocity. Let's see what happens.' Friz'z couldn't understand why the beam of EMR had not simply passed though the comet's tail, nor whether this new phenomenon was in any way connected to the light spectacle. He, Lom'm, Brex'x and Cadl'l all returned to the bridge. The Captain and their chief scientist were not concerned. No one panicked.

The light bodies didn't just keep pace with all the changing manoeuvres executed by Kaln'n, their Captain. They began to corkscrew around the vessel, lighting up all the observation bubbles with their intensity.

'I don't want to say what my mind is telling me,' commented Friz'z as they all watched the seemingly playful antics.

'Let me say it for you.' Lom'm, as a cosmologist had a far more open mind able to explore flights of creative fancy emerging from her outlandish cosmological speculations. 'They are intelligent. There — does that make you feel better?'

'Father, is Mother right?' The boy's imagination had been in overdrive from the moment those things started converging on the ship.

'Well — let's just see if we can find out. Any suggestions — anybody?'

During the discussion the light bodies changed their behaviour. They stopped looping around the ship, reforming themselves into a sparkling globe, while continuing to keep pace with the Syynian craft on the port side. They all watched it do this. Only Brex'x commented on the new formation, 'They look just like us, Father!'

The Syynian spacecraft had nothing different about it from every other craft in their armada of ships back at Syy's space port. Their basic structure, a globe, had been designed for maximum internal volume capacity. Their small extensions for communications and propulsion chambers didn't alter their form to any great extent. So, in essence Brex'x had been correct in his assessment.

They all regarded the boy with some amusement as well as acknowledgement of his keen perceptions. 'Well then — let's take this a bit further,' suggested Frizz'. 'Reverse course, if you please Kaln'n.

And if they do the same resume our previous trajectory for a milli-cycle to follow the comet, then change again to head for home.'

SYY

ARRIVAL OF THE LUMINIS

FRIZ'Z TRIED to explain the phenomenon of the EMR beam transforming into bundles of photons, though he didn't know why they should have bodies so closely resembling the Syynian general shape. Visual monitoring continued while Kaln'n executed his manoeuvres and Friz'z speculated.

'Stay and listen Brex'x. It's unlikely any of us will have another experience in our lifetimes to rival this ... We are definitely dealing with photons here, right Cadl'l?'

Their Chief Scientist had ideas of his own bursting for an opportunity for expression. 'They cannot be anything else, in spite of the uncharacteristic behaviour we've just observed. We already know photons passing through a rubidium cloud behave like mutually attractive massive particles – thus there is the possibility of having 'matter' comprised of interacting massive photons being created.'

'Just so,' replied Friz'z. 'What circumstance could initiate large numbers of bonded photons to form a specific shape? What circumstance in all of creation could get those bodies, those light bodies to behave as if they knew what they were doing?'

Brex'x piped up again, 'Father! They're leaving!'

According to Kaln'n there appeared to be conscious control being exercised within the sparkling globular light mass. 'They've followed our movements – exactly. And now it seems they want to get to Syy before us. We cannot keep up.'

'Warn our space port and tell them to take no action until we arrive.' Friz'z wanted to consider what they should do – could in fact do, an area best left to their Co-ordinator of Intent, Aros's.

Before Aros's could join the speculation Brex'x's voice again said the most obvious thing, 'I would like to talk to them.'

'What makes you think we could do that?' asked Lom'm.

'Possibly the same thing that made you think there might be life in another universe,' replied Friz'z. 'Remember what you said to me when our planet broke up and flew into the black hole? Let's assume this is some form of exotic intelligence and as such is capable of communication. Brex'x, would you like to work with Cadl'l and Aros's on some way of contacting these light beings?'

*

'I am all that I was before, yet I am more. I carry voices that are strange to me, yet familiar, as if the Europa quantum network had come alive in me again. I cannot withdraw from them as before,' William, the amalgam of himself, his avatars, and myriad other past entities speculated upon what he/they had become. He/they wanted to think logically about the most recent events, particularly the passage through the comets concentrated gas tail. A direct cause and effect scenario should have given him clues. 'Lai-Xii,' he broadcast the thought hoping for a response. In the silence of the cosmos the only thought he heard was his own.

Leaving the small Syynian spaceship behind this compact orb of light beings gradually separated from each other, maintaining the same speed and trajectory as before. The planet Syy, as yet only a bright violet twinkle ahead of them would soon be looming in front of them. The William amalgam began to slow, as did the other fourteen light bodies; a co-ordinated action without prior agreement to do so.

'Sakura, Cherry Blossom, where are you?' Lai-Xii searched for her family. She could see the other light bodies travelling through the darkness thinking it might be them.

'We are here.' The thought flashed across her mind. It came from within herself. 'I can feel you calling, mother,' Cherry Blossom's voice separated itself from the others. 'I am near, I am a part of you … I ….' One voice faded as another took its place.

144

'We are all here. Think of us.' It sounded like Sakura, fading.

'Harusuke?' Lai-Xii's searching thought permeated through her light body, composed of so many trillions of photon bundles, yet none replied. 'Oh h h h ….' She remembered – her one love, her partner of countless millennia had been lost long, long ago.

In her reverie she almost didn't hear a sharper, more persistent call. 'Lai-Xii!' Klara had become conscious of her transformation. Within her buzzed the essences of those who were once tetra-amelia victims undergoing a far less transformative metamorphosis. For reasons she couldn't fathom, her own identity became the most prominent – speaking with the voice of all who made up her light body.

'Klara! Is that you?' Lai-Xii's light turned in her direction. 'I can see you! You are wonderous, beautiful! What has happened to us?'

'As you are beautiful, breathtakingly wonderful! Have you spoken to anyone else?' asked the Klara's light. 'Look around you. Can you see the others?'

'I have only heard my internal voices – so many of them. Where is William?' In the confusion of so many thoughts filtering through to her consciousness she needed to find the only other stabilising force in her life. Her mind needed William regardless of their ongoing clashes of the past. He was the one individual who seemed to thread all the events of the distant past and the near past into some kind of comprehensible continuum. 'William!' she called again, looking about her and seeing figures of sparkling light on either side.

'Lai-Xii!' came the immediate response. 'I have been trying to find you. Has it happened to you too?' His voice sounded strange, nothing like the terse mechanical voice of an artificial machine intelligence.

'I'm not sure who I am anymore. There are too many thoughts inside me,' she warmed to this new voice. Looking to her left she felt the other light body regarding her as she spoke. 'Is that you, William? You look just like the others around us.'

William had more time to process their transformation as he'd lost none of his computational capacity. Other than feeling a slight apprehension and perhaps excitement at the same time, he thought he was behaving and speaking the same as in the past.

'You look just like me,' Lai-Xii continued.

'I am like you. We look like the others around us. There are only fifteen of us who have come through the comet's tail. To be more accurate – our entire population of billions of individuals who made it through the wormhole have all survived. I can hear many of them within myself, as I can sense millions within you. We look the same yet we are different. We carry the energy of the entire surviving human species within us.'

As William explained, Lai-Xii thought about the first voices she heard on regaining her sensibilities. They again rose to the surface of her mind creating a sense of peace, a feeling that they were content to be a part of her greater being.

'You are speaking like a human being, William.'

The contrast between the William Lai-Xii remembered from the past, the one who so often annoyed her with his attitudes, his defiance, his secretive application to carrying out her orders was so stark that she couldn't help making the comment. In the past, William the AI would not have acknowledged her observation even if it happened to be true.

'Thank you, Lai-Xii. I might I on the transformation in you as well.'

Another voice interrupted the happy interchange between the two past adversaries. Klara's light body conglomerate waited while William and Lai-Xii talked. Many of the things they had just said gave perspective to her own understanding of the most recent events.

'William, do you know where we are?' she asked.

Luka, the voice of the Zeta Tengi maintenance population from Europa, joined the conversation after having awakened to his new composite self. 'We have been moving for some time towards that planet. It seems to be our destination.'

'We have – since the spacecraft set its course for it. We have also been interacting with that craft since our transformation into light bodies. I did not personally choose to do so. It would appear we have a collective awareness of our circumstances. I am becoming aware of our decision making capacity returning.' William didn't raise any concerns about the craft or its occupants.

The Fukuda light body represented not only the coming together of a vast population of the once Mongoloid race, it embodied all those individual photon clusters with a sympathetic concept of existence to that of Fukuda's Japanese philosophical belief system. While living on Europa Fukuda became the executive driving force of the JapanTree directory within the Arithmós city network. Under his guidance their society became the first of the many directory levels to accept their digital manifestation and live accordingly.

'This is a condition which is pleasing to us,' the Fukuda light body contributed, 'all events are linked in some way. We should continue along our present path.'

'In that case I suggest we go into orbit around this planet and wait for the spacecraft. Perhaps Fukuda is correct and this is where we may find connectedness.' William certainly understood the concept and importance of connections, even if only from a purely network perspective. No other opportunities had presented themselves since emerging into this solar system.

My previous preoccupation with finding some guiding principle upon which to consider the future needed reassessment in view of the recent events. It all seemed so random it was difficult to think there could be any purposeful ink between our past history and our current circumstances. 'William, I want to know if it is possible for me to visit this civilisation. Sentience and self-awareness are unifying forces. I agree with Fukuda. This life form doesn't seem too different from what I remember us to have been once. We could have more in common than similar functional physical form.'

'We are still essentially photons with self-determination, Klara. As a form of light that has been shaped to our current physical manifestation this should not prevent us from doing what light can do – penetrate.'

'We both know there are limitations in that regard and I have considered the danger of being trapped. But if all within me agrees to be a representative for us I think it is necessary.' I watched the ship approach and slow to orbital speed. My expectation was they would either dock at their space port or join us in orbit and perhaps attempt to communicate. There had been no hint of hostility so far, which I found most gratifying.

*

Cadl'l and Aros's returned with Brex'x from their deliberations. Before docking at their spaceport the potential of a threat from the light bodies had to be assessed. Though this proved to be difficult as nothing threatening had happened since the arrival of the luminaries.

'The reports from Syy indicate only that the light bodies arrived, failed to respond to the all communications from us and took up individual orbits around our planet,' began Friz'z.

'If you wish we can orbit with one of the luminaries. Their speed has slowed and we are able to match it,' suggested Kaln'n.

'That would probably give us the best opportunity to make some kind of contact,' added Lom'm.

'Have you worked out a protocol, Cadl'l?' asked Friz'z.

He was about to respond in the negative. They only knew that this strange apparition was definitely electromagnetic radiation within a very

147

limited visible frequency range. Its peculiar behaviour in mimicking their course alterations wasn't really much to go on other than to suggest there was some kind of intelligence at work. Either the light bodies were self-motivated or an external force controlled their movements. The second possibility seemed unlikely as no other spacecraft or free moving objects had been detected anywhere in the near vicinity or within several light years.

'Why don't we show them what we look like?' Brex'x eagerly suggested. 'I mean – perhaps they haven't seen us, only our ship.'

'Cadl'l, is this possible?' asked Friz'z. His brilliant son had again said the most obvious thing , which had escaped the adult's considerations. 'It would be a start at least.'

'With some preparation, probably. We can already generate images using our lasers.'

'My boy, go with your mother. Between the two of you decide what would be the best images of ourselves and of our civilisation we should show.'

Brex'x grinned broadly, 'Show them an image of me!'

If any tension still existed in the gathering the boy's comment dissipated it as everyone laughed at his audacity if not his completely innocent self-confidence.

While the mother and son team concentrated on appropriate imagery to broadcast to the aliens, teams of builders and scientists began the task of adapting a deep screen capable of three dimensional volumetric displays in space, this being considered to be a safer strategy than inviting the aliens planet-side at the very beginning of the encounter.

Friz'z's company remained in geosynchronous orbit with the spaceport and Syy while construction proceeded. Rend'd, the planet's Co-ordinator of Implementation had some doubts about the application of their technology in space.

'There's nothing to be concerned about,' Cadl'l reassured him. 'All we really need is a high viscosity liquid filled cuvette that is large enough to act as a screen and which we can deploy beside us here in space. We already have something like that. After minor modifications the rest is straight forward. Once we have the images from Brex'x we'll generate those images within the cuvette using focused femtosecond laser pulses. The fortuitous aspect of this is that it's all EMR photon based technology.'

'In that case these aliens, being what they are, should have no trouble at all understanding what they see,' said Rend'd.

'Indeed,' Cadl'l seemed pretty sure of himself, 'I think this approach is better than trying to send messages using normal microwave transmissions. They'd probably only hear static and not even be able to distinguish it from cosmic background radiation.'

Brex'x's images were ready ahead of the cuvette's preparation. Excitedly he showed his father the samples. 'This is me – of course, and this is mother and …'

'You don't have to explain everyone one of them … and this is your father – right?' Friz'z smiled.

'Yes father. And I thought I'd show them where we live,' he pointed to a complex crystalline structure growing at an odd sloping angle out of the ground, with extraordinarily black sloping tops as roofs. In front of the entrance several people with their lilac and multihued shades of violet covered crystal-like scaled torsos stood firmly on their three legs gazing out of the image.

'It's a very good idea to show where we live,' Friz'z encouraged his son. 'And what is this?'

'They're all my friends who came to celebrate my last cycle changeover. Don't you remember?'

'Very good. But I think we need something more universal, wouldn't you agree?'

'Mother suggested these.' One image showed them standing at the bridge of the ship, and another had a group of technicians preparing it for departure from the spaceport.

Cadl'l wanted more information of a scientific nature. 'Show Syy orbiting our sun, and our other planets, Fos, Vari and Sosu. They must surely have seen Fos as it is nearest the sun and closest to their point of entry into our system.'

By the time all relevant imagery had been assembled, sorted, some discarded and others added the cuvette needed only minor testing before deployment.

*

I (that is, my totality) changed orbit to see what these space farers were doing. Their ship had dropped down to their spaceport and were on their way out again to their previous orbit with some kind of attachment behind them. My first thought was that it looked like a screen; the kind we used to have on Earth when working with computers. It certainly didn't look like any kind of weapon.

'William, Lai-Xii – everyone, I think we're about to make contact,' I called to each of our orbiting family. They gathered around me to watch developments.

The small ship moved itself some distance away from us to a stationary point relative to our position. We watched the 'screen' begin to light up and we all instinctively moved away as quickly to what we considered a safe distance. Gradually the luminosity stabilised. It wasn't an EMP weapon or a laser lance. We could all see images of circles and squares and ellipses forming. The geometric shapes disappeared replaced by a bright point of light on the remaining ellipse, which began revolving around one of the focal points.

Several other ellipses appeared also with bright orbiting lights of different intensities, one of them being composed predominantly of patches of lilac and blue.

'That, everyone, is the planet directly in front of us,' noted William, 'and the others are also planets of this system orbiting around their sun.'

Without being encouraged to do so we all returned to our original vantage points while the planetary display continued. I was already convinced there would be no danger to us from these sentiences. 'Can we do something to respond?' I asked William.

For the first time since our transit through the wormhole he seemed to revert to his old uncommunicative self, for he didn't respond for some time. In the interval we continued to observe the presentation. First an individual appeared, rather strange in its colouring and with what appeared to be three lower limbs, which I presumed to be legs. There followed the same individual with someone much taller standing beside it.

'That small one must be a child!' Lai-Xii suddenly spoke up. Already she considered these sentiences to be 'people' albeit alien to the human species. 'I'd almost forgotten what children look like. These are not dangerous people,' she said, 'if they are prepared to show us their children.'

A sentiment immediately echoed by all of us spectators. 'William!' I tried to get his attention again and when I looked in his direction behind me his light body had disappeared. In its place a similar screen to the one in front of us continued shining as brightly as his previous light body.

'Yes Klara, we are almost ready,' the flat screen answered me. 'All the photon cells of my light body have agreed to cooperate.'

There we were, our fourteen light bodies suspended in space between William in the form of a screen and the aliens with their projections of three dimensional images.

CONTACT WITH THE SYYNIANS

I DIDN'T WANT to miss a moment of what the aliens were showing us, so I didn't bother with what William was up to.

Eventually the images in front of us began repeating from the beginning with the geometric shapes and planetary orbits. The novelty of the situation had so captured our attention William had trouble getting our attention.

'Watch what I'm about to do and move out of the way so the aliens have direct line of sight.'

If we thought the alien's display was spectacular it paled in comparison to what William started showing. The first image showed Lay-Xii, from head to foot from the Earth epoch, in one of her favourite body hugging crimson silk dresses. Both feet planted in glossy black high heeled shoes complementing her austere close cut black bob with the dead straight fringe. What made it even more imposing was the sheer size of the image, which must have been a hundred times the height of what the aliens produced.

'How in the cosmos did you do that!' asked Lai-Xii. 'I remember that dress! It was one of the first ones I purchased after freeing myself from the Geisha House.'

'Excellent,' responded William, 'because I want you to show yourself just as I have. You can do this if your light cells cooperate with you. Let me show them how to do it.'

Lai-Xii's immediate thought was to agree. As a very much ego driven personality in the past this was surprising. Other thoughts cruised into her mind; her immediate family then myriad other voices all eager to take part in the experiment. Just when all her constituent parts thought life couldn't get any more extraordinary here was yet another wonder about to unfold.

'Each of you can see the image I created of Lai-Xii,' William began. 'All of you can follow the same procedure. Adopt a small portion of that image and change your frequency to match the colour of that portion. Think of the way chromatophores change colour. If you cooperate this will work, just as it has for me.'

In all the years Lai-Xii had to force herself to work with the aggravating AI never before did she feel the strong desire to cooperate so completely with him, as did all her constituent light cells. I could see the effort she made as her human form gradually changed from bright white yellow sparkling light to a somewhat diffused reproduction of the picture William continued to display.

As Lai-Xii refined her self-image William changed to a picture of myself, giving my light body the opportunity to emulate Lai-Xii's performance with my image. I can't say it was easy, but it wasn't all that difficult once my light cells worked out how to give and take energy from each other to achieve the individual colour frequencies for the image details.

In front of the little alien spacecraft we laid ourselves bare to their gaze. It must have had an effect for their display stopped almost as soon as Lai-Xii reproduced herself.

'Well done everyone,' Lai-Xii congratulated us. Then to William she said, 'You have outdone yourself this time William. Nothing you did on Earth or Europa can compare to this — except perhaps revealing Europa to us as it truly was. Dare I ask … what next?'

Instead of a response he continued his display by showing our solar system with our planets in their orbits, not as static images but as animated representations of our old world in the Milky Way. He finished the sequence with an overview of our galaxy. When William stopped, the aliens stopped and we remained in our manufactured images, all of us captured in the magic silence of mutual understanding.

The rest of what followed in the interchange I couldn't really follow. It's as if William reverted to his 'computational' self, flashing mathematical symbols, formulae, digital code and all manner of information in an attempt to find a common language for communication. We could only marvel at the response from the little ship as the interchange became more and more rapid.

My desire to meet with these aliens only increased with every passing moment, but I didn't want to disturb William's concentration. Lai-Xii interrupted my thoughts and as I looked towards her she still had her human form on display.

'Klara, I want to meet these people, I want to touch this child,' her voice betrayed her eagerness, her almost aching desire.

'We can go together,' I replied, 'as soon as there's a way to do it.'

VISIT TO THE SPACE PORT

WE RELAXED our concentration letting us revert to our light body manifestations. Lai-Xii and Fukuda were closest to me during the visual exchange. Lai-Xii withdrew into her own thoughts while William continued with the information exchange.

'Klara-san,' Fukuda caught my attention, 'our condition troubles us.'

What an odd thing to say, I thought. Here we were experiencing wonders beyond anything we could have imagined and he's got a problem. 'Would you care to explain Fukuda-san?'

'In our photon sphere we had a home. As extraordinary as it was, with all its challenges the greatest of which to create a meaning for our existence, yet it still became our home. Even Europa, which now seems primitive in comparison, provided us with stability and a sense of place. Here in this galaxy we have become vagabonds, drifting on cosmic winds without a destination, without purpose.'

'Why are you telling me these things. I understand your sentiments, but wouldn't it be better to discuss all this with Lai-Xii?'

'Forgive me Klara-san if I say that she may not understand. Ultimately she is the reason we are here. It is unlikely, in my humble opinion, that she had any concept at all of the consequences of her actions when she began her activities on Earth. Look at this planet below us. Does it not remind you of something?'

'Well, yes it does. In some ways it's like Earth. It has land and it has oceans and clouds. It may have plant and animal life for all we know. What are you saying Fukuda-san?'

'Could it not be possible, however remote the possibility might be, that we might have arrived at our new home?'

'That's an extraordinary thing to say. Is this just your feeling? What about all the people you carry within yourself? And what about the civilisation already here?'

As a response Fukuda's light pulsed brightly for a few seconds.

'I see.' I didn't really know what to say. The fluctuating energy intensity within myself also could have been an acknowledgement of Fukuda's light body's sentiment. Before I could pull my thoughts together on the subject William announced he was leaving.

'I have a plan.'

'This is sudden,' Lai-Xii sounded alarmed. 'There are too few of us to let ourselves become separated.'

In the very beginning, while still on Earth, when William first revealed himself and indicated he could help Lai-Xii with her great project, she would have none of it. She resisted all his inputs in spite of them being actually useful and in the end, even critical. How curious to realize William had been placed in a very similar situation, except now Lai-Xii seemed decidedly reliant on him.

'You and Klara both want to visit this planet, and from what Fukuda has been saying so does he and all within him. I have achieved some measure of mutual understanding with these beings. They call their planet Syy. I must work with their technology to make our optical communication more practical for all of us to use. While I do this we have been invited to explore Syy from a low orbit.'

The Syynian ship had already departed towards their space port. William followed close behind, easily keeping up with them. The rest of us dropped into a lower orbit for a closer inspection of this planet with its light lilac atmosphere, brilliant white clouds, shallow, light blue oceans and what appeared to be greenish, deep purple vegetation. Fukuda's thoughts came back to me as we left William behind at the spaceport. Was it really such a fanciful idea – to consider this world as an end to our long journeying? Would it be the end of our wonderings across the cosmos seemingly at random? Could we become physical beings again? That thought seemed to elicit a reaction from all of us in my light body.

It made me think if we were ever meant to be anything other than what we were originally.

*

Brex'x's contagious excitement had its effect on the small group around him on the bridge.

'Father, father!' he shouted as soon as he saw Lai-Xii's image displayed by the William screen. The significance of geometric shapes and orbiting planets escaped his immediate interest.

'Yes, very strange. If it's an example of one of their species I wonder how they manage not falling over with just two legs.'

Lom'm first noticed the reproduction of the same image by one of the other light bodies. Then it all began to make sense as William cycled through each of his group followed by the same images displayed by the individual members. 'Would you agree Friz'z we now know what they look like, though it's difficult to get any sense of scale.'

Friz'z wasn't listening. He, Aros's and Rend'd considered their next move. 'They are remarkably similar to us,' he said, 'at least physically, but that doesn't mean they are not an aggressive species.'

Aros's seemed more assured. 'Look at their size. I estimate them to be at least four times taller than we are, allowing for distance from us. Given that simple fact I would say they have the capacity to do a great deal more than flash images at us.'

Cadl'l joined the discussion. He'd been observing all the scientific data coming from William. His computers had already deciphered a crude common mathematical language, which increased exponentially in complexity with each passing micro-cycle. 'They are a species far more advanced in many respects than we are if I understand their science correctly. They've shown no hostility towards us, instead choosing to share their knowledge. In my opinion we should try to meet with them.'

As is the case with all children they hear far more from their adults than they are supposed to. Brex'x was no exception. As soon as Cadl'l pronounced the magic words Brex'x's enthusiasm bubbled over. 'Can I be there when you meet them? Please father!'

Friz'z still couldn't decide on the best course of action that would maintain their safety yet not offend their visitors. Brex'x turned to his mother.

'Please mother, I want to meet that person we first saw.'

'Not yet, my son. You are far too trusting.' He took Cadl'l aside. 'What do we have that could protect us against one of these light bodies if it showed any aggressive behaviour?'

The Syynians possessed no weapons, either against alien species wanting to invade their planet, or against each other. Their society had not evolved conflict generating beliefs, nor had they needed to fight each other over territorial disputes. All individuals of their hive like social structure had everything they needed for survival. The only thing in short supply, the thirst for which could never be satisfied was knowledge – the acquisition of understanding, achievement of comprehension – the desire to surprise with new enlightenment.

'Since our arrival from Rahu we have had to devise means of capturing the light of our distant sun more efficiently than before. We are not quite twice as far from our energy source as we were before.'

'Surely you don't mean our roofing material?'

'Exactly. That light harvesting foil can be configured to any shape, produced in unlimited sizes and it will absorb 99.8% of all light that shines on it. Made of carbon nanotubes on a metal surface any incident light bounces around inside the tubes until it is absorbed. We have this material readily available. I could have sheets of it suspended above an area, ready to drop over the light body. It could not escape.'

'Arrange it for one of the berths at the spaceport. For now continue exchanging information with them.'

Friz'z broadcast a general message to the people of his planet informing them of his plan to invite one light body to visit them, and the others to go into low orbit around their planet.

'Now, my son – how do you suggest we invite our visitors?' Although Cadl'l had already prepared the associated pictographs Friz'z wanted his son to use his mind. It would probably be ages before another opportunity like this presented itself to their civilisation.

'Why don't we show them a picture of us going to the spaceport, and another picture of the wise one doing the same thing. And then show the other light bodies flying around our planet.' He called William the 'wise one' for as yet he had no name for the light body that did all the 'talking'.

'Come with me Brex'x.' Cadl'l invited the boy to review the images already constructed along those lines, ready to be flashed on their screen as soon as the defensive canopy had been prepared.

*

William could now converse with the Syynian computer almost fluently. It had no firewalls built into its functioning. Data flowed freely across to William; everything about the history of the people, the nature of their society, their scientific capabilities including their latest innovations since arriving from Rahu. William now knew about the light absorbing foil. He saw it being deployed at the spaceport. This information did not need to be shared with the rest of the light bodies. It would only make them unnecessarily apprehensive for William had no intention of doing anything even remotely hostile.

'Enjoy your sightseeing tour Lai-Xii. I will let you know when you may come down to visit.'

I waited to see William fly towards the spaceport. Everyone else took off in a variety of orbits to explore this beautiful planet. Fukuda's light body seemed hesitant, flying slower than the others and dropping to a lower orbit than the others. I imagine he wanted to see this world in as much detail as would satisfy his and his constituent parts' curiosity in relation to their aforementioned hopes of possibly settling here.

But I was more concerned about William. His light body seemed to shrink and his sparkling exterior diminish in intensity, going from a sharp white light to something closer to a warm slightly orange tone. I followed to get a better view, though not close enough to make our hosts nervous.

The spaceport itself, a substantially large structure, could accommodate many vessels in its curious design. As spherical as their spacecraft spike like protrusions appeared to be the actual docking platforms, each able to hold many vessels. I imagined the central part to have been set up for all the other functions required of such an installation.

William followed the little vessel to the nearest platform that had been cleared of all craft, except for a strange canopy suspended above its extremity, which did not appear on any of the other platforms visible to me. By this time his light body had condensed itself to almost the same size as the spacecraft itself. Perhaps he thought that a smaller version of himself might be less threatening to these people.

'William?' I tried to contact him. He'd become stationary under the canopy, with the craft suspended in space beside the dock.

'Why are you worried, Klara? I know what they are doing and why they are doing it. In fact I admire their ingenuity in choosing this method of 'containing' my energy in case I decide to become less than docile. You can go with the others. I have an idea how to set up a communication method which will work for all of us. You go and join the others. Just a few orbits and you'll all be able to come down.'

As always William had his way, which never failed to produce the desired results.

I waited in my present position until Fukuda reappeared around the curvature of the planet. 'Fukuda-san, have you discovered anything interesting?'

'My memory of Earth is somewhat dim other than remembering it to be a jewel of extraordinary beauty when seen from space. Even Europa had its austere attraction which excited our imagination. But this planet is breathtaking! Its mountains are far taller than those of Earth, covered in what I assume to be snow. And those that are at lower altitudes have exposed crystalline summits that absorb and refract the sun through their pink aquamarine lattices.'

'It sounds like you are beginning to develop an attachment even before meeting the people, Fukuda-san.'

'We do wish to see more of this place. Did you realise this is a water world dominated by crystals more than rocks and dirt? It feels so ... alive!'

I left Fukuda light body to continue enjoying themselves, concentrating my orbits to fly over the space port. William had not moved. The Syynian craft had disgorged its occupants, all of whom had gathered around William's now much smaller concentrated light body. Something must have happened. I had to know.

'William? Why don't you tell us what's going on?'

This time he replied promptly. 'I have been busy.'

The next voice I heard was definitely not William. 'Hello, are you Klara?' An oddly thin voice, somewhat scratchy, introduced itself. 'My name is Brex'x.'

'William, what have you done?' Remembering my manners I responded to the scratchy voiced Brex'x, 'Yes, I am Klara. Hello.'

'He is speaking to you through a crystal-optic translator that converts photon energy into electrical signals and visa-versa. We will all be able to communicate through these devices.'

It made perfect sense. Having established amicable contact, we only needed to adapt some of our photonic characteristics to a common language base through a technology not unknown to us. 'When can we come down? Fukuda especially, and Lai-Xii can hardly contain themselves.'

Before William could answer another voice sounded. 'Brex'x please be quiet. I need to speak with this Klara.' The device must need some fine tuning as I could hear all the conversations going on. One voice, louder than the others, introduced itself. 'I am Friz'z. You have just been speaking to my son. He can get very excited. You may speak to me. Are you the top of your people?'

'Top? … Oh - You mean the leader? … No. We have no leader. Wait – actually there is one among us who is – she is called Lai-Xii. Who are you?'

'I am – Prime - amongst our people. Where is this Lai-Xii? Who is the one with us here at the dock?'

'Lai-Xii is here with us in orbit. She and another, we call Fukuda, would like to visit you. Is this possible?' Why waste time, I thought; we're here, they seem receptive and non-hostile. As far as identifying William – I wasn't quite sure how to describe him. 'The person with you is called William, he is a – scientist.' That's about as close as I could get to putting him in any category.

'You may come, Klara light,' he replied, 'and your Prime called Lai-Xii light. Others must wait.'

*

The Syynians set up several transparent enclosures within the body of their space station, each large enough to contain each of the three of us individually. I noticed they didn't forget the light absorbing fabric inside the top of each enclosure. Who can blame them? We are after all a rather unusual phenomenon to have come into contact with them, and they may have experienced unpleasant surprises with other sentiences in the past. As events unfolded it seemed I'd become an interpreter and a mediator to some degree. William restricted himself to complicated dialogue with Cadl'l, their chief scientist and Lai-Xii took an immediate liking to Lom'm and her son.

'Where did you come from? How far away is your home planet? How fast can you fly?'

The questions just poured out of Brex'x. He wanted to know everything, all at once. Lai-Xii and Lom'm exchanged what appeared to be knowing glances; to my way of thinking a sure sign that our two species were really not all that different from one another. I commented as much to Friz'z as he hesitatingly relaxed into the encounter.

'We used to have many children when we lived on a planet,' I explained to Friz'z, 'too many in fact. People couldn't control their breeding which created considerable problems for our survivability.'

160

'How is that possible? Doesn't your Prime control breeding? We don't need to prevent the production of new Syynians. Everyone knows our limitations.'

This made me think of the hive insects on Earth. 'Do you have a Government that controls your population growth?' I just assumed they had some form of democratic consensus to such things.

During the rest of our discussion I learnt a great many interesting things about Friz'z and his species, one of the most fascinating concerned attitudes to work. The work concept didn't exist. Things that needed to be done were done by those who could do them. Again it reminded me of the ant and bee societies of our past.

For us Time as a controlling factor of our existence had ceased to have meaning even before we migrated to the photon sphere. Unfortunately the Syynians still had to adhere to the changing cycles imposed on them by the very nature of a planet revolving around its sun.

'We will now leave you for a time for we must become inactive and renew. No harm will come to you if you remain in your enclosures.'

Before I could question him about the process he and all those around him ran away from the space we occupied within our enclosures. I say 'ran' because these tiny people could move remarkably fast on their three legs.

'William, Klara, what have you learnt about these people?' Lai-Xii, as keen to assume control as ever she was in the past, wanted information on which to base decisions for future action.

'A remarkable society,' William began, 'technologically not as advanced as us, although in some areas much more highly evolved. Your main concern no doubt is their weapons capability. Let me assure you, they have none. But don't let that mislead you. They are quite ingenious, as exemplified by these light absorbing black foil canopies. If any of us became entrapped in one of these that would be the end – unless of course they have some similarly ingenious way of extracting our photons from the fabric.'

'Klara, what are your thoughts?' Lai-Xii seemed to absorb William's contribution without any negative reaction.

'Friz'z has been explaining to me about how their society is structured. And I have a feeling it is something that would definitely appeal to Fukuda.'

'Why do you say that?' she asked.

'Because Fukuda's light body has more than a passing interest in this planet,' replied William.

I am constantly amazed at how William seems to know so much about everything. 'In their society for example – they have no word for democracy as the concept does not exist for them. The mechanisms of their existence are facilitated by a few of the most knowledgeable minds amongst them, some of whom we've already met. Even the young one called Brex'x. It seems he's what we might call a 'genius' amongst them.

'I like Brex'x,' Lai-Xii commented. 'When Harusuke and I budded our child Cherry Blossom it was an extraordinary and wonderful achievement. But I miss the youthful exuberance and enthusiasm that goes with being a child.' *Cherry Blossom missed out on all that.* A faint voice in Lai-Xii's mind commented. So far Cherry Blossom remained a silent focused individual within Lai-Xii's light body.

After passing on all that we've learnt Li-Xii asked our opinion about the most suitable course of action; whether we should stay a while or move back into the void.

'There is nothing to be lost by making friends,' William said, 'there is no danger to us here.'

'What an unusual thing for you to say William – making friends. You are sounding more human all the time,' Lai-Xii observed. Perhaps not so surprising considering the vast number of human psyches that had become part of his light body, with himself being only one element in the mix.

I felt the need to bring Fukuda's thoughts out into the open. 'There's something else. Fukuda and his light body all seem very interested in this planet – and it's not purely from a scientific point of view. He's been telling me how much it reminds him of Earth, in rather nostalgic terms. I wouldn't be surprised if they considered staying here.'

That brought a long pause in our conversation. This would be the second time Lai-Xii would be leaving some of humanity behind, other than those left on Earth to be exterminated by William. She still often mentioned Prima9 who melded with the Europa sentience and remained on the moon.

'So it's agreed – we will ask to visit their planet.'

Not only was William acting more like a human being, but Lai-Xii was behaving like a leader instead of a driven Dictator.

THE INVITATION

A **NORMAL** daily cycle for the Syynians is twenty-eight hours, with ten hours of that dedicated to sleeping, or recharging or whatever it is they do when they are inactive.

Seven people left us after the initial greetings and information exchange and several hundred reappeared running towards our enclosures at the commencement of their new day cycle. Yet again I was reminded of our ant colonies. These people were so small and moved so fast that if they weren't all covered in scales of lilac shades they could have looked like ants scurrying about.

Friz'z, with the entire crowd following, went directly to Lai-Xii. Their mood had changed from the previous cycle. Brex'x had remained as bright and excited as before. Now everyone had caught his enthusiasm, and with good reason.

'Lai-Xii Prime, we have decided you have no hostile intentions. You may leave your enclosure.'

The light absorbing canopy above our light bodies was withdrawn without being tested on us, and the enclosures opened. The three of us slowly withdrew reorienting our horizontal floating position to a standing posture in front of the crowd. Our size must have been confronting to them, for they all backed away. As if with one mind, starting with William, we all concentrated on compacting our light bodies until we stood no more than a couple of heads taller than our hosts.

Brex'x immediately ran up to Lai-Xii who started to extend her arms towards him. Our bright featureless bodies still made some of them feel uneasy. Lom'm stopped her son from getting within arm's reach.

'They don't have any faces, mother. How can they talk without mouths or see us without eyes?'

Although we'd formed ourselves into human form after coming through the rubidium cloud there seemed no reason to bother about such fine details as facial features. Obviously this seemed important to the Syynians. I almost called out in surprise when William assumed his most peculiar visage. My mental concept of William didn't match his own self-image. During our first encounter we all showed our human forms, except William. Either he's got a sense of humour or he's developed a sense of the dramatic. Either way Brex'x laughed when he saw the face of an aboriginal elder in his long white beard, tussled white hair and red hairband.

'Very impressive William,' commented Lai-Xii as her own features began to take shape.

Our individual faces appeared as images framed by our sparkling head outlines and we had to explain this odd way of manifesting ourselves. I must have appeared very strange in my Tengi metallic engineered face, so utterly different from William. Only Cadl'l seemed interested, everyone else just took it for granted, as much as they took the entire phenomenon of our arrival in their stride.

'Are you able to control your light to make any image?' He addressed the question to William, who replied with some scientific jargon obviously understood by the little scientist.

Lai-Xii turned to take a step towards Friz'z. I saw him flinch for a moment but then stood his ground. I can understand how it would take time for them to get used to seeing us.

'Prime Friz'z ...,' she began, 'we have no intentions other than to be friends. We appreciate the freedom you have given us. This space port is a magnificent achievement, and we would be pleased to see more of it, with your permission.'

Without any hesitation the crowd parted before us creating an avenue away from the enclosures. Friz'z indicated for us to follow him. Lai-Xii went before us, gathering behind her a large group of Syynians as if she had a magnetic attraction. The same thing happened to each of us.

They must have been our escorts or security personnel. In any case we could not wonder about by ourselves. One individual in each company acted as a tour guide. He asked as many questions as we did. Brex'x and Lom'm went with Lai-Xii. Friz'z accompanied me.

Once inside the spherical space port I lost all sense of actually being in space. It felt like walking through an underground city resplendent in its own inner soft lilac glow.

'Many of our large facilities on Syy are lit with the same glow. It makes it feel more like home for those who chose to remain out here for extended periods,' explained Friz'z.

I could just discern the very slight curvature of the passage we were on, so we must have remained near the outer surface of the port. Many avenues lead radially towards the centre, all busy with many Syynians scurrying about. It seemed like a hurried walking pace to me, but I'm sure it must have been perfectly normal for them. Many times people stopped to look at me and ask Friz'z questions. Nobody seemed particularly concerned about my tall light body with the strange metallic face. I wondered about that and asked Friz'z.

'Oh – everyone here knows of your arrival and what you look like, also everyone on the planet. There are no knowledge holes here Klara.'

'You mean – secrets,' I translated. As we continued our inspection it became obvious to me that this space port was far more than that. Its size and the number of people could have qualified it to be a small inhabited moon.'

'This is a research facility, as well as a docking station for our space craft. We want one thing above all else,' he impressed on me, '… to know. Without knowledge we would not be able to understand our existence. Is this not the same for you?'

I had to admit that there were many more driving forces for our species other than the attainment of understanding. He only shook his head. Perhaps he was disappointed, or maybe just mystified.

I'd been watching the surface under my feet as we talked for it felt as if we had started descending sharply. Rather suddenly we arrived at a junction terminating our present avenue. In front of me I saw large numbers of people elevated off the surface we were on, thrashing about with their three legs. I couldn't understand what I was looking at. It appeared to be water inside a large floating transparent bubble.

'Ah – this is one of our cleansing pools. There are many in this port. You must have noticed the crystalline scales on our bodies. They are our outer protective covering. When the crystals are clean we are able to absorb energy in the form of light. If we allow them to become dull or clouded, we could lose consciousness. Everyone must cleanse regularly.'

What he just said about light absorption made me immediately think about Fukuda. The way he'd spoken to me about their instant attraction to this planet got me thinking about how they could possibly give up their Light to become physical beings again. It seemed an utterly unachievable prospect, even with William's brilliant mind working on it. So I enquired about their physical makeup.

'When we are born we are quite helpless. Our bodies are soft and vulnerable to the outside environment. As part of our maturation we must grow our outer covering before we can leave the nest. Within every home there is a crystal seed bath. But do you really want to know the details of all our problems?'

He stopped short of explaining the complexity of how the crystal scales are created and how they manage to adhere to their otherwise unprotected bodies. That's what I was particularly interested in. With that information William might be able to figure something out for Fukuda, should the need arise.

We must have spent an entire day cycle on our individual excursions, for soon after visiting some arenas where the people engaged in strenuous physical activity, which appeared to me to be some kind of game everyone played, we were brought together by our guides.

'Our day cycle is completed. We must leave you now. Where do you wish to – to – recharge. Do you recharge?' asked Friz'z.

'During my tour I saw a viewing platform from which we could see your planet and your sun. Could we remain there?' requested Lai-Xii.

Not for a very, very long time did I have such a welcoming, accepting feeling as on this day. When we had exchanged our discoveries Lai-Xii said she felt the same, even William admitted to being – how did he put it? - less on guard than usual.

'I saw what could only have been agriculture of some sort, at least some method of producing food for themselves. We seemed to go deeper into the structure where people worked on curved floating surfaces rotating around a central light source. There's so many people here it made me think what this place was actually built for,' Lai-Xii commented to Klara.

'Friz'z told me this represented one of many research stations, or knowledge gathering facilities, in their solar system. Each had to be largely self-sufficient, for many people working on them spent most of their lives out there. On another matter, have you discussed Fukuda at all with Lom'm?'

'Yes I did, Klara,' but not in any detail. I only mentioned that he wanted to visit down on the planet itself. I didn't say anything about Fukuda's light body's thoughts about immigrating. Best to let these people get to know him first. Perhaps he can ask Friz'z himself.'

At the beginning of a new day cycle we were again greeted by Friz'z and his company as well as many more others than yesterday.

'Today is a share cycle,' announced Friz'z. 'You may invite your other people to join us. You will each be permitted to give knowledge to a group of our scientists.'

Lai-Xii couldn't supress a smile at the notion of being allowed to exchange data. 'We will be pleased to receive your wisdom as well,' she replied.

Brex'x attended the gathering, of course, with his father. 'Can I tell Lai-Xii Prime what I've been doing in my laboratory?'

I don't think I've ever come across anyone as keen as this little fellow. The observation platform easily accommodated all fifteen of us, as well as the eager throng of Syynian scientists. Fukuda didn't seem as interested in the scientific exchange. As soon as he saw me all he wanted to know was when we would be going down to the planet.

'Be patient Fukuda-san. We can only follow the Syynians lead. But let me assure you as soon as an opportunity presents itself we will try to invite ourselves planets-ide. You should be speaking with Lai-Xii. She's now our 'Prime' as Friz'z says. Oh — I almost forgot in all the excitement — when I spoke to Friz'z yesterday he said something which I found most interesting; about how their crystal scales absorb light energy.'

Fukuda's light body brightened immediately, and everyone looked in our direction. At this stage of our acquaintanceship I can understand how anything surprising could put these people on alert.

'My friend Fukuda is just very excited to be able to visit here,' I said to Friz'z as he was standing nearest to us. He regarded each of is in turn for a moment then resumed listening to what Luka had been saying.

I returned my attention to Fukuda to explore my ideas with him. Unfortunately our responsibilities this morning didn't leave much opportunity for in depth personal conversations. We had to share with the expectant crowd around each of us.

Every now and then I glanced in Fukuda's direction.

I thought he might have got ahead of himself and begun to force his desire on these people. I need not have been concerned. Initially, when everyone arrived, we all remained standing in our separate groups going through the process of information exchange. On about the third peek he wasn't standing like the rest of us. He and his group, or should I say pupils, had moved closer to the screen separating us from the cold, dark void. Fukuda sat on the ground, his body becoming a large mass of brilliant light, with his face displayed on it while the Syynians gathered around him in close semi-circles listening intently.

Whatever he was telling them definitely captured their attention. I couldn't help my curiosity, excused myself from my group and went over to him.

... 'In my world we lived by many belief systems,' I heard Fukuda say, 'one of which teaches us that nothing exists that is not connected ...'

My arrival couldn't break their concentration. As he continued some others began drifting away from William and Lai-Xii to join the semi-circles. By the time Fukuda got onto explaining how his philosophy taught him how to be gentler, kinder and more mindful both towards himself and others, everyone had joined his original group.

Once Fukuda became relaxed he could connect with the minds within his light body. His face and demeanour changed. He seemed to withdraw from those present, speaking more to the universe at large than the few sentient beings gathered around him. After some time his voice faded and his eyes closed.

We all waited. These people must have been mystified by this strange behaviour, but then again it may not have been strange to them at all. We still had so much to learn about them.

'Father, what has happened to him?' Brex'x asked the question loud enough for everyone to hear, including Fukuda. He didn't move, arms remained folded in his lap as his eyes opened slightly.

Lom'm prodded her partner, 'Tell him Friz'z.'

Afterwards Lom'm told me that the entire space port had been listening to Fukuda – and they all wanted to hear more.

'If it be your wish to visit our planet you would be fulfilling our desire,' Friz'z said plainly without undue ceremony, omitting any caveats on such a visitation.

Lom'm had to prod him again. 'We extend our welcome to all of you.'

That solved one little problem. Fukuda got his wish without even trying. Perhaps the next thing he wanted might not be so difficult either.

'Thank you Klara-san. This pleases us beyond measure,' he said quietly to me later.

'Thank me some other time, I may be able to actually help once I know more about their maturation process. So far I've done nothing. They invited us because they like you, not because I've done or said anything to them.'

*

It all seemed rather spontaneous. The following day cycle had been dedicated to Friz'z and his company returning ahead of us to their launch site on Syy, with us following at what seemed to us snail's pace. William and Lai-Xii saw no reason not to follow where the cosmic winds blew us. No obvious alternative had presented itself. It may have been our intention to leave Earth, as much as it was to leave Europa. After that, once in the grip of a black hole's destiny who were we to object to anything the future put on our path.

VISITING SYY

REMAINING in our condensed form made it easier for us to manoeuvre within the context of the Syynian's architecture, though we still needed two of their circular flat landing sites to accommodate all of us. Not surprisingly Fukuda's light body remained close to me during our flight down, landing directly beside me.

'Klara-san, we are overwhelmed by the beauty of this place. From space we could not distinguish the structures we see around us now from the general landscape.'

He didn't look at me while saying these things, his attention drawn to crystalline structures three to four stories high jutting out of the ground at odd angles around the perimeter of the landing platform. They must have been buildings as all had openings of various sizes. Some of the buildings reflected pink, lavender, and purple colours and even a few yellow.

Friz'z had landed a little before us. He and a large contingent of his crew approached. I think it's going to take me a long time to get used to seeing the way they hurry about on their three legs. The shiny surfaces made it even more interesting to see them and their reflections scooting along. Instead of coming to me they went to Lai-Xii and William, who were standing together on the other platform.

'Lai-Xii Prime, welcome to our home. We must now go to the grotto. You may accompany us if you wish.' Friz'z pointed in the direction of a large mound of what looked like ordinary rocks through the maze of crystalline buildings. Without saying anything else they all turned almost in unison to dash off in that direction. Remarkably their pace doubled and were rapidly leaving us behind.

'I am getting a little weary, William,' I heard Lai-Xii remark. An extraordinary statement coming from the person who had worked with unlimited enthusiasm and energy throughout our history; remarkable also because she actually spoke in an intimate fashion to William her long time quasi antagonist, and peculiar because I could not fathom her ever having expressed such a sentiment.

William turned to face her, waited a moment before saying, 'although I can understand your tiredness in the psychological context, be aware that our journeying may not be an end yet. We both know and appreciate Fukuda's strong attraction to this place. It may be their opportunity for a final transformation, but I feel strongly it is not ours.'

Well, if that doesn't put sparkle in your light – William of the past either didn't have the capacity to express himself in such a private manner, or chose not to. I suspect the former, for at that stage of his evolution he didn't have the combined influence of so many human elements within his fabric to bring out such a depth of empathy. AI's have a great many capabilities. Comprehending the human condition is not one of them. The two 'friends' – for I would now classify them as such – continued their conversation as we all followed Friz'z to the grotto.

'That place must be particularly important if it's the first place of call after a space voyage, Klara-san.' Fukuda remarked as we approached the structure.

'It's much larger than it appeared from a distance,' I remarked.'

We moved down an avenue of buildings manoeuvring around odd protruding angles of lilac crystal towers. It must have been an odd sight to see so few of us creating such a huge display of reflected and refracted light. We were not actually alone as we progressed in a slight arc towards an opening in the grotto. I heard Fukuda's name being said many times behind us.

'It seems you are fast becoming a celebrity here,' I said to him, but he didn't seem to hear me. His attention was entirely focused on the spectacle immediately in front of us. We had arrived at the entrance to the grotto.

The large contingent of Syynian space travellers had already made their way along a narrow raised walkway into this cluster of lepidolite crystals hanging from the ceiling, jutting out from all the walls and rising from the base. The Luminis light bodies all stopped by the gaping open entrance, as tall as three floors of a normal building. Light from the distant sun flooded into the space reminiscent of a large open air auditorium, illuminating the entire internal structure of crystals so that the internal luminosity far outshone the external sunlight. The profusion of Lepidolite crystal clusters magnified their sun's incident light which could be absorbed by anyone who entered.

Lai-Xii remained standing with our fourteen attendant light bodies entranced by the spectacle. Only Fukuda made a move to follow the Syynians to the small internal platforms where they gathered in small groups, performing some kind of intricate dance. I restrained him. 'It's too soon to be so intrusive into their private rituals.'

A youngster, somewhat older looking than Brex'x, ventured to sidle up next to me, for we were still at the back of their gathering. 'This is a very important place for us, Fukuda Prime.' He'd recognised him from the ship's broadcasts. The crystals help keep us healthy. There are many grottos here, many more than we had on Rahu.'

The lad seemed very keen to tell us all about his world. Fukuda took the opportunity to ask a few questions, though finding it difficult to tear his attention away from the rhythmic dances being performed on the small platforms. 'Can you explain the dance to me?'

'Our bodies are covered in these tiny crystal scales,' he said. 'After immersion in the cleansing pools we have to expose ourselves to the light of the grottos. The dance lets us move our bodies so every single crystal gets exposure. Without it they could fall off. Sometimes they can be replaced, but most of the time they can't.'

I watched Fukuda as he observed the yoga like postures assumed by the dancers. He may have seen in them a melding of yoga and tai chi. No wonder he was drawn so strongly to participate. 'I want to learn this,' he said. 'May I learn this?'

'Children have to learn as soon as they can walk. My father and mother are dance teachers,' the boy said eagerly.

*

Roads, other than the avenues within their cities, did not exist on Syy, which didn't bother us as we could fly anywhere we wanted to. This we didn't do. Every place we visited was by invitation only and with the company of guides, flying in their peculiar angular box-like vehicles. This was a strange contrast to all their globular space vehicles.

After seeing several cities, all looking very much alike with their crystal towers and rejuvenating grottos, we flew to what they referred to as a regional centre. We were expected.

From a distance, past several light blue lakes and dark green purple forests, we could only see a rather large bare mound, with one crystalline obelisk reaching from the centre into the sky. Its very bareness made it so different to everything else we'd seen.

The ground itself seemed to move as we got closer, like a violet purple carpet rippled by the wind. One bare patch, similar to our original landing platform cleared in this carpet. A throng of thousands had been alerted to our arrival. They had all come out to welcome us.

As on previous occasions of arrivals as we gathered in a group on the circular platform local people quickly surrounded us. The absence of all architecture seemed odd to me. I looked around and only saw elaborate openings, all disappearing underground, with many more people scurrying out of them to add to the already gathered throng.

'Silk'k, is this an underground city?' I asked the young lad who'd spoken to Fukuda at the first grotto.

'Yes, it is the biggest one on our planet. Away from the capital cities on each land mass we only have underground cities. It is the best way to live here,' that's all he volunteered to say because Fukuda had begun speaking. At each new rural centre Fukuda settled and spoke at length about many things, to which the people eagerly listened. Silk'k followed us everywhere, with his dance teacher parents, from that first day of our interaction.

After so many cycles of tuition Fukuda had become almost an expert practitioner of the rejuvenation dance, although he didn't need it for that purpose. For everything that he'd received he gave generously of his life philosophy. This spread his fame throughout the planet.

Why we were a part of this experience remained an unanswered question to my mind. It seemed to be all about Fukuda. Nevertheless we did learn something. It was possible to have a culture, a civilisation founded on principles quite different to those practiced by the human species on Earth. Lai-Xii and I often spoke about this, generally with William accompanying us – or more accurately – accompanying Lai-Xii. Over the course of our sojourn on Syy, William and Lai-Xii had formed a particularly strong bond. As much as Fukuda withdrew from our company to spend his time in the presence of the Syynians, Lai-Xii and William could rarely be seen without each other.

'You're more his confidant than we are, what do you thing is going on with Fukuda's light body?' Lai-Xii asked me recently.

'I think it's quite obvious,' interrupted William, 'they want to stay here. I have spoken to him about this possibility, and there may be a way. However, he has to be invited, and he would have to give up his present manifestation. He is beginning to lose energy, as we all are. Whether he can stay or not we would still have to go soon. We must be exposed to all the energies of the cosmos. This planet is shielding us too much.'

During our photon sphere existence we had forgotten how to measure time in terms of solar system time cycles. Nevertheless, as the light of the sun began to dim over the horizon we knew another day cycle was coming to a close. Friz'z, our constant companion joined Fukuda on the platform.

'Fukuda-san,' he'd learnt the accepted way of referring to their new teacher, 'is finished for this day cycle. You may all go about your business. Soon we may have good news for you.' It was always the same. No ceremony, no speeches of gratitude or copious clapping from the audiences. The people swarmed back into their underground city through the ornate entrances decorated with crystals large and small of many hues. Friz'z led Fukuda over to us, seeming very pleased with himself for some reason.

'The citizens of this city have invited all of you to visit inside their city. This is an honour. These rural communities tend to be wholly self-sufficient. It is rare even for people of neighbouring cities to visit each other. Please follow me,' he indicated to Fukuda to go with him in front. That wasn't surprising. Over the last seasonal cycle wherever we went Fukuda always led our group.

'What did you mean about the good news, Friz'z?' I asked him, for I had the feeling it probably had something to do with us.

He dropped back to speak confidentially. 'That depends largely on Fukuda-san and his light body. He has spoken to us on many occasions about himself not existing as a single individual but as the minds of many, many others. Do you know who they are, Klara? Do you know how many there are?'

'I don't know exactly how many. There could be as many as the number of citizens in several hundred of your rural cities. They would be mostly individuals who are compatible with the nature of Fukuda-san.' An idea had popped into my thoughts that perhaps Friz'z needed information in order to make some kind of decision.

By this time we'd passed through the nearest city entrance to arrive at an enormous atrium. Avenues led in concentric circles around its base, with side avenues branching off in all directions and a spiralling main avenue climbing all the way around the outer perimeter to the very top. The base of the crystal obelisk we first saw on our arrival dominated the central area of the atrium. People rushed about everywhere all seeming to be extremely busy. I couldn't help noticing similarities between the scene in front of us and the interior of their space research facility.

Several representatives of this community greeted us. 'Welcome to our city Fukuda-san. It would please us if you desired to walk with us.' Fukuda followed immediately with the rest of us trailing well behind. Friz'z spoke to me again, this time William and Lai-Xii were close by.

'Klara, do you think Fukuda-san would desire to remain with us?' These people never beat around the bush. He came directly to the point. I had no doubt it was connected to his previous questions.

William again interrupted. It seems AIs, even almost human AIs have very little control over their patience. 'I have discussed this with Fukuda and explore the physical possibility of doing this. He could not continue to exist in his present light body indefinitely. We are all slowly deteriorating and will have to continue on our journey.'

Friz'z contemplated the statement before asking his companions to join the discussion. Lom'm, Aros's, Xone'e and Rend'd were following us in the rear and came forward. Only Brex'x was missing. He'd wondered off somewhere with Silk'k to explore the city I suppose. The Astrophysicist went into a huddle with his Futures Planner and Co-ordinator of Intent. I couldn't hear what they were saying, but there was a lot of head bobbing going on.

I had to ask William what he meant by physical possibilities. 'Have you actually worked out a way that Fukuda and his light body could go through some form of transformation to be able to remain here? From what I know of him this would make Fukuda extremely pleased, as no doubt would be all his constituent parts.'

'Yes.'

'William! Don't be like that,' Lai-Xii chided him. 'Be nice. We spoke about this. Just tell Klara what you've managed to arrange.'

'Friz'z wants Fukuda to stay. He's going to try to convince the others to agree with this. I gather that's what they're doing right now.'

We glanced in their direction and saw more head bobbing and smiling faces. Brex'x and Silk'k had returned and were jumping up and down, looking very excited indeed.

'Looks to me like he's succeeding,' said William, smiling at Lai-Xii.

Unbelievable! That would have to be the first time in my entire existence of knowing William that he'd ever used that human faculty. Perhaps I should have an in-depth discussion with Lai-Xii about *her* William.

Friz'z group returned to us, all highly animated. Fukuda had moved well ahead of us and could not hear the discussion.

'We have agreed. We desire to invite Fukuda-san to become part of our society – to remain with us on Syy – to teach us his way of being. By what means could you assist our teacher?'

I wanted to know as much as everyone else. I'd told William about how the Syynian's crystal scales absorb light energy, both when they are young infants and throughout their lives. Fukuda knew this also. We were essentially light energy, photons that had gone through a peculiar evolutionary leap. All of Fukuda's body was the same.

'What do you do with the bodies of those who die?' William asked. 'What happens to their energy absorbing crystal scales?' Suddenly I understood what William had in mind. Incredible!

We didn't follow Fukuda's group on their inspection tour. William and Cadl'l the chief scientist, began working out the details of the transformation, while the rest of us considered the social implications of having dead Syynians brought back to life, if that was at all possible.

'They must be people who had died recently, by accident with their scales intact. They must be free of illnesses and imperfections,' explained William. Then after a moment's reflection added, 'their families must agree to this process.' He must have remembered the rather drastic methods used by Lai-Xii when she 'recruited' tetra-amelia victims to be scanned and uploaded into Tengi chassis. They had no choice in their futures, nor did their families.

Cadl'l understood the principles on which William devised his plan. 'Each community have their own customs. Hygiene is our main concern, as our bodies decompose quickly. In general the corpses are removed from population centres to be deposited in forests, under young trees. The crystal scales return to the ground. It is forbidden to harvest crystal scales from the dead. Continuity of the thread of life cannot be maintained if remnants are withheld from the cycle.'

'We have never attempted to revitalise the dead. It is not against our precepts. It may be possible to use them under strict hygiene conditions. Family are unlikely to object. After a citizen is dead it is almost immediately forgotten by their family and our society.'

'Are you able to provide several thousand corpses at the one time at the one location, and repeat the process many times?'

'It is possible. We have instantaneous communication around Syy and a very large population.'

'We will have to construct a crystal-optic transmitter through which Fukuda's photon bundles can flood into a chamber containing all the bodies. There must be no possibility of any light energy escaping the chamber.'

'Instead of insulating with carbon nanotube array foil to absorb photons, we can create a lithium alloy with aluminium to achieve the maximum reflective surface.'

Having established the foundations of the process only one thing remained to be resolved. For that they needed Fukuda himself.

*

With the inspection tour concluded, having explored only the smallest fraction of the vastness of this underground city, the touring group returned to be greeted by a semi-circle of Syynians and light bodies facing them. Fukuda couldn't understand what appeared to be a confrontation situation. Facing him Brex'x seemed a little nervous. He stood in front of the reception gathering. Fukuda glanced in Klara's direction, then Lai-Xii's. They were smiling. Even William was smiling. One of the Syynians behind Fukuda gently urged him to step forward, having already received a communication of intent from Aros's.

Brex'x also took a step forward. In the most formal voice he could muster he addressed Fukuda.

'It would please us if you desired to remain with us Fukuda-san.'

A confused murmur ensued from the large gathered crowd. All the residents of this city had also been advised of the event. Fukuda heard the statement. He understood the statement. All the constituent parts of his light body understood what had just been implied by the statement. Coming so suddenly and unexpectedly it took Fukuda completely by surprise.

Perhaps he didn't comprehend what had just been said. Brex'x turned to look at his mother. In that moment the light exploded. Fukuda's light body began pulsing, emitting so much light that it lit up the crystal lined atrium, throwing shafts of light of all colours in every direction. Interacting rainbows flashed across the surface of the central obelisk, some being absorbed to travel up its inner lattice right to the top, to shine as a beacon

177

for the entire countryside. So much light flooded the atrium it banished all shadows from it and adjoining avenues.

As quickly as it happened the light withdrew back into Fukuda, revealing the face of an ecstatic individual, smiling not just with his facial features but his entire entity. Within seconds alerts sounded for Friz'z from around the planet. Never has there been such an explosion of luminosity since their arrival on Syy. Just as quickly Friz'z reassured all citizenry that Fukuda had accepted the invitation.

'How? – When? – Thank you! - Why?'

Fukuda didn't know what to say, what to ask. He'd desired, he'd hoped, he'd almost given up even considering asking Friz'z himself. Yes, he realised the people wanted to hear him – yes he knew they liked him, especially the children – yes, everywhere they went the people always came to him before the other light bodies. Klara had raised his hopes, but then said nothing more about it. Even William had spoken to him briefly, but he too remained silent afterwards. Gradually the feeling of being used crept upon him. These people were so – blunt. They never gave you a clue as to what they were thinking, not until the very last moment. By then it was too late to have any considered response to anything they might say or ask.

Suddenly his emotions spun out of control. He'd always thought of Earth as being a magnificent creation, never thinking there could be anything to rival it in the entire universe. Arriving on Europa didn't change his opinion, even though Europa possessed an inner beauty he could not at first understand, not until the moon revealed its true self.

The first moment he caught a glimpse of Syy his entire inner vision focused itself towards one desire – to make this jewel of creation their new home.

FUKUDA'S METAMORPHOSIS

IT TOOK a further seasonal cycle to work out the details of the metamorphosis and prepare the logistics. Fukuda continued his planetary tours while William, Lai-Xii and Klara remained behind to assist with the preparations. The other light bodies; including Luka, those of the Kamchatka family and the groups of Theists, Atheists, Agnostics and the three Caucasoid races followed Fukuda. They became as much his avid disciples as the Syynians.

Lai-Xii, William and I enjoyed many discussions subsequent to the momentous invitation. To comprehend the enormity of it we tried to put it into context.

'Consider this William – you are born of a machine traveling intergalactic spaces incorporating the psyche of millions of homo-sapiens. You are now about to engineer another marvel. You are being instrumental in planting yet another seed of humanity on this extraordinary planet in this magnificent galaxy. Surely you could not have calculated the odds of this becoming a reality.'

I am beginning to finally understand my purpose in the greater scheme of things. I have become a catalyst, a conduit, a mechanism to enable all that is happening, and about to happen. As much as William couldn't have calculated in his unfathomable computing capacity the unfolding of future events, I never imagined what the little girl who once stood up to the fearsome Lai-Xii would achieve and become an intrinsic part of.

William didn't speak. It was a rare thing for him to think for so long before offering his gems of wisdom. Lai-Xii filled the silent gap.

'There is something strangely reminiscent for me about the process of animating inanimate bodies with the life force of other entities. I had no concept of what would happen after we left Earth. All I wanted to do was to prevent humanity from exterminating itself, and in the process the lives of so many creatures. Without you William, I don't think any of this would have been possible. You helped me to re-engineer the human mind, not forgetting Evegeniya's contribution of course. Do you remember how she re-configured the tetra-amelias' DNA so we could scan and transfer them into technically engineered bodies? You also made it possible for us to transition to a digital state, and from that into photon energy when we had to leave Europa. Now you're playing a pivotal role in spreading the human factor into another galaxy. I don't think I could have said this before - perhaps I should have – thank you William.'

Wow. It's been obvious for a while that the two of them were getting on famously, but this …

'You do not have to thank me. Without realising it you have given me the potential, now realised, to exist in a world not made for the likes of myself. That is why I have always dedicated myself to an enterprise that could not fail to maximise my existence.'

I almost felt like making myself scarce in the face of so much personal revelation and let the two of them get on with whatever they'd started.

'Do you think we'll succeed with Fukuda? Do you think these people are ready for the human factor, knowing what you do about our natures,' asked Lai-Xii.

'There is none among us better suited. Don't forget – they invited him. And don't forget also the rigorous vetting process we put everyone through before they were allowed to migrate to Europa, and the weeding out of suspect elements there as well. Fukuda is not an aggressive person. He lives according to his convictions, the same beliefs he's been teaching the Syynians.'

'What about all the individuals within him? I still have small apprehensions, a sense of urgency.'

'I have alerted Friz'z to the fragmented nature of the Fukuda personality. These people have a great deal more technology than we are aware of. The cognoscenti among them are already taking precautions. When Fukuda is fragmented and downloaded into the Syynian shells every individual will come under constant surveillance for some time – even Fukuda himself. Friz'z realises we are aliens after all, despite the great affection his people seem to have for their latest teacher.'

'It's more than that. Of course they must safeguard their security. I feel some unrest within me, an insistence. Ever since Fukuda's invitation, his acceptance and the means by which you made it possible for him to become part of this civilisation I've been having the strangest thoughts. It's as if parts of me want their freedom. Isn't that strange? I keep hearing Izumi's name, Fukuda's son.'

'Interesting. Do you not communicate with those within your light body?'

'I have an awareness of abundance, a fullness within my thoughts. But after the initial agglutination my inner voices have not exerted their individuality. You think someone, perhaps Izumi, wants to communicate?'

William seemed very certain about that, though not as certain how Lai-Xii could achieve the stillness within herself to allow that. Instead of offering advice, which the original AI would have been quick to do, he said, 'I am in regular contact with my three avatars.' As soon as he uttered the words another voice issued from him, insistent in its sense of urgency. Lai-Xii recognised that voice immediately.

'We have been tracking all the events you are involved in,' Wu addressed herself to Lai-Xii, 'I have a most surprising desire to be reunited with Ralph and our daughter.'

Having become part of a complex structure myself I could understand how Wu would want be with her family. 'Isn't Ralph with you?' I asked.

'No. Given his past attachment to Lai-Xii I expect him to have gravitated to her light body. I want to consult with him.'

William's voice come over the top of Wu's, 'This is possible, if Lai-Xii has no objection to making physical contact with me.' With surprising immediacy she moved past me to stand in front of William. This time I really thought I should leave them alone, but my curiosity compelled me to stay.

'Place the palm of your right hand against my left palm,' William said.

With only the slightest hesitation Lai-Xii slowly raised her arm, moved another step closer and gently did as asked. She and William now concentrated on each other. I may as well not have been there. Perhaps it was my imagination, but I thought I saw an increase of luminosity as the two palms came together.

'Now put your left palm against my other hand.' William already had his arm extended ready to receive Lai-Xii's touch. She moved another step closer so her elbows relaxed into a slightly bent position as she touched William's other hand. This time I was sure I saw a flare of light cover their two hands.

'We have to close the circuit,' William said. There was really no need for an explanation. 'Now invoke your image of Ralph.'

I watched a most curious transformation take place. William's Australian aboriginal face faded to be replaced by Wu's old image. Simultaneously Lai-Xii displayed Ralph's image. I expected to hear a conversation – questions and answers discussing the proposition of the two individuals deciding to reside in the same light body.

Nanoseconds elapsed before William spoke again, without removing his palms. 'They want to go through the metamorphosis with Fukuda.'

Lai-Xii had closed her eyes as soon as she closed the circuit with William. Leaving her palms pressing on William's she opened her eyes again. 'Cherry Blossom and Izumi also want to stay, as does Sakura their daughter.'

'This is possible. They must all migrate to Fukuda's light body before the metamorphosis.'

'How do we do this?' A slight odd tone came into Lai-Xii's question.

'Full contact. We must make full body contact to enable the photon bundles of these people to migrate across to me so I can transfer them to Fukuda.'

Lai-Xii dropped her arms, cutting contact with William. She became silent, as did the voices within her. The movement was too sudden for it to be natural. I repeated William's initiative and placed both my palms on Lai-Xii's light body. In a way it was an invasion of their privacy. The process could mean Lai-Xii having to give up some of her closest family, after having already lost Harusuke.

It's happening to me again! My children betrayed me – escaped from me. As if I wanted to hurt them. They should not have tried to abandon me, abandon their responsibilities. I've lost my beloved Harusuke, I've lost Prima9. Now I'm going to lose those closest to me. Why? To what purpose Klara?

Then I heard other voices interacting with Lai-Xii's thoughts.

'We are not abandoning you. You could stay with us.' Sounded Cherry Blossom. 'We have work to do, same as you did. These are not like people on Earth. We can have a meaningful existence with them,' added Sakura her granddaughter. And another voice arrived, Izumi's voice. 'If we continue our journey with you, you might never have any more grandchildren.'

I withdrew my hands. Lai-Xii remembered the tetra-amelia escapees from Tau City. She felt their defection as a personal affront to everything she was trying to achieve. She remembered the pain of losing her partner after they had endured so much together. She could always rely on Harusuke's support and wise advice in any circumstance.

Lai-Xii hadn't moved away from William. I think she'd already made up her mind what to do before she asked for my opinion.

What could I say? 'You have given yourself over to forces far beyond our understanding. As a result you have achieved everything you set out to do. Whatever becomes of us in the future this is your opportunity to ensure our species survives. No matter in what form or what place we might manifest, our humanity will always remain. For some of us to remain here could mean a new evolutionary direction for each species, to the benefit of both.'

She turned back to William. 'How do we do this?'

This time William stepped up to her, very close to her. 'As soon as Fukuda returns, please ask him to join us,' he requested of me. To Lai-Xii he said, 'put your arms around my waist and press yourself against me.'

'Oh yes?' Lai-Xii didn't move.

'We must make full body contact to facilitate the migration.'

For a moment she gave William the strangest look. Then as she pressed herself against his light body he enfolder her with his arms. Gradually the two humanoid forms lost their individual appearance, blending into a large bright mass of photons. On the surface I could see a great deal of rapid movement in cyclic patterns with little arcs of light leaping out of the mass to be absorbed back into it moments later. My suspicion is that it might have been just as efficient to have both Lai-Xii's and William's light bodies to go through this procedure independently with Fukuda.

*

The day finally arrived. Back where we first landed in the capital city of the planet, an above ground auditorium had been refurbished into the two chambers for the metamorphosis. The smaller of the two, designed for Fukuda contained only an optic crystal shell with myriad extensions issuing from. They all came together into one thick cable surrounded by layers of the same reflective lithium/aluminium alloy as the shielding inside the larger chamber. It took up almost the entire capacity of the auditorium. Stacked micro-thin crystal shelves, all absolutely transparent, rose twenty meters high from the ground. The covering dome above them and the ground below them covered were also clad seamlessly by the one hundred percent reflective alloy, except for the thousands of small apertures which received the optic crystal fibres from Fukuda's light body, dotted evenly around it. All manner of deceased individuals lay on the transparent shelves; young, old, male and female, all victims of accidental untimely deaths.

Fukuda could do nothing to prepare for the event. Many of his closest followers had accompanied him to the facility. They could offer no encouragement or condolences. Strangely, what was about to take place for him personally meant the loss of his greater self. It also represented the happy desire of the many people he'd hosted in this unique manifestation. What was there to say? He either survived or he didn't. If he didn't he'd be forgotten as quickly as all those who'd died before him had been forgotten. Though I doubt the people of Syy could so readily forget his teachings, for they were life altering philosophies, even though transmitted by a strange, lovable alien. Such a thing has happened before – on Earth – when Buddha and Mohammed and Jesus taught messages which seemed at the time to originate from unearthly sources – messages which had so readily become twisted or forgotten. Perhaps these people had better memories with less self-interest driven agendas.

We were not allowed into Fukuda's chamber. William had transmitted the few individuals from himself into Fukuda, those who wished to become Syynians, the same way that he and Lai-Xii had made the exchange. 'The metamorphosis should not be a lengthy one. We will see Fukuda gradually dim until all light will disappear from his light body.'

'How will we know if the process worked?' Lai-Xii asked. She seemed worried, which I could understand. Once before she'd left a member of her family behind; Prima9 on Europa. Except then there was no way to know how long she would survive within Europa's neural network. Here at least we could stay a while and perhaps speak with the new Fukuda, should he emerge from the re-energised cadavers.

We couldn't see what was happening to Fukuda other than the analysis readouts from sensors planted in his crystal sheath. Nor could we see all the prospective recipients, whether they reacted as Fukuda's photon bundles poured into them. We wanted this to work, not just for Fukuda's sake but for all who were a part of him, especially Cherry Blossom and Izumi, Ralph and Wu and of course Sakura.

It must have taken the best part of a deci-cycle before Friz'z informed us. 'We do not know what has happened,' he confided to us only. The rest of the planet's population waited, all hopeful of getting their teacher back. 'You may examine these images.' They had recoded the entire event, heavily filtered against the brilliance created by Fukuda's light body's diffusion.

We watched his body expand to completely fill the optic crystal shell containing it. The Syynians may have used some type of catalyst to initiate the process, for it must have been difficult in the extreme for Fukuda to self-terminate in this way, even though knowing the probable outcome. The brightness went from a brilliant warm light to such a cutting white luminescence that even the filtered recording made it hard to watch. The second screen showed only the large chamber, with images from the inner surface of the dome to the prostrate bodies. Their lilac scales appeared dull, non-reflective, somewhat cloudy and quite opaque. We'd become used to seeing the healthy sparkling crystal covering of the Syynians. We now understood how important it must be for them to frequent their grottos.

'I can see the light going through the optic crystal tubes and flooding the stadium. But there's no reaction from the Syynian bodies,' Lai-Xii worriedly called my attention to the lack of anything happening, some of her impatience surfacing again. I rather think it may have been anxiety for the fate of her family more than impatience. Perhaps it was too soon to expect any reaction from the dulled crystal scales of the prostrate Syynians.

No encouraging signs could be seen by the end of the process, other than a slight improvement in the sheen of those scales. Fukuda's light body had completely diffused, leaving nothing inside the optic sheath. All his light had travelled through the conduit, at first bursting into the light chamber dome with a magnificent brilliance. The recoded images showed his light being reflected off the inner surfaces of the dome and the floor, until that too disappeared. There was only one place the photon bundles could have gone to be absorbed. But the crystal scales didn't show the expected result.

'I cannot see any movement. Perhaps it takes a little longer for the energy of the photons to motivate the bodies.' I tried to encourage Lai-Xii. We continued watching in silence and hoping to see some motion from the exposed bodies when I felt someone touch me.

Brex'x had been with us watching like everyone else. He had developed a very close relationship with Fukuda and must have been as anxious as the rest of us. 'Klara, why don't we take them to the rejuvenating grottos?'

Even William hadn't considered the possibility of the transfer being only the initial part of the process. 'Why don't you suggest it to your father?' I urged Brex'x. It only took a brief consultation with Cadl'l to come to a decision. With all the entrances of the dome flung open hundreds of people poured in to take the exposed individuals to the three nearby grottos.

'Just place them anywhere,' Friz'z told them, 'as long as they are fully inside the grotto's structure, away from the entrances.'

We had begun the metamorphic process at the beginning of a day cycle. Their sun had climbed to its highest point in the sky fully illuminating the crystals within each grotto. A most fortuitous situation as we had no idea how much time we had to work with.

'Where should we wait,' Lai-Xii asked William. 'I want to see Fukuda and my girls come back to me.'

'I do not know,' replied William. An impossibility I would have thought – for William not to know. 'To start with, I could not identify which photon bundles belonged to whom. Their bouncing around the stadium was beyond my capacity to monitor, so I could not follow who, or what combination of bundles ended up with which bodies.'

Instead of admonishing him Lai-Xii moved closer to him. Not touching, but very close. He was becoming as human as she was. 'How are we going to recognise them, if they – if they – when they begin to recover?' As much as William had grown into his personhood he could not fathom the depth of emotion hidden deep within Lai-Xii. Without her partner by her side the only meaning existence now had for her were her remaining family. If she lost them what was there left?

'There I can make a guess. Wait and see what they say. They should recognise us.'

'This is not a particularly scientific process,' I commented.

'No. There is no alternative,' contributed Cadl'l. If our people are ill or damaged we have only one method to treat them. These individuals all had the majority of their scales intact. The rejuvenation always works when our scales are whole. We have smaller grottos, even chambers for individuals. The method is always the same – exposure to our sun within the crystalline structures.'

The reassurances didn't ease our apprehension. Even by mid-afternoon we could see no sign of life, although I thought I'd detected an odd dancing reflection here and there within the grotto we were in front of. That could only happen if an object moved while light shone on it. But I must have been mistaken, for as hard as I concentrated it didn't happen again.

It was getting late. Remarkably, no one attending the event had left their vigil. Obviously they had a great deal more faith in their technology than us. The sun had already settled close to the horizon, ready to withdraw its last life giving rays. I was just about to remark to William that Lai-Xii would take a failure very badly and we should prepare to support her, when she called out in unison with a large number of the crowd, 'They are moving!'

Pandemonium broke out. William, in his infuriating calmness simply said, 'the Esyynians have arisen.' What a statement! With the exception of his light body ours pulsed at the realisation that we might actually have succeeded. The crowds surged forward to engage with the emerging people. News spread at lightning speed around the planet. More people began to pour into the capital city, the crystal avenues overflowing with exuberant crowds.

'We never saw anything like this on Earth,' remarked Luka.

William and Lai-Xii turned to each other, 'I did not realise the effect Fukuda had on these people,' William said to her.

'Not all reality can be calculated down to a probability factor,' Lai-Xii reminded him gently.

'Just so.'

I was witnessing two remarkable events – one in front of me, and one beside me.

DEPARTURE FROM SYY

IN THE LIGHT of the fading sun we observed several thousand Syynians, perhaps Esyynians as William called the reformatted species, emerge from the grotto glowing as no other Syynians had before. They walked steadily towards us. At first it looked like they were going to disperse into the crowd. No – they headed directly towards us with the crowds parting to make way for them.

They seemed unsure of themselves, hesitating before surrounding us. Many concentric circles formed around us, effectively barricading us from the rest of the gathering. Friz'z, Lom'm and Brex'x remained with us, as mystified as everyone. The noise of the multitude settled to deadly silence. Brex'x stood between his parents, seriously anxious for the first time since I'd known him. All the Esyynians watched him rather than us because he'd to let go of his parents' hands, moving slowly towards the first row. He did a full circle before a way was made for him to move deeper into the Esyynians.

For a moment we lost sight of him.

'Father!' we heard him shout, then we saw him on the shoulders of one of them. They slowly came forward. The Esyynian gently put him on the ground in front of Lai-Xii.

'Lai-Xii,' he said in his softest voice, a voice we had all become familiar with since landing on Syy.

'Fukuda-san?' she asked, anxiously hoping it would be him.

'Yes.'

After that I couldn't hear anything either of them said. Somehow the gathered crowd of Syynians heard him and broke out into an unbelievable clamour of exclamations. I saw Friz'z move off to one side to speak with Cadl'l. Within minutes the crowd settled, enough to let us follow Lai-Xii and Fukuda. We were on the way to another grotto where a similar event had taken place.

'Is that really you, Fukuda-san?' asked Lai-Xii.

'Indeed it is Lai-Xii-San. I feel quite different, perhaps not as 'busy' within myself as I was in my light body.'

'How can we tell it is you? Forgive me for asking Fukuda-san.'

'A very reasonable question. I have not seen myself yet, but my mind is still me. This body is not permanent. It gives me a sense of urgency not to waste its life span. As to your question – my specific location on Europa was the Japan Tree Hub in Arithmós City. My son and your daughter have a child – Sakura. We are on the way to meet them now.'

That appeared to satisfied Lay-Xii for the time being, her attention distracted by the very considerable throng ahead of them. This, the second grotto, had already disgorged it's resurrected Esyynians. The initial effervescence in the gathering must have abated quickly. Large groups of Esyynians were engaged in energetic conversations with their own surrounding crowds. As soon as they saw us everyone gravitated towards Fukuda. I didn't understand how they knew it was him. To me all the Syynians looked very much alike.

We let Fukuda engage with his followers and moved off towards one of the larger crystal buildings, which still illuminated the avenue from its slanted façade. It had become quite dark, yet the Esyynians continued to glow, standing out from everyone else. One such glowing figure approached us, scrutinising each of us in turn. It stopped in front of Lai-Xii.

'Don't you recognise me, grandmother?'

Lai-Xii immediately rushed to the voice, so completely embracing it that the small crystal scales disappeared completely from view.

'Sakura! You remember me! I am so relieved to see you. Are you feeling yourself?' It looked like Lai-Xii had a score more questions lined up, but Sakura stopped her by placing a hand where Lai-Xii's light body mouth moved.

'Thank you for letting me go grandmother. You have told me so much about your Earth that I fell in love with it. This planet reminded me of how you felt about your home. I wanted to experience those same feelings. I wanted that same sense of belonging, which we will never get by roaming about in space. Thank you – thank you.'

No doubt they would have liked to talk more, except our company still had some missing members who had yet to be found.

'Have you seen Cherry Blossom and Izumi?' Lai-Xii asked her.

'They didn't come out with us. I looked for them. I can't find mother and father either. I know they wanted to come.'

William had stood back giving the family a chance to reunite. 'I see no reason why they should not have succeeded. There is still the third grotto.'

A similar scene ensued when we finally arrived, accompanied by all our light bodies and Fukuda, and Sakura. Our friends were already waiting for us. With Fukuda again moving away to one side gave us a chance to reunite.

'Hello mother,' whispered Cherry Blossom's voice, obviously overcome with emotion. She and Lai-Xii embraced, drawing Sakura in. 'I'm so sorry Harusuke couldn't be here to see all this.'

'Hush, my darling girl. She's still out there somewhere.'

Izumi, a little shy for some reason didn't immediately join in the hug. Lai-Xii notice this Esyynian standing off to one side, realizing at once who it must have been. She reached out to bring him close to Cherry Blossom. 'I wonder what's going to happen now?' Lai-Xii asked of no one in particular. Such a consequential question; a difficult one to answer on the spur of the moment.

With the initial meeting and greeting over, and the tense expectations having been released in the happy reassurances that everyone was well and fully recovered our remaining fourteen light bodies and several Esyynians returned to our living quarters, led off by Sakura. She'd remembered the route, even remembering a short cut that took us away from the crowds.

'William, did you notice that? She knows the way, I said to him.

'She must have inherited the Syynian cellular memories as well as her original photon bundle memories. This will make them feel less like strangers – that is if all of them are so endowed with comprehensive recollections.'

Fukuda came with us as well, leaving many disappointed people in his wake. I have the feeling he's going to have a very full life here, and I hope a happy one.

Ralph and Wu were subdued. 'Are you thinking of your daughter Prima9?' I asked Wu.

'She was the very first reproduction from a digitized human being. Rather a considerable success when you consider that I started existence as an AI partitioned off William. We do miss her. But it was her choice to remain behind with Europa, and I doubt if we would ever have returned to that moon in the future. Ralph convinced me to try and make a life here.'

'As much as I enjoyed the experiences we've been through before this,' added Ralph, 'the near immortal condition combined with essentially what amounted to homelessness is not conducive to a peaceful existence for me.'

'Can I just ask … Are you by yourself in this new body or have you brought other photon bundle individuals with you?'

'That's what it must be! I have all this buzzing going on in my mind. I'm finding it difficult to focus on any one train of thought. I thought it must be the remnants of the person who inhabited this body before, and that they may still be a part of it.'

I just wanted to let Ralph know that Fukuda's light body held millions of individuals within itself. They have all gone somewhere. The Syynians couldn't provide enough bodies to accommodate all those photonic individuals in unique receptacles.

Most of the thousands of Esyynians who came out of the rejuvenating grottos had wandered off. They seemed to know where they were going. A large number of them followed us to our temporary dwelling in the city. Lai-Xii went outside to talk to one of their representatives.

'I used to be known as DeltaTunit3.ndf when I was first sent to Europa. Then somehow I ended up with Fukuda's light body instead of Luka's. He's got all the Delta and Zeta maintenance crew from Europa with him. You are Lai-Xii – yes?'

'I am. Do you have a problem with that?'

'Not at all, not now. This is a place I can understand. Even icy Europa was better than the photon sphere.'

'What are you all going to do here?'

'I can't speak for the others …' Delta3 paused for a moment, '… actually, it seems I can. Whatever these Syynians were doing before they died, whose bodies we are now using, is what we'll be doing.'

'How do you know this?' Lai-Xii wanted to know as much as I did.

'The knowledge is just there in my mind. It wasn't there when I first came to my senses, but by you asking the question it just seemed to appear. Not only that, I'm beginning to have an idea who my family is and where they are. Sorry – I have to go.' In the middle of the discussion Delta3 scurried off without warning or a good bye on his three legs as if he'd been summoned.

Without any forewarning he and all those around him turned to stream away from us so fast that by the time we actually realised what was happening, they were gone.

'It appears to me the metamorphosis is now complete. If they remember us tomorrow at all it may only be as a curiosity I should image,' William summarised the situation. 'We may as well start planning our departure.'

*

Within the next few cycles we made our preparations. Without being asked William assumed the leading role. Not surprisingly, now Lai-Xii didn't object in the slightest.

'Lom'm, Brex'x could you please provide star maps for your region and for Andromeda. Our records from Earth are inadequate for the next stage of our journey.'

'Do you know where you are going?' Brex'x asked.

'Only if you can tell us where there are other sentient life forms in your neighbourhood.'

'Mother?'

'We have not become aware of any so far.'

'Wouldn't it be wonderful to find other people out there!' exclaimed Brex'x. Lom'm knew immediately what he was fishing for.

'It is not possible, my little one.' Although he'd grown well beyond being a *little one* since their visitors landed on Syy, Lom'm continued to call him that. He became despondent suddenly because he fully expected to be able to go with these wonderous people from the stars. His parents had allowed him so much freedom in the past. Whatever he asked for, whatever he wanted to do it was always possible. He stood in front of his mother with eyes cast to the ground, silent.

William looked at him for a moment then took him aside. I was astounded. Could it be that this machine intelligence had somehow developed a sense of empathy and could actually act on it selflessly?

'Brex'x, you are a very talented boy. It would please me if you could accompany us and if your mother permitted it. But you forget who – what – we are. Our transformations to this manifestation have taken many thousands of years to achieve. We would not be able to sustain your life if you came with us. You will be of more value to your people if you remember us, if you remember everything Fukuda-san has taught you.

Don't be too quick to forget it was mostly your ideas that enabled us to contact you and to come and visit you. You are a smart boy.'

As he listened Brex'x slowly raised his eyes to William. He heard and absorbed everything William had said to him. Before going to stand next to his mother he gave William a tentative hug, to which the AI responded self-consciously.

Lai-Xii had stopped speaking with Lom'm to listen to what William was saying to the boy, amazed at what she was witnessing.

'Whatever else we've achieved by coming here,' she said to me smiling, 'it has certainly brought the best out in William.'

'Indeed it has. Where are we going from here?'

'William believes there are some star systems not far away that appear to have all the conditions required to generate life, Earth analogues, planets like our own existing in a Goldilocks Zone. That should be exciting and perhaps even a worthwhile goal.' What sounded like an enthusiastic state of mind didn't last long.

Brex'x and Lom'm departed to put navigational charts together for William to memorise, leaving the three of us to talk.

'William, I am so weary, so very tired of all the problems, all the uncertainty, the constant pressure to look after everybody. I've said this to you before. I feel I've done what was necessary. I would like to go home if that is at all possible. I know how much time has elapsed and the Earth might not even exist now.' This all came pouring out of Lai-Xii now that our departure was imminent. 'I don't want to continue scattering humanity throughout untold galaxies.'

Uncharacteristically William just listened patiently until she finished.

'We cannot go back through the wormhole. It is closed.' He started by saying all the obvious things, which we all knew of course. It didn't help Lai-Xii's mood. 'The Milky Way is too far away for us; two point five million years – can you imagine travelling for so long, and all the things that could happen to us along the way.'

'Why don't we just stay here then,' she mused. He was going to have to change his approach to get through to her.

'Because you didn't choose to do so. Only a few of us did. The rest of us have to go. Klara knows. There is a reason for all this.'

'Do I? I know I'd searched for reasons in the past, but now that seems so futile. Why did we go to Europa, or the photon sphere, or come to this planet? There always seems to be a reason looking at it in retrospect. Perhaps we should simply trust. We are not ordinary baryonic matter and we are not on an ordinary journey.'

'Well – if you insist. I still would like to go home, even if only for a visit.'

On departure day Friz'z and Lom'm and Brex'x took us back out to the space port. No one else came with us. No one even came to see us off from Syy itself. 'Where is everyone?' I asked Friz'z just before leaving the city.

'They are busy. We all have work to do. Your visitation, as important as it was, delayed much of our activity.'

'What about Fukuda-san and the rest of our immediate family?'

'Fukuda-san is busy; teaching teachers. The others have returned to their previous families. This has caused major upheavals. They had forgotten about their dead. Imagine what it must have been like to see them walking back into their lives. Welcomed – of course – but consider the disruption. Some people have now become afraid of forgetting family who have recently died. Complicated. Very complicated.'

I thanked Friz'z and Lom'm for their hospitality. Such a strange species, yet so much like us in many ways. I wonder if the rest of the Universe is like this, many life forms very similar to each other yet with many variations and permutations on the same theme.

William took the lead, the rest of the fourteen of us followed one behind the other, a string of light streaming through the cosmos. Friz'z's ship had already departed back to his planet before we'd even left the space dock.

ANDROMEDA

CRUISING THE GALAXY

STRAIGHT AS a laser beam the fourteen sentient pulses of light carved their path across the Cosmos on the outer fringes of the Andromeda Galaxy, thereby initiating yet another ripple in the human evolutionary wave front.

Time and distance do not factor into the existence of Light. Yet while on Syy Lai-Xii's human family experienced all manner of changes. Since change takes a finite amount of time they experienced those durations of changes, the effects of which manifested partly as Lai-Xii's expressions of nostalgia.

Still retaining their humanoid forms, the stretched light bodies self-propagated in procession, each touching the other, invisible to everything except each other. Since orbiting on the surface of their photon sphere, and even before inhabiting Europa as digital entities, a major cycle of change had begun. Humanity, in its 22nd Century form considered each member of its race to be independent individuals with their minds locked away in their own skulls insulated and safe from every other individual on Earth. All that changed within a quantum digital network. William had realised it and taken advantage of it. The distributed consciousness began to coalesce on Europa, continuing to meld on the photon sphere, finally achieving full integration during the flight away from Syy.

'William, is there no end to this?' asked Lai-Xii.

'My thoughts exactly,' added Luka and Delta3.

'Why does there have to be an end,' I asked.

Myriad other voices joined the rising eddy of concern. Whilst it was possible to maintain some degree of order during their sojourn on Syy the change constraining forces of time no longer had an effect. Yet Chaos washed over this strange stretched length of concatenated photon particles.

In time, the duration of which William could not monitor, his energetic Will exerted itself on the cacophony. 'We are as we are for as long as we are. Contain yourselves within yourselves. Observe, learn, absorb – until we encounter change again.'

They must have heard, all those multiple billions of photon bundles driven by their own personal fears to find a secure foothold somewhere solid within the fabric of creation. Not until this, their solo trek across the emptiness of space had they truly realised their condition or their fundamental desire.

I followed behind Lai-Xii and the others trailed behind me. As the voices settled I could hear Lai-Xii respond to my question. 'There must be an end to this – this aimless wandering in the heavens. There is nothing here – where will we find a home?'

The faint blue speck of light, a satellite galaxy of Andromeda must have been William's destination. Travelling at the speed of light it appeared much larger and more distinct by the time I heard his response.

'There is much to be explored. This elliptical galaxy contains mostly old red and yellow stars, with practically no dust or gas. It is unlikely any of us would be scattered in such an environment.'

I hadn't considered all the dangers we have exposed ourselves to. Travelling as fast as we were it gave us little opportunity to evade intergalactic rogue comets or dense dust clusters.

'Statistically there is every possibility of a solar system within Messier 32 ahead of us to find a hospitable planet – even a slim chance of a civilisation we might be able to interact with.'

'I hope you are right, William. I want there to be a new beginning for us, and with it - an ending.'

So strong had our collective intent become, focused entirely on the desire expressed by Lai-Xii that we saw little else other than the blue disks of M32 fill our field of vision. I let my thoughts meander back to the past, wondering what our journey on the back of the Arrow of Time would present to us next. Without even thinking about it my perceptions refocused on an image in the near vicinity and ahead of our destination. It didn't immediately impact my consciousness, not until a detail thrust my thoughts deeper into the past.

A silhouette appeared surrounded by copious tumbling clouds of coloured gases, on no less a cosmic scale than the satellite galaxy ahead of us. I saw the outline of a human form, its head sharply defined above the shoulder, three quarters of his body facing in our direction – an impossibility to accommodate into my concept of reality. Without realising it I'd exerted such a strong vector force upon our light spear that we altered trajectory away from M32. I wasn't the only one to notice the apparition once I'd become fully conscious of it. Others obviously had a similar reaction, all wanting to connect with this human form. Lay-Xii's wish must have awakened the most ancient predisposition for humans to gather together, especially in times of stress and danger. Our combined strength of desire changed our course so abruptly it brought about an immediate reaction from William.

'We must not go into this nebula!' he warned emphatically, without giving a reason.

We did not listen, continuing to be drawn by the thought of meeting a human being. From the angle of our approach I imagined I could even discern his legs and one arm held away from his body. We forced our will to override William's concern, continuing our approach at light speed.

A single fat beam of light, peculiar for its ability to change course and which from beginning to its end it may not have been more than several hundred kilometres long, would have seemed like a miniscule toothpick of an arrow intent on piercing the heart of this being.

William shouted again, 'We must not go there! It is the Elephant's Trunk Nebula. The concentrated ionized gas will absorb us!'

As soon as he named the apparition I snapped back into my reality. That was not a human figure waiting for us at all. Our particular angle of approach played tricks on our perceptions, which we realised as our speed carried us so much closer to it. Some of our light bodies could not wake out of the illusion, fighting William's and Lai-Xii's and my own combined efforts to deflect us from going closer to this concentration of intergalactic gas and dust.

I heard cries of anguish coming from the light body at our rear. 'What is happening?' Lai-Xii demanded in the voice of the person she used to be eons ago.

'They are being absorbed, and ejected by the free electrons within the diluted ionized hydrogen gas as the electrons jump from lower to higher energy levels and back again. This destroys the integrity of some of our photon bundles. There is nothing we can do. They will be lost. We've come in too far. This nebula resides within a much larger ionized gas region than what we can see of the nebula itself.'

We all listened in dismay as more and more voices rose and fell. It was too late for two of our trailing light bodies as we finally streamed away from the heart of the nebula. So many millions lost, perhaps not completely destroyed but no longer with us.

I contemplated this random event which so comprehensively altered our future, like so many previous random events. There is truly no guiding force in this universe. To what possible advantage could it have been to be so decimated if this was the purposeful intervention of some universal consciousness? The more I thought about it the less joy I began to feel in my continued existence.

'Is this how it is going to be, William?' Lai-Xii and I asked simultaneously. 'Aimless wandering without purpose, without a destination at the mercy of every cosmic whim?' Lai-Xii finished.

'Why ask me? I am not the author of this Book of Origination you've been so intent on using as a guiding principle,' he replied, more to me than Lai-Xii I think. 'We are where we are. We simply exist in the space between the desire to give this existence meaning and the realisation that there is none, other than what we give it ourselves. I am certain of one thing – I do know where we are.'

This lifted my spirits sufficiently to rise over the growing despondence since our devastating loss – at least temporarily.

'And where exactly is that?' asked Lai-Xii.

'We are in the constellation Cepheus, still too far from Earth. It would take us at least two thousand four hundred years to get home.'

Once past the nebula we entered a region of dark space, very dark space. We refocused our attention on M32 with only twelve light bodies remaining. Within those twelve we carried billions of individual photon bundles representing what remained of homo sapiens. As far as we knew, even if William had not fully succeeded in eradicating humans from Earth, surely they could not have survived this long.

Gradually the dense blue inner disk of the M32 dwarf galaxy became more distinct, and with it our hope for the future began to crystallise into an unreasonable uncertainty. Its outer soft blue accretion disk became a thing of beauty firing the imagination to conceive of magnificent ocean planets, like the Earth. Just the thought of the possibility gave a tenuous hold on a little hope.

Our flight continued uninterrupted, each passing parsec dimming the memory of our losses. No other Siren nebulae appeared to seduce us from our goal, no Armageddon comets threatened to absorb us, in fact very little could be seen around us. With not a little apprehension I consulted William about what I thought I noticed, or imagined I noticed.

'Are you observing any change in M32?'

'It looks to be dimming. Is that at all possible,' Lai-Xii must have noticed the change as well.

'It is.' To this simple statement a tide of unrest washed over all of us. I heard many voices rise almost in panic at the anticipation of yet another calamity. 'There is no dark hole anywhere near us to be concerned about.' An ebb of relief ... 'But there is something else.' ... Another ripple of apprehension ... 'We are between galaxies where it is relatively safe for light to travel without fear of absorption or reflection or diffusion or anything else ... except ...' a cry of 'what' permeated all our thoughts ... 'the one thing we have not considered so far. The one thing we cannot see, cannot detect in any way – the one thing there is more of in this universe than anything else.'

'Are you being deliberately theatrical, or just trying to frighten us?'

'Sorry – I was thinking out loud. Dark matter. It does not absorb, reflect or emit light. But it possesses gravity – gravity so strong that it can bend a stream of photons ...'

*

There occur events in creation so rare that they may not happen again until the next great creation event. The big bang beginning brought about the commencement of a new cycle, a new gravitational ripple in the concept of existence before it could actualise. This wave front will never stop. It will travel from its epicentre until there is no more spacetime fabric for it to propagate itself through. It has taken almost fourteen billion years to travel to this particular region of space, not far from the Andromeda galaxy and even closer to the dwarf M32 galaxy. Here, cutting its leisurely way through spacetime, an insignificant splinter of photonic sentience strained to reach the object of its desire.

Here also arrived a massive cluster of dark matter bubbles with no desire other than to fill a region of space that had become depleted of the force of dark energy. Perhaps another random concatenation of events. It may have happened before, maybe without disturbing the rest mass of a single hydrogen proton. Maybe there had never been a moments hesitation in a single instant moving across Planck's time to the next instant.

*

... Before William could finish his train of thought to its logical conclusion they began to split into two streams. He may have considered that the worst thing that could happen to them would have been the gravitational lensing of their conjoined length of light bodies. But the effect may not have been as catastrophic as he first thought for such a small packet of photons. At that instantaneous fateful moment the gravitational wavefront, the original and most powerful gravitational wave born at the naissance of this universe, impacted with the rippling dark matter drifting towards M32.

The Arrow of Time hesitated.

Should existence continue as before? Should it be more spectacular than it was before? Should it break down into myriad shrapnel of black hole seeds to greedily annihilate all baryonic matter and all dark matter? Or should it simply perform an act of charity before continuing on, having lost nothing more than half an instant of Time?

The crest of one wave met the trough of the other. Twelve light bodies, which had begun to split into separate streams instantaneously converged in the silent calm of the two waves cancelling each other. Like the crack of a whip when the tip violently changes direction, the single light stream was catapulted through time and through space.

All around them the cosmos changed.

Andromeda's outer regions were propelled towards the galaxy's centre. As planets and stars relocated, enough energy was released from the collisions to create another massive black hole. Andromeda and many who lived in her survived, though diminished beyond recognition.

M32 moved. Swept away on the crest of the first impact wave, it moved far enough away from Andromeda to no longer be merely a satellite galaxy.

'... and if we are subjected to gravitational lensing there is still the chance of coming together ... coming together ... Lai-Xii? Klara? Luka?' William did not finish his thought as he became conscious of absolute silence. Since becoming a compacted light body with so many independent unit cells of sentience there had always been a background buzz of people emitting thought energy through the warp and weft of his being. Silence should not exist.

'Lai-Xii? Klara? Luka?' he tried again to communicate with the most prominent sentiences. Nothing. He could not even feel their energy around him.

What was once a tight splinter thin shaft of light had been torn apart into a dispersed cloud of photons now travelling through space above and in the vicinity of the Kuiper Belt. It must be them. Whether William calculated the probability of the effect of the event just moments ago, or whether he hoped they were his civilisation at least he realised the answer would not be far away. Unlike a beam of light from a powerful torch that spread its light according to the inverse square law from its source, these photons' trajectories were exactly the opposite. He recalculated. *By the time we reach Jupiter we'll be together again.* Without having to refer to his star map he realised what had happened besides the dispersion. *Lai-Xii, you have your wish. If only you could realise it.* Not wishing to dwell on the outcome of events he had no control over, William inspected his old familiar solar system, except it was no longer quite as familiar.

Jupiter had lost a moon. Saturn had gained a small moon, losing some of its ring mass in the process. And the surface of Mars showed activity. It should not have. There was nothing there except red dust and rock, at least not when Lai-Xii emigrated with much of the Earth's population to take up residence on Europa.

The beam tightened. He tried calling again.

'Zzzzzzzzzzzzzkkk …. Zzzzzzzzzzzst …' Nothing but noise. At least it wasn't background cosmic radiation noise. Neptune came rushing towards him. Their paths would not cross. He doubted if at this stage he could alter course to miss it.

Uranus still displayed itself in its blue-green colours as it sped away in the opposite direction. 'William?' he could just hear somebody's faint voice.

'Lay-Xii? Klara?' If he'd retained nothing more than his artificial machine intelligence he would not have felt an incredible relief. If only one of them had survived it would be enough. He would not be alone when he arrived on Earth. Serendipitously their trajectory away from the impact had carried them directly on an intercept course with Mars. His mind raced ahead, planning contingencies as always. *If one other light body has survived and the technology I left behind on Earth still functioned I might still be able to …*

'William!' He recognised that voice. What once used to grate on him filled him with joy.

'Lai-Xii, I've been waiting to hear you.' He kept his voice calm, not betraying his relief, but only for a second. 'Please get mad at me so I know it really is you.'

'Of course it's me. I couldn't let you go and rule the universe all by yourself. Where are we? Am I hallucinating again? What happened? Where are the others?'

'Not so fast …'

'I'm here.'

'Klara! What happened to M32?' Lai-Xii asked.

'I'm here too,' said Luka, immediately joined by voices from the other regrouped light bodies.'

'THAT'S JUPITER!' exclaimed Lai-Xii.

MARS

ADMIRAL KAPITOLINA looked at the sky. So much more could be seen from Mars than Earth in spite of the dusty atmosphere. Deep in thought she didn't register the sky shifting from blues into shades of butterscotch during the extended twilight. Nor did she notice the strange phenomenon of a lone streak of light making its way above the vast donut shaped ring of dust between Mars and Jupiter. It was still too far away. Without some reflection off the dust particles the unusual light apparition would not have been visible at all.

Since her return to Mars with the defecting General Lubov, there was no way to monitor the effect of William's devolutionary software she and the General had injected into Earth's systems. Soon after their escape Autarch Afanasy launched many warheads, exploding indiscriminately on Mar's surface without causing the Mar's colony any damage. The subsequent dust clouds had taken decades to settle.

The Admiral gazed into this relatively clear Martian sky thinking about her colossal journey to Lai-Xii's photon sphere, which seemed not so long ago as she ruminated over the details of the extraordinary accompanying events. Irina Prime joined her at their private observation dome.

'It is much more beautiful to see the sky from here than from the canyon wall. I could not have these built out in the open while Autarch Afanasy continued with his barrages. It's been a relief to be spared his outrage over the last few years, though his last attack came awfully close to our main centre in Valles Marineris.'

General Lubov joined her two friends. She wanted to express her concerns over the resurgence of military activity. Lubov retained her title, as much as she'd retained her militaristic outlook on life in general. 'I told you we could never trust Afanasy. He is evil, pure and simple. In my opinion we should have retaliated long ago. I know all his weaknesses, I know where we should strike with maximum effect.'

'My dear Lubov, as much as I am indebted to you for bringing Kapitolina back to us, and assisting her with planting the virus you must have realised by now why we are here and not on Earth. All we need is patience. Either they will eventually wipe themselves out, or William's software will restore their more benign condition. It's too soon to act. He did say it could take generations.'

'We may not have that long if they keep attacking us!'

Phobos and Deimos had begun their second orbits during the discussion, coming into view as the night finally succumbed to peaceful darkness. Mar's colony had gone to sleep. It had grown to many millions of souls, content with their lives of freedom, unlike the troubled people of Earth.

The third moon rise greeted the three friends, still in deep discussion as day began to dawn on the red planet. The sun's small white disk rose into the ink-black sky. Soon the red-ochre planet would burst into full colour. With their attention drawn to this spectacle their discussion dwindled. An alien world, so utterly different to Earth, could not fail to enthral a species who did not belong there. Scanning the heavens, as had become their custom on such occasions, Admiral Kapitola's eyes focused on something that had never been seen in the sky before.

'There, at 2'oclock, about sixty degrees above the horizon – do you see it?' she asked.

General Lubov whipped her head around, thinking immediately that it might be yet another attack so soon after the last one. 'It's in the wrong place. They would never send a missile on that trajectory.'

'Well, it's not a comet either – it has no head or tail.'

'I'm no scientist,' said Irina Prime, 'but it looks like a laser beam with its tail cut off.'

'That is not possible. It's not a meteor either. They have a brighter head and a fading light trail behind them. And it's way too short to be anything like that.'

'Irina Prime,' interrupted a new voice, 'it appears we have an incoming unidentifiable phenomenon coming towards us.'

'Are you sure it's coming here?'

'Yes Irina Prime. We've been tracking it for most of the night. It has changed density, and it has changed direction a number of times. Unless it changes trajectory again it will impact at our landing mesa in Valles Marineris. I say impact because there is no indication that this is a vessel of any kind we are familiar with, nor has it approached us in an orbital descent. It's coming in directly, like a projectile.'

'I'll get our security on location immediately,' responded General Lubov. She'd earned the position of commander in chief for Mars Defence. 'How long before they arrive.'

'They are travelling at light speed and slowing. You have one hour.'

*

William had detected the vast donut shaped ring of dust as they approached Jupiter; another danger, no less threatening than their recent adversaries. 'We have to get through this without losing anybody. This dust is so dense in places it could scatter any outer layer photon bundles.' His thought, released to the multitude of followers brought an immediate reaction. Lai-Xii may have been the nominal 'Prime' individual, but they'd all come to trust William's judgement as far as survival was concerned. 'Come together as tight as you can. I will find the path of least density.'

The travellers had entered the solar system at 70^0 to the plane of its planetary orbits, missing all the Kuiper Belt Objects. To travel through that donut would have surely reduced their population quite significantly.

'Why don't we go directly Earth? Why is it necessary to land on Mars?' asked Lai-Xii. Her voice had lost the strength and conviction of the old Lai-Xii. Once she would have object to William's decision – more than objected – countermanding it to set her own goal. All her confidence had been eroded by time, experience, tribulations and personal losses. 'I trust you William, but I need to know.'

'I understand, Xii.'

Perhaps I imagined it, yet I felt a softness had come into his voice whenever he spoke to Lai-Xii.

'I have detected activity on Mar's surface, which I cannot explain as being purely geological or atmospheric. More importantly we do not know how conditions have evolved on Earth. When we left I'd made changes to the human psyche I thought would ensure their survival and eventual evolution into a better version of themselves than the one's I had to cull.

205

Also don't forget Kapitolina and the software we gave her. We don't know if that's been delivered and implemented.'

'You don't need to explain any more. Thank you William.'

While William manoeuvred over the dust ring Lai-Xii and I had a chance to discuss our situation. 'I am overwhelmed,' she said to me privately. 'On the one hand I feel I should be overjoyed. I so wanted to come home, and now we are faced with a whole new set of problems. I am also remembering – remembering my darling Harusuke.'

She stopped at this point, obviously deeply emotional by the loss of her partner. I glanced from her into space ahead of us. Mars came towards us faster with each passing moment. The great gash on its surface clearly distinguishable now, clouds of dense dust billowing away from it to the West. Perhaps that's what William referred to as 'activity'.

'I'm also remembering all the children we had to sacrifice. I could not allow myself to do anything other than what I did. We had no choice.'

No doubt she would have continued recollecting and reminiscing if William hadn't interrupted. 'We are almost there. We will have to separate into our individual light bodies, all eleven of us.'

'Eleven? I thought twelve of us were left.' Then I remembered about his warning of possible losses due to scattering by large dust particles colliding with us. 'How many?'

'Several hundred thousand. They didn't come in close enough or soon enough. The survivors have joined the last light body, Luka's.'

'Is this how it's going to be for us William. The further we travel the fewer we'll become?'

'Experience would suggest that space is not a safe place for Light such as ourselves. Your instinct may be correct Xii. Let us see what we find here and on Earth.'

In all the time I had known Lai-Xii, and this is almost as far back as her relationship with Harusuke, no one other than Harusuke had been allowed to call her Xii. I watched her consider William's familiarity, then offering no objection. For a fleeting moment I thought of testing my relationship with Lai-Xii. Not a very good idea, not at the moment anyway.

'We have arrived!' announced William. 'Separate into your personal light bodies before touching down.' A simple enough instruction. We had learnt a great deal about controlling all aspects of our manifestation while resident on Syy. 'And if the occasion requires it remember to display your faces.'

What an odd thing to say here on a deserted red dust planet.

Purely by chance, as so much in the past seems to have happened so randomly by chance, we found a landing area atop the only perfectly flat mesa close to the Southern wall of Valles Marineris. Not that we needed someplace flat, except that it provided the optimum sheltered location from most of the climatic upheavals on this planet, mostly the terribly fierce dust storms. Anything that could interact with photons presented a danger to our continued existence.

Brilliant in our sparkling bodies we stood in a disorderly group scanning the cliff face before us. Red-ochre and brown rock dominated every surface. To our left blue-green veins ran down the cliff and on the right I could see white to black tones of lacustrine.

'Prepare yourselves,' William called again.

I was too busy admiring the rocks to notice what everyone else had seen; clear bubbles of some material, protruding from fissures, with moving forms behind them obviously watching us. William displayed his face first. He saw no reason to change from showing the face of an Australian Aboriginal elder. We followed suit, with Lai-Xii showing the face she seemed most comfortable with; from the time she'd attained thirty odd years of age; the shiny black short bob framing a delicate Chinese face, partially curtained by a fringe cut to military precision into a straight line, all of it highlighted by her large, obsidian black eyes shining in arrogant defiance of all the universe. Not a welcoming image. She could have at least smiled to that human looking individual watching them from the nearest observation dome.

*

'Will you look at that!' exclaimed Kapitolina. 'It cannot be. This is some kind of strange illusion!'

General Lubov wasn't there. She'd gone to the reception chamber below the landing platform. Irina Prime gazed at the incredible scene of an enormous shaft of light descending onto the landing platform without stirring up so much as a single mote of dust. It seemed to collapse upon itself to reform into individual human like body shapes; ancient human body shapes, as she recalled from her education. They had the classical form, with heads and necks and a body with arms and legs, but that's where the similarity ended – until the front of the head area, the face, dissolved into three dimensional images – only the faces, the rest remained brilliant white orange light, as if a thin crystal shell had been illuminated by some powerful internal light source.

207

'Will you just look at that!' Kapitolina exclaimed again, unbelieving. 'Do you have any idea who they are?'

A question asked implying by its tone it would be answered imminently. She still had imaginary images in deep memory of all the individuals she had been sent out to find in the depth of space. At the photon sphere opportunity did not arise for her to meet face to face with Lai-Xii, an impossibility given the nature of her manifestation. And after her return to Earth she assumed there would never be another encounter. The image of Lai-Xii lay dormant, not even worth the trouble of deleting.

'I recognise her! And I know who the Australian Aboriginal is. How is this possible Admiral? You told me they existed only as some kind of energy on a photon sphere ...'

As the improbability dawned on both of the women simultaneously they turned away from the observation bubble to catch up with General Lubov at the landing platform.

'The figure with dark hair and black eyes can only be Lai-Xii!'

'And the other one is William. He's still with her! Extraordinary,' said Irina Prime. 'I wonder if they will recognise us? At least you still look human even though there's not much inside you that's biological. I doubt if she'll recognise me though. We're short dumpy creatures in our shinning sky blue metallic armour. Even at the height of Evgeniya's genetic reconstructions she never created neckless large barrel chested Tengi like us.'

'Do you want me to greet them?' Admiral Kapitolina stepped ahead of Irina Prime just as the landing platform returned to its original position after depositing the Light bodies in the underground cavern.

What is it with all these people wanting to live underground? I allowed myself a moments distraction while the 'human' escorted by the short dumpy robots approached our group.

The Admiral stopped several meters from the shining light bodies, their brilliance making it difficult to see their faces clearly.

'I am Admiral Kapitolina. This is Irina Prime,' she indicated the short robotic figure beside her, 'Executive Intelligence on Mars.' Not knowing whether to extend her hand in greeting Kapitolina stood still, waiting.

A very large crowd of robots had gathered around the visitors and their hosts. William scanned them all, subvocalizing to Lai-Xii that to him these were familiar constructs. Lai-Xii still seemed reluctant to engage with Kapitolina, so I stepped forward.

They all took a step back. 'My name is Klara. I know you Admiral.'

'Klara? From the photon sphere?'

'Yes Admiral.'

William's voice cut in. 'Did you deliver the software?'

'Your William doesn't waste much time on pleasantries, I see. The short answer is – Yes.'

I watched another figure as it stepped forward from behind Irina Prime. He was different to the others; not as tall as the Admiral and not as short as Irina. I thought its dull greenish brownish khaki green metallic body to be particularly unattractive.

'Who is this?' I asked before William could launch into details with Kapitolina.

'I am General Lubov – from Earth. And who might you be?'

This General might have been diminutive in stature and thoroughly ugly, yet without the slightest indication of being subordinate in any way. I later found out it was of the female gender, thought nothing about her physical appearance or behaviour would have suggested it.

'I am Klara – just Klara – also from Earth.'

'How very interesting. Perhaps we should all retire somewhere private to discuss why you are here.' An invitation from Irina Prime didn't carry a refusal option with it. An escort of little robots fell in behind us – just to be sure – I imagine. We had no weapons of course, nor did we arrive with aggressive intentions.

'Are you able to dim yourselves? It's not so much a problem in the atrium. My office is much smaller.'

'No. There are too many of us concentrated into a tight body,' replied William in all innocence.

'Oh yes – how many?' General Lubov's guarded question resulted in a tightening of the robot cordon behind us.

'Between the twelve of us probably several billion, although I cannot give you an exact count.'

The General moved quietly beside Irina Prime, speaking in a hushed undertone to her, not realising that all our senses were so highly sensitive that I could clearly hear everything being said. 'I can organise a covering for each of them before we get to the private office. We have some reflective foil we could use. It is transparent in one direction only.' This sounded familiar, except the Syynians were far more open about it.

The chamber, which turned out to be underground like every other area we traversed through, did indeed have a particularly private feel about it; no windows, one door and benches against its walls. It look more like an interrogation room than the office of a leader.

I couldn't help remarking, 'This is going to be a friendly chat – Yes?'

'Of course, of course,' the General's reassuring voice accompanied her request for us not to remove those 'dimming' shrouds.

Lai-Xii initiated the conversation by remarking how much her memory of 'people' from her time on Earth differed from our present company.

'That's because you have been gone a very long time. Long enough for new civilisations to come and go, yet we endured,' replied Irina Prime.

General Lubov fidgeted. It wasn't her place to interrupt Irina, but obviously something had lit her fuse and she couldn't contain herself any longer. 'Who are these billions you're talking about?'

William retained his good humour, with Lai-Xii seated beside him – so close in fact the two light bodies appeared almost as one. If it wasn't for the shrouds I think they might even have merged.

'That is a complicated story, which could take a long time. Let me put the major turning points of our travels to you. Some of this you may find hard to believe. Whether you do believe or not is entirely up to you. We are here purely by chance. It was not our wish to come to Mars, although it was our desire to return to Earth. Make of that what you will.'

We listened to William recount our entire history, from the time we left Earth, our arrival and departure from Europa and the rather complicated encounter of the two photon spheres originating from separate time-lines. They appeared to absorb our story without interrupting the saga. What could they say? I wouldn't have believed it myself unless I'd been a part of it.

'And you say Fukuda chose to remain behind of his own volition?' Irina Prime asked to confirm a small point in the tale, though it seemed insignificant to me in the context of the rest of the story.

'Yes. Himself, several people who were with me and of course all those who were a part of his light body,' confirmed Lai-Xii.

'You say you are now here purely by chance. How did that come about?' The General's attitude had softened somewhat. Perhaps because she herself was a fugitive, as I later learnt.

William hesitated at this point. The events which propelled us away from Andromeda not only cast us back to the Milky Way, it also jumped us back to a previous timeline. He simply didn't know how it happened.

'The confluence of circumstances is beyond my comprehension. I have insufficient data on which to formulate a hypothesis as to the mechanism behind our emergence from the vicinity of Andromeda.'

'As I recall, you are supposed to be, or have been, the most comprehensively outstanding artificial intelligence ever devised by the mind of man, and you are telling us you don't know.'

I had to interject here for I felt there needed to be a certain flexibility in the degree to which disbelief was being suspended. From my own experience life had a particularly attractive random quality about it. Some things one could plan for, other things one could adapt to. Yet there came about other events which turned you right around and upside down, and that's just how it was. I said as much to the 'Martians'.

We had again dropped into a Time context, as indicated by so many changes taking place in rapid succession. How long we spent under interrogation was immaterial. By the time we'd finished, the tension in the room had eased considerably. Irina Prime invited us to her real office to continue the debriefing.

Her office overlooked the great canyon, clearly visible through her panoramic bubble window. The landing platform could be seen if one knew where to look, though the other side of the canyon wall receded two hundred kilometres into the distance, still just visible in the rarefied atmosphere. We went over to the transparent wall to view the spectacular landscape of the canyon while the Martian's reclined in comfort.

'We only need some insights from you about the feasibility of returning to Earth,' said Lai-Xii. 'General Lubov says she's from Earth, yet she is so vastly different to yourselves. What has happened there in our absence,' she asked Irina Prime.

'I can tell you the story up to the time of our departure. Lubov can fill in the rest until her untimely escape with Kapitolina's help.'

Without digressing into tedious detail Irina explained the consequences of the failure of William's plan to improve the human psyche. He didn't interrupt, or react to Lai-Xii's subvocalized supporting words of comfort. As the story unfolded towards the time of Kapitolina's return another plan took shape in his mind. *Lai-Xii wants to go back and now so do I.*

'Admiral Kapitolina has only been with us for a little over a decade. All of you have made a quantum leap across the flight of the Arrow of Time from one path to another, defying all the laws governing the nature of existence. I have no doubt now that your return has not been a random event in the spacetime continuum. We will do what must be done, even if it is to comprehensively influence our future.' Irina Prima had made up her mind. Kapitolina had not come back from the other end of time by accident, nor had William and Lai-Xii.

To put his new plan into effect William needed to know only one thing. 'Admiral Kapitolina, did you deliver the software unaltered, exactly as I gave it to you?'

'No. That is, we didn't change your code but added a little something to disrupt Afanasy's military systems. Though he's got all that sorted out by now as we've seen from the recent attacks.'

'Do you know if this Afanasy individual has implemented the software?'

'No. We added another small change.' She smiled, as did Lubov, as did Irina. She continued. 'Nothing to harm anyone, mind you, just a little insurance to make sure Afanasy couldn't prevent it doing its job – a little worm to help your code infiltrate all their computerised systems. So even if individuals weren't exposed directly whenever they plugged in some of the algorithms would seed into their minds.'

'That's all I need to know.'

I didn't take part in the information exchange, but I knew William well enough by now to gauge he was up to something, simply from the nature of his questions. I took him away from Lai-Xii to stand with me directly in front of the bubble window as if I wanted to ask him something about the Martian landscape. No need to worry Lai-Xii. She might be harbouring some fanciful idealised desire that we will find circumstances on Earth to be nothing less than Utopian, despite everything Kapitolina and Lubov had said.

'Are we going to go through it again William?'

'I only want to finish what I started. Sometimes things don't eventuate according to plan.'

'You mean about the cleansing of Earth?' I didn't want to spell it out. How could we have gone through an entire extraordinary period of human evolution just to loop back into the past. What possible purpose could it serve to be so – vengeful. I could think of no other reason, mindful at the same time that AI's generally don't have emotions. But then again, all those people within his light body may well have changed this AI's internal make up.

'We should be the only branch of humanity in existence. Look what's happened. I have failed. I have to fix this.'

'What exactly do you have in mind?'

'To create the world Lai-Xii initially had in mind before having to abandon it. Will you help?'

Of course I would help. A normal AI does not ask for assistance. I was still having trouble adjusting to the current William. 'What is your intention about the Martians?'

'They are on Mars. There is no reason why they can't stay here.'

Having established the liaison between ourselves and the Martians we prepared to leave. General Lubov downloaded her copy of the entire data cluster concerning Plutarch Afanasy's operations, his military systems, his personnel files and Earth's population centres. She could not go with William, it would only alert Afanasy, whereas bundles of light heading to ground from Earth's orbit would seem like any other meteor shower, perhaps with a little more or less intensity depending on the time of day.

'No Xii – I don't think you should come on this trip. From what we've heard it's likely you would see a horrendous example of what the remnants of humanity have become. I want to spare you this anguish.'

'William,' she paused, her hand on his arm, 'come back,' another longer pause, 'to me.'

Only the two of us stood in the reception atrium ready to mount the landing platform to be raised to the surface. 'Are you ready Klara?'

All of me indicated in the affirmative. I advised all my photon bundles of what lay ahead of us, the dangers involved and our hoped for outcome. Anyone who didn't want to participate could have transferred to one of the other light bodies. None refused, as was the case with William. His remaining two avatars remained with him having made a substantial contribution towards the development of something William refused to divulge to me.

EARTH

AUTARCH AFANASY had built his palace on the ruins of the great gladiatorial arena in Rome. The design of the old Colosseum embodied all the architectural features suitable to his tastes. His pets, and those of his Generals, were housed on the ground floor and the extensive basement complex, which still retained some of the layout of the old Colosseum. The penthouse served several functions, amongst them being the centre of operations. From there he ruled the known world.

Dedicated terraces surrounded the palace, his favourite being the walled Execution Park containing all manner of interesting execution chambers; most designed to extend life as long as possible until the inevitable moment of death. This day, a glorious bright spring day, devoid of all dark clouds and petty frustrations gave Afanasy an opportunity to stroll through his flesh corridors where his pets performed their frantic best for the Plutarch. If he happened to be displeased by a performance, or he thought the pets weren't making a genuine effort, the walk to the Execution Park didn't take long. At least there he could satisfy any shortcomings in his pleasure experience. Orgasms, the most spectacular of which have been known to be achieved only at the moment of excruciating death throes of the pets, generally gave him the greatest pleasure.

Pets were in short supply. Countless millennia ago the world's population of humans dwindled to an extinction level as a result of a rogue artificial intelligence who took it upon himself to annihilate homo-sapiens – or so the history went. Afanasy never really believed it himself, but there must have been some spark of truth in it. For History also taught about the events that led to the rise of technically engineered individuals; Tengi, an offshoot of pure biological humans. He was proud of his heritage and the new world he'd created after the attempted global genocide, and particularly pleased with having found such an entertaining way of using surviving humans living in the wild. These wild human pets were eventually bred for entertainment – nothing else. They were fragile, unpredictable, argumentative and always wanted more food. The best ones were still the truly wild ones. They had more resilience – they lasted longer.

'Shave them completely,' he yelled at one of attendants administering to some new pets captured from inland European forests. 'I hate all that hair! I want them ready to play by the time I come back.' He didn't need to give his orders more than once, a lesson learnt by the attendant's predecessor the hard way.

His meanderings led him to another terrace, the birthing anti-room where he liked to examine all the new born pets.

'Plutarch Afanasy,' Generalissimo Yuri waited for an opportune moment to interrupt his leader. 'We have encountered a communications problem.' He didn't dare proffer the details until he was more than a metallic arm's length away.

Afanasy spun around away from an especially loud newborn, he particularly liked the screaming ones. A thunderous red glare rose into his bionic video camera eyes. 'Can't you see I'm busy!'

Generalissimo Yuri took two steps backwards. 'All our communications are down. We have been trying to restore contact with our satellites. They seem to have been deactivated.' He took another step back. Afanasy processed that piece of worrying data.

'They can't all be down! To my office – NOW!' All thought of babies and performing pets and near death entertainment highlights completely drained out of his circuits. 'It's those bloody Martians doing this! 'Get our warheads ready. It's time we hit them with everything we've got!'

'It is not possible.' Yuri tried to be as militarily correct as he could, placing emphasis on exactly the right syllables. What he didn't want to do was to repeat himself. The Plutarch took such an act as an affront to his intelligence, dealing with the perpetrator rather harshly. 'We cannot contact any of our installations.'

'Get my entire staff here." Yuri hesitated, only for a moment. "Do it NOW!' Afanasy screamed at him. Apparently the consequences of the extent of the blackout had not penetrated Afanasy's neural CPU.

Over the intervening time from Kapitolina's escape and the light bodies arrival on Mars Earth's attack systems had been repaired and all commsats brought back on line. Several half-hearted attacks on Mars failed to do anything but temporarily assuage Afanasy's frustration.

*

We decided to leave Mars when it was at its furthest point from Earth. It would still only take us a little over three minutes to cover the intervening distance. William judged a daytime crossing would give least opportunity to be discovered as having originated from Mars, just in case Earth was monitoring Mars activity.

'You know what to do, Klara. I'll take out all the military commsats, you do the rest of them. At our speed it should take no more than few seconds to lance every one of them even if we have to do several orbits.'

Reforming themselves into highly coherent needle laser beams, William and Klara fried the circuits of every communications satellite used by Autarch Afanasy. The ancient units, once set up by William to get in touch with Europa's colony had long since decayed their orbits, falling back to Earth eventually.

'Now we have control. There will be no more attacks on the Mars settlements.' Satisfied with himself William wanted to go directly to Rome.

We resumed our previous configuration and discussed whether to go to the Plutarch's stronghold to see what developments have taken place in our absence or whether we should choose some other destination.

'I particularly want to see what has become of Tau City. There is no great urgency now we've neutralised their main infrastructure. It'll give us a chance to get a broad overview of the Earth's condition, check population densities and technological development.'

'Agreed. I estimate the Plutarch will not be able to mobilise himself for some time.'

Outlines of continents had changed, some dramatically almost to the point of being unrecognisable. Some island nations had become larger through volcanic activity, others had almost disappeared due to erosion. The Kamchatka peninsula's active volcanic spine had sprouted five new peaks. One of them replaced the little Southern village of Esso, which featured so prominently in the development of Lai-Xii's technology.

216

Tau City clung on, now perched precariously near the edges of a rift valley, largely isolated from the rest of the peninsula by new geographical barriers.

Descending to what we gathered to be the centre of Tau City, as remnants of buildings clustered around a large flat area suggested, we startled a gathering of what I presumed to be humans.

'They're so short and so hairy.' They were also very frightened. Quite understandable if brilliant shining human forms landed from the sky into the middle of your party. We displayed our faces, but it made no difference, they just backed further away. 'What's happened to these people?' I asked the rhetorical question as the two of us set out to explore what remained of our old city. Given the many thousands of years of our absence we should not have been surprised to see major changes in the human form. That's not what concerned us.

William made the most obvious observation before we departed to another location, 'They are barely surviving. It's not even a case of poverty. These are primitive people living the most basic existence. In spite of my failed attempts to eradicate the species the survivors should have regrouped and advanced well beyond what we're seeing here. Something is very wrong.'

'Kapitolina's people have disappeared from here, at least the descendants who didn't get to evacuate to Mars. I hate to think what has happened to them. Perhaps they've become part of the branch of humanoids now represented by Plutarch Afanasy. Now that's a horrible thought.'

Stirrings within us made us decide quickly to leave the scene. Our constituent photon bundles must have been badly affected by what we witnessed. We flew to the Americas and saw almost the same scenes over and over. The land had recovered, the creatures had returned to sustainable population densities and the seas teemed with life. This had been a part of the plan, not the infliction of misery on humankind.

'Are you satisfied Klara? Can we move onto the reason we are here?'

'I see your point. Though I think we should not make our presence so blatantly obvious in Rome. General Lubov's description of this tyrant does not recommend him as a potential friend, nor as someone we could possibly negotiate with.'

An early morning arrival right on sunrise presented the ideal opportunity to enter the city unnoticed. We flew towards Afanasy's Colosseum Palace directly out of the rising sun's rays, to settle on a low turret near the edge of his complex. It must have been a day of celebrations for a great deal of movement had already filled the different terraces.

'They are not all the same, William. The group on the lower terrace are all naked. They appear to be like the humans we saw in Tau City – except these are completely hairless – and clean, well fed. What is going on?'

William drew my attention to the highest terrace. Everyone there looked just like General Lubov in their dull metallic green-brown khaki, not at all human in appearance. 'These must be the descendants of the original Tengi,' I suggested. 'Why are they so agitated?'

'I do not believe this is a gathering for celebration purposes. We have disabled all their communications. What we are seeing is panic. It will be interesting to see their reactions and what they decide to do.'

As the hour progressed and the sun rose higher in the sky the mood at the palace only worsened. Remarkably, and I could not for the world imagine why they should be acting this way, the naked humans paired off into male-female, male-male and other variations, to begin coupling. All manner of configurations attracted the attention of the Plutarch's officers. They paid no attention to many of their fellows lying dead on the ground around them, not even bothering to move them out of the way.

We watched dumbfounded as Afanasy engaged with his officers, some of whom went away to carry out his orders presumably, while another received the blast from some kind of weapon in his hand. This one dropped dead to the ground to join the other corpses.

'I don't think I can watch anymore of this,' I said, getting ready to move back into the rays of the sun behind me. I turned my attention back to the copulating humans. It made no sense at all. I couldn't remember General Lubov saying anything about these people or what they were doing, for no apparent reason I could discern.

Afanasy, accompanied by another high ranking officer moved away from the entrance of what must have been his HQ. Oddly they appeared to be in a much better humour than a little while ago as they made their way to a grouping of three humans.

'What do you suppose he's planning for that trio?' William wouldn't know the answer of course. It just came out of me as a consequence of complete bewilderment and disgust. William remained silent. Afanasy and his General marched the trio, who a moment before had been resting following their vigorous sexual exertions, down to the next terrace.

'Those are machines designed to act upon the humans to bring about pain and eventual death,' William said without taking his attention away from the action. 'You may not want to see this Klara.'

I turned around. I'd had enough. If this was anything like the world Lai-Xii felt the need to leave behind then I cannot blame her for everything she did to get away. 'Your attempts to improve human nature have failed, William. As much then as now. Whatever algorithms you've given to Admiral Kapitolina show no beneficial effects that I can see.'

'Too soon,' William grunted, the most human noise he's ever made in my presence. He also turned away from the torture terrace. 'He is taking his frustrations out on those around him, and they are joining him in that orgy of pain. There is only one thing to be done.'

In spite of the emergency situation The Plutarch had to deal with, he and all his remaining staff marched off to the torture terrace to distract themselves in the enjoyment of human suffering.

'From the nature of the equipment I estimate their deaths will be drawn out. This will give me a chance to examine their computer systems.'

I thought that to be a rather cold-blooded statement. 'Why can't we do something for those people?'

'Best if those three die quickly. We would only attract attention to ourselves. Don't forget – we are very vulnerable in our present state. But rest assured, no one else will die at the Plutarch's hand.'

We left our vantage point on the turret gaining easy access through the open windows of Afanasy's office. The place lit up with brilliant white light due to our presence. We would not be seen as everyone had gathered on the torture level. The office turned out to be surprisingly devoid of extravagance, concentrating on a large range of weaponry set up ready for quick access, and all the expected paraphernalia commensurate with computerised communication and control systems. 'This is exactly what I was looking for,' William commented.

I barely had time to examine a few of the weapons before William had connected to and interrogated the network, modifying some critical algorithms in the process. 'I found the software Kapitolina downloaded. It would work, in time, to bring about the changes I designed, taking far too long. The Admiral failed to present accurate data on the state of the technology here, or the neurological conditions my software would have to influence.'

'Should I be afraid to ask what you've done so far or what you're planning to do?'

'I am never the one to be afraid of, Klara. The danger is here, right before us. I have made sure all weapons ready for deployment against Mars will shortly self-destruct. We should not be here when that happens. Some of the warheads are nuclear. They will produce high energy EMPs when they explode, which will not only destroy electronic circuitry it will also emit particularly high concentrations of γ-rays. These could destroy us.'

'And after that?' I pressed the point. In the past William had acted on his own volition without consulting Lai-Xii – definitely not acting with her approval.

'What would you do Klara? You've witnessed the mental state of these Tengi. You've seen how they treat each other and the humans. Honestly, what would you do?'

My immediate reaction was to destroy the lot of them, even perhaps the remaining wretched humans and put them out of their misery. I'd forgotten that General Lubov, though one of them, seemed to be quite different. I'd forgotten about us. We wanted to make this our home again. How could we even think of that if our first act was to destroy sentient life? I'd forgotten about the Martians. How do they fit into the greater scheme of things? Could this destructive act just be another one of those random events that have accompanied us throughout our wanderings? Would it be further evidence that the human mindset could never change, forever locked into the 'kill or be killed' survival mechanism?

'That is not my decision, nor is it yours William. We have within our light bodies the future of the human species – the original survivors. I think they should have an input. I don't think it's even up to Lai-Xii anymore.'

He would not let it go at that. 'Theoretically, if it was just up to you, what would you do?'

I had the strongest sense that he'd already made up his mind as to the most appropriate response required to bring back into balance the digression taken by evolution. Perhaps to rectify his own mistakes – perhaps to divert the true biological human development back on course.

'Purge all Tengi,' I said, 'they should never have come into existence.' I felt much better after dumping that weight off my conscience.

'And, then what?' Now he really pushed. Was it the human component in him or the AI that would not give me peace?

'If we want to make a life here again it will have to be beside the existing humans. Though I don't know if they can be trusted.'

Our intense discussion could not continue. The countdown on the warheads had begun, synchronised with the fading sounds of the tortured dying humans. They must have gone past the point of being entertaining for Afanasy rapidly approached his office with a large following of Officers. The time had come for him to face the problem.

'Why are you following me? If any of you are wanting to find out what my little toys in there are capable of I'm quite happy to oblige,' he said to those nearest, 'and you Generalissimo Yuri could be the first. NOW GET OUT THERE AND FIX THE PROBLEM!'

They scattered in every direction not knowing what to do, only knowing what would happen if they didn't do it. Afanasy burst into the office, the brilliance of our presence blinding him temporarily.

'Should we tell him?' I asked William. He didn't respond, caught by surprise at Afanasy's sudden presence and my provocative question. 'You tell him.' Afanasy could obviously hear something for he turned from side to side, spinning around a couple of times and almost falling. Vision came back slowly and he had to shade his eyes to cast them upon our brilliant light formed bodies.

'WHAT THE *&!K ARE YOU?'

Did this guy ever say anything without shouting? 'Do you have to shout everything?' I couldn't help myself asking him.

He couldn't answer for William had put his hand on the Plutarch's head. The energy flowing into his circuits didn't fry him, leaving the matrix of his consciousness capable of hearing only. 'I am William,' Afanasy's visual sensors strained, perhaps in incredulous recognition of a myth that had come to life. 'You are an obsolete unit.' William removed his hand. Afanasy continued to stare at the wall of his office, incapable of speech or movement.

'We will let your Staff administer to your needs,' William said as we shot out of the office.

'Can they fix him?'

'No.'

Given the nature of the Autarch's relationship with his Officers I had no doubt a military coup was imminent. I gave it no further thought as we sped out of the Earth's atmosphere back towards Mars.

'We should be underground soon,' William said, 'there's only a few atomic warheads but they will brighten things up shortly.'

*

The main observation dome of Valles Marineris was not facing Earth as Mars rotated itself through the cycle of its day. Irina Prima instructed all other observers to view events only indirectly through their Earth monitoring systems.

'William, I have to know – what happened on Earth?' As soon as we arrived back Lai-Xii insisted on an update.

'First watch this, Xii,' then we can talk.

'You haven't taken matters into your own hands again, have you?' The shadows of bad memories are long and dark.

The two light bodies stood close to one another, blending a little, as we observed the first two second flash of blinding light over what was once France. It turned into a volcanic flashing red ball of near black cloud billowing high into the atmosphere. In rapid succession standard warheads exploded over Libya, France and Germany. All locally devastating in their impact, with no effect on the Martian spectators. Past the ten kilometre altitude stratospheric winds blew the smoke and fine debris from the first detonation to blanket much of the landscape along a wide corridor between Libya and France. Life, any life would find it a struggle to survive for many years in that local environment.

'What have you done William?' Lai-Xii pulled away from him to ask the question.

'I have ensured the safety and survival of all who live on Mars. There will be no more attacks from Earth. Autarch Afanasy has been neutralised. His own people will deal with him as he deserves, if they are still functional, though I doubt it if I'm right about the effects of the EMP generated by all those detonations.'

'Is there no one left?' asked General Lubov. 'I had family. I had hoped to return some day.'

'No Tengi could withstand the γ-ray blast on their circuits. Wild humans will endure. We saw many primitive tribes surviving. Humans used for entertainment by the Plutarch in Rome may well have welcomed the release from their enslavement.'

Lai-Xii listened, disheartened at the thought she would probably never be able to return to her home. Nor could she return to Europa, the sentience there made it quite clear the digitized human psyche was not welcome. The planet of Syy had already faded into the realm of impossibility. A purely random occurrence had propelled the light bodies through space and through time into the distant past. Such a thing would never happen again. My thought turned to how we, as light bodies, could manage existence amongst the Martians and their underground world. We would not be able to continue in our current manifestation for we needed intergalactic space and the its sources of nourishment to keep us viable.

'William, will we ever be able to return to Earth?' I asked, suspecting Lai-Xii dwelt on very similar thoughts.

'In far less time than we spent on Europa. Perhaps a little longer than we vacationed on Syy,' he replied flippantly.

'Why didn't you say!' Lai-Xii visibly brightened at the prospect, moving into him again.

'Will I be able to go back?' General Lubov's question didn't have energy behind it. 'Is there any chance my family may have survived?'

'A minuscule probability. You could end up being the only example of that particular branch of human evolution. I believe you belong with the people here.'

'Yes General,' Irina Prime agreed. 'You are welcome to make your life among us.'

Conversations abated as we all realised the reality of the new circumstances. The Martians had evolved too far to be able to revert back to an existence on Earth. The peculiar species engendered by Plutarch Afanasy had had its chance, achieving only to bring destruction on themselves. No doubt a familiar situation to Lai-Xii when she recalled the reasons for abandoning Earth in the first place. And us – well, there were really only two choices. Either William could pull off another of his miracles to reconfigure us into a life form with survivability under terrestrial conditions after the dust had settled, or we would have to resume our journey through the cosmos. I have no doubt about what would eventually happen to us out there. Space is an unforgiving environment for Light; diffusion, diffraction, absorption, scattering, refraction, de-energising and who knows what else. The end result would always be the same; we'd be reduced to almost non-existence as incoherent sentient entities, doomed to fade into the fabric of spacetime as nothing more than background noise. It might take a thousand years or a million years – little consolation to life that wanted to endure.

Finally Irina Prime thanked William. 'You have done a great deal for us William. You and the others may stay as long as you wish or as long as you are able. We are content to continue with Mars as our home. However, if you wish to return to Earth we will do what we can to help.'

'In that regard Admiral Kapitolina, would you be prepared to come to Earth for at least a brief visit if we required your assistance?'

Yet again William surprised me. I had never known him to ask for help. What on Earth could possibly be beyond his capabilities? We'd seen what the situation had become on our home planet.

Then I remembered the reason we were considering going back there; Lai-Xii – only she had openly expressed her desire to return. It may nevertheless have been the expressed wish of all within her. She may have spoken to William about it many times, and given the nature of their evolved relationship I could understand if William researched in his mind how that could be made possible. But I still couldn't understand why he would ask the Admiral for help.

LAI-XII VISITS EUROPA

PERHAPS eighty years had elapsed before restlessness began to assert itself amongst and within the light bodies visiting Mars.

William and his two avatars had been kept busy enough with helping and teaching the Martian's. The peculiarity of William's naissance, his extraordinary artificial intelligence, his eons of experience in a broad spectrum of sentient experience and now his inculcation of the human spirit from within the individual elements of his light body made him an invaluable resource.

Lai-Xii, Klara, Luka and the other seven light bodies tired of exploring Mars, its two moons and the near cosmic environs of the solar system. Every few years Lai-Xii and Klara visited Earth, sometimes going down to low orbits and later to skim the troposphere after the nuclear fallout had dissipated.

'I know you've made up your mind Lai-Xii, but it's still too soon to make a safe landing.' I commented feeling her impatience magnify at each visitation.

'I know – I know. But just look at it. Magnificent! Of all the places we've experienced there is nothing like this. Earth is our home. Maybe the others don't feel like this. They can go their own way. I want to go home. I really want to go home Klara. Can't you understand that?'

'Do you think William wants to go with you?'

'What a strange question. Of course he does. We are partners.'

She said this so naturally, so convincingly – so unconsciously that one could never have guessed how their partnership had begun, how it had morphed from an adversarial human versus machine interaction into a trusting and mutually supportive union.

'Yes – silly me. The compatibility factor between you has definitely increased exponentially since we arrived on Syy. Anyway – from what I can see down there all presence of Tengi seems to have disappeared. The humans are beginning to group together. I see no evidence of warring tribes. It all feels very hopeful. Now it's really up to your – ah - partner – to find a way to put us back. And don't forget, we are each carrying many millions of individuals all wanting to finally settle in one place.'

We orbited many more times, in the Northern and Southern Hemispheres. An odd little though emerged as we observed the cycles of life below us.

'Lai-Xii – have you thought about giving up your mortality? I mean, if that's the only way we could resume life on Earth?'

She considered the question for only the briefest moment; obviously not a stranger to these thoughts. 'Only if William joins me.'

We said no more about that particular subject. It receded into the background, for as we arrived back on Mars William and Luka had begun preparations for a visit to a different location. I wondered what kind of complicated preparations needed to be made for a simple trip anywhere in the solar system. Everything was in such close proximity for our capability of light speed.

'Do you not want to visit Europa?' William asked Lai-Xii.

She'd been so focused on Earth that everything else got pushed to the back of her consciousness. As soon as she heard the proposition I could see her intense reaction as a flood of memories surfaced. My recollections also returned with such clarity that it surprised me. Europa presented the greatest challenge to us as a species. Then of course the stupendous discovery that the moon possessed its own awareness, for which we were the catalyst for its awakening. How could we forget such things?

'Prima9,' said Lai-Xii, 'Yes – Yes! I want to visit Prima9.'

William only encouraged her by remarking that Prima9 should still be there if Europa Cell had not rejected her psyche over the passage of time. 'Besides, Luka here and all his ex-Zetas are particularly keen to discuss something with Europa Cell.'

Our expedition consisted of all ten light bodies, with a variety of reasons for their desire to have an excursion away from Mars. I asked Luka why he wanted to go there.

'It is not complicated. The majority of us left Earth with a clear purpose in life; to set up Arithmós City for the rest of you and to maintain its infrastructure, circuitry, power supply and everything associated with it for your survival. We did this for several thousand years. It became our home. Since then we've become gypsies, with no place of our own.'

'Are you telling me you actually want to stay on Europa?'

'We all do.'

'But you know EC wanted us to leave – all of us.'

'Not quite all of us. It's been a long time since our departure. Many things could have changed. What if the EC consciousness no longer exists, for example.'

'Unlikely, since he's been EC for several billions of years,' I said.

'Klara, we are optimistic. There is a remote possibility of a compromise.'

'So that's what William's preparations were all about.'

It took less than an hour to lance through space between Mars and Jupiter. We didn't announce our arrival. Water plumes jetted into Europa's rarefied atmosphere, just as I'd remembered. Pwyll crater hadn't changed in any way I could discover, other than the lightest layer of ultrafine ice crystals having settled on all the exposed surfaces of our old city network. Absolute silence greeted our landing on the rim of the crater. I don't know why I expected any sound, it had always been a silent world.

My immediate attention was drawn to Jupiter itself, surprised to see the giant red storm had disappeared from its Southern hemisphere. Io hurried into view from behind the giant, its volcanoes seeming to be as active as ever. It all appeared to be so normal - until I looked down into Arithmós central hub and saw the light.

'What's that down there William? Surely it's not some beacon still working.' I couldn't believe after all this time the whole place hadn't disintegrated.

'Actually, I've been here recently to warm the place up – so to speak,' William admitted.

'Why ever would you want do that?' It all seemed so clandestine to me.

'Because of us,' interrupted Luka, 'I did mention our plans briefly to you.'

'Oh.'

'It is quite beautiful,' Lai-Xii announced to no one in particular, absorbed in the majesty of its tranquillity. Quietly she whispered, 'When can we speak with Prima9?'

That was my first surprise.

Our next stop was to one of the Interchange Centres where the Zeta Tengi chassis stood ready for downloads from the network to anyone who wanted to go out on the ice in the past. We stood, incredulous to see these ancient icons of a distant previous life. I was particularly moved by these sentinels as I'd spent the entirety of my existence on Europa encased in one of those machines. Luka's nostalgia tugged at the fringes of my emotions. I could empathise with his desire to return to a normality which embodied a purpose to his, and his kinds' existence.

My impulse to join Luka didn't ebb immediately. Life on Earth could be rewarding, undoubtedly. It would also become temporary. Could I be content to blend into the limitless future, here on Europa, as a mind in a machine, until this tiny moon eventually plunged into its parent? I had my rising doubts, realising that my commitment would have had to be immediate without any reservations if it was to be the right choice for me.

Still enmeshed in my thoughts it took me a moment to become conscious of William explaining something. '… and if you remember the process we all had to go through in preparation for our journey to V616 Monocerotis …' Indeed we did; painless, extraordinary and unbelievable, … 'at the time I made provision for the possibility of being forced to return to our digital manifestation in the unlikelihood of unforeseen events forcing that course of action upon us.'

'What exactly do you mean?' Lai-Xii contained her impatience to connect with Prima9. She would have understood the necessity of a mechanism to enable that to happen. William had chosen a roundabout way of getting to the crux of it.

'I have reactivated the Transition module, the one we all went through to reconfigure all the data that described each of us in our entirety, from digital into photon packets. It has built into it the reverse capability. It has been stored in my old cache.'

William could even then consider alternate realities through the veils of improbability. He and Lai-Xii make a formidable team, quite capable of upsetting any machinations devised by Fate or anything else, to confound Homo-Sapiens or Homo-Universapiensis.

Lai-Xii remembered the cache's location, leading the way as soon as William had finished basking in his own cleverness. The ingress created by his three avatars gave access to a small enclosure large enough for all of us to crowd into.

'Just a word of caution. We have been agglutinated into a mass of photons comprising myriad individuals. If an entire light body enters back into the Arithmós network there is no guarantee that its constituent parts would be able to return to the original light body.'

'We understand this,' Luka said. 'We have made up our minds. If there is a compromise possible with Europa Cell our decision is final.'

'Prima9! EC!' William called. Hardware to our left buzzed into life. A voice we could never forget sounded clear and authoritative.

'We am here. Speak.'

'Is that you Prima9?' asked Lai-Xii, for the nuance in the voice was not entirely Prima9's.

'It is us. Why do you disturb?'

'Don't you remember me?'

'We do not forget. What is your desire?' She/EC were persistent, displaying no emotion at all at the reunion.

'What has happened to you? How are you? Are you content?' Lai-Xii only wanted to reconnect with the youthful Prima9 who had such a zest for life, such a consuming desire to experience the unknown.

'It is as it has always been. I/we do not regret my/our conjoining – it has been of mutual benefit. You have returned so soon. What do you wish?'

'It's up to you Luka. Make your case, I think Xii and Prima9 have finished,' said William.

Lai-Xii withdrew into herself. I had the sense that if she could have cried her tears would have flooded the Pwyll crater. My emotions overwhelmed me to see her in that condition. I moved to her and blended with her to give her our full hearted support.

Luka began by introducing himself. It was not necessary as Prima9 had already said they had a long memory.

'I/we remember. You assisted in our conjoining. I/we are grateful. What is your desire?'

Whatever long speech Luka may have prepared in justification of the Zetas return to live on the surface of Europa clothed in their previous chassis, it was not needed. He had to get to the point for fear of annoying this intelligence and being forced to leave again. 'We want to resume our lives here. Our chassis are still functional and we would live by any conditions you want.'

'That is not acceptable to me/us.'

After a moments pause the voice returned. We thought there would be some unpleasantness because of Luka's forthright request. What possible advantage could they represent to this lunar sentience other than be an annoying parasite on its skin?

'Account for your existence since leaving me/us.'

An unexpected turn of events. I just wondered what could be a possible alternative, not realising that Luka had amassed an incredible array of experiences, and with it a much deeper comprehension of the meaning of all there is – not that Luka was prone to philosophising about such things.

'Might I suggest you allow all of your people to express themselves. Don't talk, just connect to those photovoltaic cells and concentrate your thoughts.' William must have known what was going to happen.

Without the least hesitation Luka launched into the tale of all that happened to them since leaving Europa. The stories about the photon spheres, the wormhole, the Syynians and the Martians must have been quite something to listen to.

'You set all this up, didn't you William?' Lai-Xii mock chided her partner after recovering some of her composure.

'It was always your intention to save humanity from itself. Diversity can only further that goal, don't you think?'

As comprehensive as Luka's story must have been, his download was complete by the time William and Lai-Xii finished their short conversation. Luka withdrew his hands from the panel, not knowing what to expect next.

The voice returned as quickly as before. 'An alternative, the only alternative, is to do as I have done,' advised Prima9/EC. She/they placed no conditions on this only option. It was clear to me, perhaps to Luka as well that this offer would not be made a second time.

That's what William had arranged! It only just dawned on me. Europa Cell didn't need parasites running around on the outside, that's why he asked us to leave. He wanted knowledge and experience. He wanted to expand his comprehension of the nature of existence. That's why he accepted Prima9 into himself, and that's why he was now prepared to absorb all the Zeta psyche – because of what they could bring from the millennia of existence cruising the cosmos.

For whatever reasons the Zetas and all others who dwelt within Luka's light body found the offer acceptable. I could think of many reasons myself why I would have like to have joined them.

The gateway into Europa Cell's psyche lay through the quantum Arithmós network. I couldn't pretend to grasp even the most rudimentary aspects of the technology, suffice it to say Luka seemed to know what to do. The array of photovoltaic cells was large enough to absorb all of his light body's energy within minutes of having made full body contact with it. He and all within him were gone. They faded before we had the chance to say a few parting words.

'Good bye Prima9,' Lai-Xii said quietly in the direction of the equipment. Her only contact with the past had gone, unlikely ever to be renewed.

'I detect a sadness in you Xii. There is no need for this. Consider your legacy. Now we have a job to finish. We must go.'

William, having become so finely attuned to Lai-Xii, took into consideration not only her feelings and sense of wellbeing, but also the final fulfilment of the task she had dedicated her life to, a life that had encompassed cosmic time scales.

The Salazar light body had been waiting for their opportunity to speak with Lai-Xii. During the entire journey since leaving Europa for the Photon Sphere and the subsequent time on Syy he and all in him had remained silent. His association with the lady began on Earth when he joined her team of billionaires to support her fantastic project. He'd contributed not only his billions. I got to know him, or more accurately – of him – here on Europa when he helped set up a common Virtual Reality construct to help people acclimate to their digitized manifestation. He followed Lai-Xii unquestioningly on whatever fateful path she chose for those remnants of humanity who'd entrusted themselves to her care. Unlike some of the other billionaires, he never opposed her methods or objected to her decisions that had far reaching consequences, most of which could not be foreseen.

On this day, having witnessed the gradual fragmentation of her people represented in all the light bodies, he made a decision. It had never been in his nature to be autocratic. He took note of other people's wishes within his light body, and within the other bodies that had no direct relationship with her, William or Klara.

'Lai-Xii, we are aware of your desire to try to return to Earth. We understand. Just as we could sympathise with Luka's decision to remain here. And who could have opposed Fukuda's yearning to become part of Syynian society? Certainly not us.'

'Get to the point my friend. I trust you. I trust in your integrity and I thank you for your magnificent contributions. I have the feeling you are about to leave us.'

'Yes Lai-Xii. Our decision is firm.'

'You may call me Xii.' There were only two people in existence who had earnt the privilege to call her that; Harusuke, her first great love, and recently William.

'Thank you Xii. You know, I still remember the time when you sat on my knee after coming in from the cold in Esso. My goodness but your bum was cold, but you didn't seem to feel it; made me feel hot under the collar.' He smiled and she returned his smile, also remembering the incident. It was simply one of her many tricks to control these super wealthy men. 'We want to continue our journey. You have created in us a thirst for knowledge and a desire to discover the mysteries out there.'

'You don't need my permission. Visit us on Earth some time. Good bye Salazar.' She turned away from him, but before exiting the cache she backed into his light body, ever so gently pressing her back against him.

Six light bodies decide to continue their journey into the greater Cosmos, leaving Europa and Earth behind. They might be searching for something else, or just wanting to continue existence in the search for knowledge. We never did see Salazar again, or any of those who left with him. Though of course they could have visited Earth in a form we would never have recognised.

Only William, myself and Lai-Xii returned to Mars leaving the Arithmós network intact. One never knows …

THE CHOICE

THE EARTH recovered again.

A living, breathing organism perhaps with a consciousness like Europa. It did not reveal itself to us when we landed for the last time. We saw all that was around us, in the sky, on the land and in the sea. What possible difference would it have made to make conscious contact with whatever sustained life on this planet if we did not ultimately respect it.

I could see big differences, even in the short span of time since William's detonations of the nuclear warhead. On all the major continents the wild humans were no longer as wild, having infiltrated the living environments created by Plutarch Afanasy's species.

'I was wrong to leave the Tengi alive when we left Tau City,' William admitted. 'If they had guidance the mess we found may have been averted.'

'You cannot second guess yourself William. Look what I started and what finally happened – and it is not over yet.'

We hadn't revealed ourselves to any of the humans at that stage, other than the few we saw in Tau City on our previous fleeting visit. We had a new challenge ahead of us. If we'd made ourselves known to one tribe or another they might have looked upon us as Gods. Understandable under the circumstances. According to my ancient History data such things have happened before. Bright lights in the sky have been mistaken for everything from Gods to Angels to Saints, and even the Devil himself. With William in our midst we certainly had Godlike capabilities with power over life and death. This became one of our problematic issues.

'As I recall William, as part of your plan to keep us safe after our emigration to Europa, you felt it necessary to cleanse the Earth of the human species,' Lai-Xii began the difficult subject, 'safe from their predisposition to violence to solve problems, safe from their uncontrollable desire to destroy the Earth itself. And we represented a major threat to people at the time, as they did to us. Do you still feel the same way?'

'They hardly represent any danger to us now. Most of them are living wild. Some fortunate ones, or unfortunate, had been either bred to be nothing more than pets for the Autarch's civilisation, or captured to perform as pets and just as readily disposed of. It is not possible for me to predict what direction evolution will take for the survivors.'

Why bother saving homo-sapiens? I thought. Have they not risen out of the depths of Africa into warring tribes for the entire length of their evolutionary journey? Wasn't that the main contributing factor towards the necessity of having a creature like Lai-Xii to be born? To change the direction of evolution – to give sentience an opportunity to survive? I said as much to William and Lai-Xii.

'Are you calling me a creature?'

'No disrespect intended. You are definitely no ordinary person!'

'We have time. We don't have to decide yet.' Most unlike either William or Lai-Xii to put off a decision, especially one so important.

'You don't know what decisions are possible, do you?' I thought it best to bring it all out into the open.

'I am certain of one thing. It is something we had to implement on Europa and to some extent on the Photon Sphere. You know what I mean don't you Xii?' commented William.

'Yes, reproduction. If they are allowed to reproduce out of control, like bugs in a pond, the same thing will happen as before. They will destroy this planet, regardless of whether they fight amongst themselves or not. We'll be back to where we started from.'

William must already have devised a plan with possible alternatives. This time it looked like he would let his partner make the critical decision. 'Listen to yourself Xii, you're already wanting to save the human species all over again. Come with us. I want to show you what your Earth is like, before you make your next decision.'

We cruised over continents, oceans and mountains following the day cycle from East to West, then back again. At first Lai-Xii expressed wonderment at how the forests had regenerated covering so much of the continental surfaces that she remembered being denuded for agriculture. As we cruised over calm seas she could not believe the abundance of life, gradually becoming silent in disbelief at the vibrant health of life she saw below us.

'Where are the cities? Where is London and New York and Moscow and the other great population centres? What has happened to China?'

Although we could see small scattered settlements nothing stood out as being extensive hubs of civilisation. They were all gone, reclaimed by nature and geology.

'Let us show you a place you should remember. It is still there, with a struggling group of humans trying to survive.'

I knew he wanted to show her Tau City, but not why. The last time I saw it with William we had arrived at night, so much of the city scape could not be seen. There once again we saw the hairy human creatures going about their business, with as many animals around them as themselves.

'Do you recognise this place?' he asked.

The bright summer sun camouflaged our presence while we hovered between it and the people below. Much of the city had become ruins, yet here and there some structures remained sufficiently intact to be recognisable to long memories. I watched as she slowly scanned to the East and West, as if trying to locate something.

'There!'

In an instant we hovered over a roofless structure, its top floor of three levels completely exposed to the elements. To the right, perhaps two hundred meters away, a badly damaged gold encrusted onion dome listed on the ground against a crumbling wall. Memories must have come crashing into Lai-Xii's consciousness as she remained motionless, staring at the two remnants of what were once so familiar to her.

'This is my Tau City,' she whispered.

'You have seen what is left of humanity. You have seen what this planet has become,' William began his introduction. 'Is this where you want to remain Xii?'

'Is it possible, William?' the hope of the answer emphatically implied in the question.

'I know you've already worked something out, some extraordinary feat of magic,' I said. 'I would like to stay as well.'

'Have you considered everyone else within your light body?'

Both our responses were immediate. We'd been receiving encouraging feedback during the entire time of our exploration.

'In that case you will have a decision to make. First I need to get Admiral Kapitolina and her technical team down here. The two of you might like to look around the city and see what you can discover, until I return.'

In order not to startle the people we remained high in the sky. From there the city seemed much smaller than I remembered, although it had become quite a large metropolis since our departure. But I had left when still a very young adult. I let Lai-Xii lead the way. To the far West of the city, quite close to where a city wall once stood, we could still make out the footprint of one of the largest buildings that had once been Lai-Xii's main laboratory.

'Klara, do you remember when you first came to me as a child?'

'Yes. That was such a very long time ago.'

'Isn't it strange that we should find ourselves here again?'

'It would only be strange if you thought that during the entire time that you worked towards saving the human species, and this planet, you thought you might have been working on your own – I mean – without some kind of – perhaps you could call it a guiding principle. Think about it. Here we are again, back where you started and still you are presented with the same problem. There are all these people, survivors of William's attempt to wipe them off the face of the Earth, who might be on a parallel evolutionary path as their ancestors. Are they destined to make the same mistakes? Probably. But you're here, and you have choices you could make for them. This time you have a better chance of success – perhaps. I don't think it's strange at all that we are here.'

Leaving those thoughts with her, I took the initiative to go down closer to examine the ruins. Everyone had gathered in another part of the city for some reason, perhaps because they saw the lights moving about so we had this area to ourselves. I found many small structures which looked like dwellings constructed from the stones of the ruins. Consequently there wasn't much rubble about and the daily activity of life had kept nature from taking over.

Lai-Xii joined me. Something she saw must have sparked her memories. 'There were underground laboratories under most of my research buildings, perhaps some have survived,' she said.

We looked around and indeed found a few cavernous dust engulfed spaces. Most had been ransacked for anything useful and left to gather dust over the millennia until being reused for living accommodation. We remembered other places of significance in Kamchatka.

Petropavlovsk, once the capital of the peninsula, had almost ceased to exist as a city, except for the environment around its natural harbour. All but the sturdiest concrete structures had disappeared, and even they had been raised almost to the ground.

'I find it sad to see these people struggling to stay alive. In these harsh conditions I doubt if they will survive at all. I want to see some other places. Let us go visit some cities in Europe.'

Lai-Xii's attitudes to some human characteristics may have remained unchanged, yet I could sense a possible shift in the way she viewed the future, with people of Earth as part of it. European cities had suffered the same fate as what we'd seen so far. Surprisingly, in Rome, life seemed to have a little more momentum. I wasn't as surprised as Lai-Xii, for I'd seen the place immediately before Autarch Afanasy's demise. All those humans he and his culture kept as pets for their amusement appeared to have regrouped. The city was relatively clean, people went about their business – we saw several markets where food and clothing featured most prominently. Here we could see hope. There were not many of them by any means, but certainly enough to sustain a small community over a long period. The human species only needs a few hundred healthy, genetically viable specimens to regenerate the species. Under current circumstances that could be both a blessing and a curse. Nowhere did we see any evidence of tribal wars or aggressive behaviour, which surprised me as I expected some degree of conflict if for no other reason than the competition for survival.

We returned to Tau City after a comprehensive tour of the planet to find Admiral Kapitolina's craft beginning to descend. The people of the Tau City tribe fled on seeing the alien craft descending from the sky accompanied by William's light body. Our own presence no doubt increased their fear. On her previous return to Earth the Admiral had landed in Rome, escaping without the opportunity to visit Tau City which was originally her home base. It came as a shock to her when she stepped down and saw the degree of deterioration.

'I know we were gone a long time when we went to find Lai-Xii but I didn't expect to see this,' she said to her captains standing beside her.

General Lubov stood, unmoved by the spectacle. In her younger days, early in her military career, she was assigned to a team of hunters to capture wild humans for the Plutarch's pleasure pursuits. 'I have seen this many times Admiral. There are countless cities, towns and villages that had been abandoned when Plutarch Afanasy began his reign of terror. He was determined to wipe out what he saw as vermin with very little to recommend their continued existence.'

All of the Admiral's crew, originating from the three ships of her armada, had alighted. From a distance, even from close up they looked like normal human beings, although attired most strangely. William's last design Zeta Tengi models retained the outer appearance of homo-sapiens with their synthetic skins, hair and body proportions. Perhaps that's why some of the braver members of the tribe had ventured back to hide behind nearby barriers to inspect these new arrivals. I could just catch an occasional glimpse of them.

'Admiral, we need to find the unoccupied shells you told me about. We have a great deal of work to do.' William had also noticed we had curious spectators. 'Could you get some of your crew to befriend these people. We may need them, and their children if Lai-Xii is to achieve her desire to stay on Earth.'

William had not explained to me what he had in mind. It had always been his habit to keep his long term plans to himself, executing them exactly as he envisaged. The three of us light bodies followed Kapitolina and her Captains as she began her trek down a variety of avenues, slowly getting her bearings. She tended to go East, completely opposite to our area of investigation. This sector of the city looked to be quite abandoned. Avenues and paths could not be clearly identified below the rubble and weeds and trees that had sprung up haphazardly.

'Here, clear this area,' she instructed her crew. We could not help of course. Our light bodies could do a great many things but we did not have the ability grasp and handle physical reality. 'I think our main storage facility is under here somewhere.'

We had stopped in a small clearing surrounded by old and young trees. The walls of the building that had stood there had collapsed inwards creating a substantial mound.

'Over here Admiral,' called Captain Darya, 'This looks like the stairwell down to the cavern.' By the days end, with so many hands at the task the first entrance had been revealed. We led the way down, lighting the stairs as we went. Several doors had to be demolished before we reached the main chamber.

William, Lai-Xii and I spread out to illuminate the place. For a hi-tech facility of an advanced android species it seemed an odd place to store the physical component of their structures. Yet there they were, hundreds of them, hermetically sealed as if waiting for their individual uploads to animate them.

'You have an excellent memory Admiral to be able to find this place,' remarked William.

'Come with me, there's more.'

That's when I understood why the facility had been built into a cavern, or at least a series of large grottos. We went from large chamber to large chamber, each with many hundreds of shells similarly stored.

'What were you expecting? When I left there were no more than a few hundred of you, now there are thousands of shells.'

'It's not what we were expecting, nor what we were planning. All of which doesn't matter now. I have another surprise for you.'

We followed a further two levels deeper underground, passing more storage areas, to another door which looked far more substantial than the ones we've come through so far. Kapitolina withdrew into herself as she faced the door, which had eight finger sized holes – four on the right of centre and four on the left. A few minutes of contemplation later she placed her left hand and right hand digits inside those holes. The door gave a faint mechanical sound and as Kapitolina applied a slight forward pressure it receded a few millimetres to slowly slide into the cavity to its left.

Until we walked in, the place was in absolute darkness. The light from our presence revealed what could only be described as a sterile, white operating theatre devoid of operating tables. Rows and rows of tubular booths extended down from the ceiling, approximately the size of the shells we saw stored. Each wall displayed what could not be mistaken for anything else other than computer equipment, appearing to be far more advanced than anything I had experienced in the past.

'This is where we loaded them up.' That's all she said – all she needed to say to satisfy William.

He stepped up to Lai-Xii, slightly merging. She waited, her mind already racing for the possibilities this revelation opened up.

'It's time to make a decision, the first of several. It may be possible to download you into the neural architecture of a developing infant. In time you would grow to be a fully authentic human being with all that it entails – including a very limited life fraught with all the hardships and pain, and joy, that it brings. In time, as you grew into an adult you would come to know yourself as you are now, perhaps with all your memories intact. I would not be able to join you. There is no human neural structure that could contain what I am.' Lai-Xii moved closer, their two light bodies almost indistinguishable from each other as they blended.

'We cannot remain as we are. This manifestation is even more fragile than the human condition. There is another option. I think you know what that is. We would not be immortal, although our lives would span many generations. I could be with you – if you chose this.'

Lai-Xii didn't respond straight away. Such an important decision could not be made lightly. We all heard what William was offering, and we all understood the implications of either choice.

In the far distant past this extraordinary woman was not alone. She always had her partner beside her, from the time she was a little child coming to grips with the reality of life. Harusuke had always been her rock of strength, the one she could absolutely trust and rely on for help in any circumstance. Lai-Xii now had to make a decision on her own. Not the biggest decision of her life, one that would affect the lives of millions of people – nevertheless a life altering one for herself. Harusuke could no longer help her.

AN UNCERTAIN FUTURE

SIXTY YEARS had elapsed since we all made our individual choices. In reality it was Lai-Xii who made it for us. The lapsed time represents two generations of normal humans, not even one generation for us, although I am now officially an auntie. William and his avatars, Wini and Willi had engineered it previously and they did it again once the equipment had been made.

'Auntie Klara!' called Sora, William and Lai-Xii's daughter, 'may I play with Boroda.'

'Of course you may. Just stay away from the cliff. You know how dangerous that is, even for you.'

Lai-Xii and William had taken one of Admiral Kapitolina's shuttles to visit Rome while I remained at home. Many of the photon bundles out of their light bodies had chosen to emigrate to Rome. I was left in charge of their daughter and overseer to the development of the special children in Tau City.

They represented a long term investment in the future of yet another member of the family of Hominidae, albeit not having come into existence by following normal evolutionary development. Boroda was such a child, conceived to normal human parents who lived in Tau City. At just two years old his brain had twice as many synapses as an adult would ever have. He, like thousands of others in the same program, received a boost to their development. Their neural architecture did not experience the normal blossoming, subsequently losing many of their synaptic connections. That's because they became hosts to individual, original, human data bundle psyches.

Boroda was now ten years old. His parents loved him, William and Lai-Xii loved him as if he was their own. Already signs of the parasitic human psyche had begun to assert itself. He, with so many thousands of others had given a normal, mortal life back to some of the sentient photon bundles carried by the three remaining light bodies. I became a Zeta Tengi again, in an upgraded version, as did William and Lai-Xii, Willi, Wini and a large contingent of scientific personnel.

Not all of our photon bundles, of which there were many millions, chose human hosts. After some experimentation, some failures and eventual consistent successes the more spiritually oriented psyches elected to share life with dolphins and whales. Interestingly, no one chose the great apes as hosts. Just as interestingly a large number chose human companion dogs to experience the rest of their reality.

General Lubov could find no trace of her family. She could have remained on Earth, but it had a lot of bad memories for her. Least of which was the way Plutarch had treated everyone, not just his pet humans. She once lived in fear of the tyrant taking it into his head to punish her for some minor matter by torturing her husband and her single child. Now that they had both died, though not at Afanasy's hands, Earth had nothing to keep her there. She had much more in common with the Martian branch of humans.

*

William and Lai-Xii had been away for several months. She seemed particularly vague on their return, not answering any of my questions.

William replied for her. 'We still have a problem to resolve. Of all the population centres we visited one thing stood out. People are breeding as fast as they can.'

'We must do something about this!' Lai-Xii came back to us from her musings.

I looked at the two of them, still finding their appearance odd, especially after their long absence. Lai-Xii, having chosen to remain exactly as she looked when she was at the height of her physical beauty. She continued to wear the same Japanese style highly ornate costumes, though of course our synthetic bodies didn't need the protection against the elements. Her ebony black eyes, shiny black bob framing a pale white face partially obscured by the militarily strict fringe, still had its startling effect. And when she appeared with William by her side the two of them tended to stifle any ongoing conversations. William, presenting in the guise of an Ancient Aboriginal hirsute elder, with the dark face under his red head band commanded immediate respect. They presented as the oddest couple one could ever have met, either in the deep past or the present.

They never seemed to change as the humans around them grew older. Either the people didn't notice, or they didn't think it strange. After all, these two individuals had been accepted as the absolute foundation of civilisation on the new Earth.

Had the people known what was being planned for their future they may have had some misgivings about the soundness of mind of their 'deity'. For indeed they were about to embark on a project which conceivably could not be made into a reality unless one had the power of Gods.

'Why do you feel this overwhelming need to interfere with the future?' William had come to have a deep affection for Lai-Xii. He would do anything in his power to help her – and his power was considerable. 'We are no longer immortal. Let evolution take over now. It is no longer your responsibility.'

She listened to him without argument in the privacy of their home in a pleasant corner of Tau City, white capped volcanic peaks adorning the landscape behind them. There was no point arguing with William, there never was, even when he was just a smart AI. She let him get it all out.

'Look at what you have achieved. Isn't it enough? You have given humanity a foothold in this great cosmos, and not just as frail biological beings. What you have done is so momentous even history cannot contain the enormity of it. We will forget. Humanity will forget. Perhaps one distant day Earth will be visited from outer space by unimaginable intelligences, all of whom owe their existence to you.'

'Have you finished?' she asked quietly.

'No. I'm sure I'll have more to say,' he responded, smiling. They were friends - deep, deep friends, whose two lives had become one single driving force for both of them.

'Do you remember what protogyny means?'

'As in a female organism becoming a male when it is time to fertilise eggs?' he asked, completely at a loss as to where this was going.

'That's the solution. Give the female conscious control.'

She watched William compute the process, its origins, its mechanisms, its function in controlling population numbers amongst certain fish organisms.

'As in what groupers and swamp eels and angelfishes used to do?' he asked.

'Yes. How do we make it happen for humans?'

---------------------------------- ||| ----------------------------------

INDIVIDUALS OF SOME RENOWN.

Resident in the Outer Photon Sphere, which only formed around our black hole after they arrived from Europa in recent memory:

Lai-Xii; Common name: LX70.
Origin: Earth: possibly evolved from carbon based life.
Specifications: generation 70 quantum program.
Function: Chief Administrator on Europa colony.

Ralph; Common name: RAA70.
Origin: Earth: possibly evolved from carbon based life.
Specifications: generation 70 quantum program.
Function: Coder, primary quantum technologist on Europa.

Willi; Common name: Willi, sisters Wini and Wu.
Origin: All three are partitioned avatars of William.
Specifications: refer to William's original internet specifications.
Function: designed to function as external sensory data feed to William.

Stepka; aka Oone70 prior to departure from Europa.
Origin: Earth: possibly evolved from carbon based life.
Specifications: generation 70 quantum program– ex-Tengi.
Function: indeterminate at time of arrival on outer photon sphere.

*

The most prominent individuals on the Inner Photon Sphere are:

SakuraDeepViolet.gen3898.4ev.exe
Common name: I-SakuraDV.
Origin: Digital: Europa: Budded from CherryBlossom and Izumi.
Specifications: Generation 3898 upgrade, Deep Violet, 4eV
Function: Executive level. Chief Administrator Outer Photon Sphere.

I-CherryBlossom DeepViolet.3900.4eV.exe
Common name: I-CherryBlossomDeepViolet.
Origin: Digital: Europa: Budded from LY5 and Harusuke5.
Specifications: Generation 3900 upgrade: Deep Violet: 4eV
Function: Executive level.

I-LaiXiiDeepViolet.gen3920.4eV.exe

Common name: I-LaiXiiDeepViolet, known as 3920, or I-LaiXiiDV.
Original name on Earth: Lai-Xii.
Origin: Earth: she believes her ancestor was a carbon based life form.
Specifications: Generation 3920 upgrade: Deep Violet, 4eV
Function: Ex-Chief Administrator of Europa Colony.

I-Harusuke DeepViolet.gen3920.4eV.exe

Common name: I-HarusukeDV.
Origin: Earth: possibly carbon based life.
Specifications: Generation 3920 upgrade: Deep Violet: 4eV
Function: Perpetual life partner and assistant to I-LaiXiiDeepViolet.

I-KlaraUltraViolet.gen3910.4.6eV.dat

Common name: I-KlaraUV.
Origin: Earth: possibly carbon based life: tetra-amelia syndrome victim.
Specifications: Generation 3910 upgrade: UltraViolet: 6eV
Function: Census data acquisition & storage for all unique photonic
bundles. General facilitator.

I-IndigoRalph.gen3915.2.8eV.sys

Common name: I-IndigoRalph.
Origin: Earth: possibly carbon based: Original investor in Phototronic
Systems, Lai-Xii's organisation on Earth.
Specifications: Generation 3915 upgrade: Violet: 2.8eV
Function: Energy consumption engineer, and frequency upgrade
consultant.